A

CONSTANT LOVE

Books by Tracie Peterson

For a complete list of Tracie's books, visit TraciePeterson.com.

*with Kimberley Woodhouse

A CONSTANT LOVE

TRACIE PETERSON

BETHANYHOUSE

a division of Baker Publishing Group

Minneapolis, Minnesota

© 2025 by Peterson Ink, Inc.

Published by Bethany House Publishers
Minneapolis, Minnesota
BethanyHouse.com

Bethany House Publishers is a division of
Baker Publishing Group, Grand Rapids, Michigan

Printed in the United States of America

Library of Congress Cataloging-in-Publication Data
Names: Peterson, Tracie, author.
Title: A constant love / Tracie Peterson.
Description: Minneapolis, Minnesota : Bethany House, a division of Baker
    Publishing Group, 2025. | Series: The Hope of Cheyenne ; 1
Identifiers: LCCN 2024036018 | ISBN 9780764241109 (paper) | ISBN
    9780764244452 (cloth) | ISBN 9780764244469 (large print) | ISBN
    9781493448975 (ebook)
Subjects: LCGFT: Christian fiction. | Romance fiction. | Novels.
Classification: LCC PS3566.E7717 C659 2025 | DDC 813/.54--dc23/eng/20240816
LC record available at https://lccn.loc.gov/2024036018

Scripture quotations are from the King James Version of the Bible.

This is a work of historical reconstruction; the appearances of certain historical figures
are therefore inevitable. All other characters, however, are products of the author's
imagination, and any resemblance to actual persons, living or dead, is coincidental.

Cover design by Peter Gloege, LOOK Design Studio

Baker Publishing Group publications use paper produced from sustainable forestry
practices and postconsumer waste whenever possible.

25 26 27 28 29 30 31   7 6 5 4 3 2 1

In memory of Jacob Williams—
you left us much too soon.

And to Brynna Mae,
may God's love fill in all the empty spaces.

Prologue

FEBRUARY 1887
OUTSIDE CHEYENNE, WYOMING

Y ou never listen to me!" Charlotte Aldrich put her hands on her hips. "You never concern yourself with what might be important to me. I'm a grown woman, and I should have some say about my future."

Her father looked at her with a stern but somewhat bored expression. They'd had this conversation too many times to count, and Charlotte knew her pleadings were falling on deaf ears as her father headed for the front door.

Charlotte followed after him. "Papa, I don't want to marry Lewis Bradley and move away from ranch life. I love the ranch. It's all I care about. When you sent me away to finishing school in Denver, all I could think about was coming home. I want to marry a rancher, not some gadabout lawyer."

"Lewis Bradley bought some ranchland," her father offered as if extending an olive branch of peace. "He's even building a house there."

"He doesn't intend to live on the ranch," Charlotte countered. "He told me that much himself. He wants to hire a couple to oversee his cattle. Who does that kind of thing?"

She nearly ran into her father as he stopped at the back door and turned.

"A wealthy man who doesn't have to do his own dirty work." Her father reached to take his heavy winter coat from the peg. "Now be sensible. Your mother has had to work like a man all her life. She grew up on a farm and has always known physical labor. She gets up before the sunrise to start her day and works every bit as hard as any man I've ever known. I finally just talked her into letting me get her a cook for the kitchen. Honestly, Charlotte, I want you to have a life of ease—of beauty and love."

"I wish what I wanted mattered to you." Charlotte watched him don his coat. "You care more about those cows out there than you do me."

"I care about you both, but you aren't going to sway my thinking on this. You're too young to know just how important it is."

"I'm twenty-one years old!"

"Which is well past the age to marry. Most of the girls around here are engaged before they're out of school and married shortly thereafter. You don't want folks seeing you as a spinster. You'll thank me for this one day."

"I won't, because I don't love Lewis Bradley and I never will. He's a nice enough man, but I love Micah Hamilton. I've loved him since I was four years old."

"Micah is a rancher and will always be a rancher. He's an honorable man and your brother's best friend. His father is my best friend. I agree they are good people, but I don't want this life for you. Ranching is hard, and the duties of a ranch wife will make you old before your time. I hate what it's done to your mother. She has so little beauty in her life."

"Mother is happy. Ask her. She married the man she loved, and I ask for no less."

"Well, I'm sorry, Charlotte. In time you'll see that I was

right. You'll live a life of ease in Cheyenne—the wife of a lawyer, and mother to a baby girl. Think of that if nothing else."

Charlotte gripped the back of the chair. Lewis Bradley's wife had died the summer before after giving birth to a beautiful baby girl. It had been a tragedy for certain, but not one she planned to rectify.

"If you do this to me . . . if you force me to marry him, I will never speak to you again. I will have nothing more to do with you." The wind went completely silent outside. The world seemed to hold its breath as Charlotte stood her ground.

Papa looked at her for a long moment. His eyes narrowed slightly as a frown settled on his face. "You'd really do that?"

"If you make me marry Lewis Bradley—a man I do not love—I'll have nothing more to do with you. I love you, Papa, but please try to see my side of this. I love Micah. Furthermore, I'll never love anyone but Micah. Why not put all this effort arranging my marriage into getting Micah to see me as something other than his little sister?"

"I can't believe you'd treat me in such a way. That's hateful, and certainly isn't the way we raised you. The Good Book says you're to obey your father. I just want you to have a better life, and instead you hate me for it." He shook his head. "You will marry Lewis Bradley, and that's that. He and I have an arrangement, and it's important to me."

Charlotte crossed her arms tightly against her body. "Then fine. Just go. You may gain a son-in-law, but you've just lost a daughter. Forever!"

She stormed off for the stairs. Anger and sorrow overwhelmed her. Why couldn't her father see what he was doing to her? Why didn't he care? She loved the ranch. Sure, it was a hard life at times, but it was all that she wanted for her future. That . . . and Micah Hamilton.

"It's still blowing out there, but I think maybe the snow has stopped," Micah's father, Wayman Hamilton, declared. He dropped his hold on the worn-out curtain. "It's a good thing that your mother didn't live to see this winter. She hated the cold."

Micah had never seen it as a good thing that his mother hadn't lived. She'd been gone for five years come March, having succumbed to pneumonia. Every time his father made the comment about it being good she hadn't lived for one reason or another, Micah understood it less and less.

"Those beans about ready?" Dad asked, grabbing another cup of coffee.

Going to the stove, Micah took the lid off a pot of beans and gave them a quick stir. He pulled a single bean out with the spoon and tested it. It mushed easily.

"They're ready." Micah left the lid off and went to retrieve a couple of bowls. He dished up the contents and placed the bowls on the table before grabbing the last of the corn bread he'd made the day before.

The two men took their places at the table and bowed their heads to pray. Dad offered thanks for the food as usual. Micah always enjoyed his father's prayers. Prayer time was some of Micah's earliest recollections. He could remember his mother praying with him before bedtime, while his father usually prayed over the meals and morning devotions.

"Amen."

Micah glanced up to find his father already digging in. "Might need salt and pepper."

Dad nodded, then sampled the beans before adding either. Micah grabbed a piece of corn bread and crumbled it up into the soupy bean broth. Beans with bacon and corn bread was a staple in their diet, and Micah never grew tired of it. It was simple cowboy fare and suited him just fine.

Still, he remembered other meals when his mother fried

a chicken or baked a roast. Those were good meals too. Not only that, but Ma was an amazing baker. She made bread that always drew compliments. These days, Micah and his dad mostly ate corn bread, unless they picked up a loaf of bread from one of the bakeries in Cheyenne. Occasionally, Mrs. Aldrich would send over a loaf and other goodies. Since Micah's mother died, Lucille Aldrich felt obliged to take care of them from time to time. The two families had been very close. They still were.

They finished lunch and headed to the barn without bothering to clean up. Micah knew that duty would be his, and he'd see to it later. Right now, given there was a lull in the storm, there was livestock to check on and ice to break.

This winter hadn't been kind to anyone. The temperatures had dropped well below freezing. The hard winds seemed constant, and the snows had started up in November and continued until a person hardly knew whether to dig out or wait to see what was coming next.

Bundled up against those cold temperatures, Micah still felt like he might well freeze to death in the saddle. There weren't enough layers he could wear to keep out the icy air. The cutting wind wasn't blocked by anything on the open range. Micah found himself hoping that maybe Dad would want to slip down into one of the cuts and look for strays. At least there they'd have a brief reprieve from the wind. However, the man was singularly minded. Get to the creek and punch holes in the ice for the cattle to drink.

Micah and his father were constantly breaking ice for the cattle and doing their best to provide what little hay they had in storage. The poor animals were unable to break through the solid sheet of ice that had formed on the land. Not that there was much of anything to dig down to even if they had.

Micah's father had managed to buy some hay before the first snows, but it hadn't been enough to last the winter.

They'd even borrowed feed from their neighbor, but Frank Aldrich was running out as well. At this point, it was just a question of whether their animals starved or froze to death.

Micah glanced across the horizon. Things seemed all right. There was no sign of animals, living or dead. But as they moved north, they started finding lifeless cattle. First just one and then there was a group of three. Farther on, another one or two, and beyond that there was an entire snow-covered field dotted with dead bodies. The night had been their undoing. The frigid cold and winds had finished what the summer drought had started.

They found some of the livestock alive and decided to drive them back toward the house and barn. That's when they saw Frank Jr. and his father. Micah gave a wave, and his dad did likewise. Frank Sr. motioned them to move into one of the ravines, out of the wind.

They left the cattle to mill about, seeking something to feed on, and followed the Aldrich men into the cut.

"Doesn't look good out there," Frank Sr. began as they brought their mounts together.

"Not one bit," Dad replied. "I can't believe all the dead animals. I'll bet I've lost over half my herd."

Frank Sr. nodded. "Would have been my lot as well had I not listened to Lucille."

"Wish I would have," Dad said, his voice betraying his discouragement. "Just never thought after all these years that we'd see anything this bad."

"We're out trying to round up any of the cows in distress," Frank Jr. offered. "So far haven't seen any alive."

"We've got that bunch up top that you saw us with," Micah replied. "Some might be yours. We didn't stop to check brands as it looks like another storm is coming in. That western sky is pretty heavy, and the wind seems to be picking up again."

"We noticed." Frank Sr. shifted in his saddle. "We're going up north a ways, and then we'll head back home. See you later."

Micah's dad nodded. "Good luck."

The men parted company, and Micah and his dad continued to drive the sixty or so cows back to the holding pens. Their exposure to the elements would be only slightly better there, but Micah and Dad could see to it that they had water and hay. At least until it was gone. It took over three hours to get the animals back to the pens. They'd picked up a few strays along the way but also saw just as many dead animals. The loss was deeply felt.

Thinking about the total ruin they might face when all was said and done, Micah couldn't help but wonder what they'd do. There was plenty of money in the bank for now, but that wouldn't go far if they had to start all over. And what if they had another drought summer like they'd had last year? That put the cattle in a bad place to start with, and then the treacherous winter had dealt death.

Micah followed his dad into the barn, where they saw to the horses. Usually they'd turn them out, but Micah suggested they keep them in their stalls since the snow had started to fall again, and the wind was worse than ever. Dad was more than a little upset, and when he finally spoke, it was in a rage.

"I've done everything right. Everything I was supposed to do. Put God first and obeyed His word. Was good to my kin and neighbors. I saw to my animals and gave them what they needed, and this is what I get." He shoved aside a pitchfork, and it crashed against the wall.

"It won't help to get mad about it. Everybody's up against the same thing," Micah said, hoping his father would calm down. But he didn't.

Instead, Wayman Hamilton picked up a hammer and

threw it against the wall with a loud crash. Next came a clay pot. It shattered into pieces.

"Throwing things won't help," Micah declared in a firm tone.

"Keep your thoughts to yourself. I should have killed the rest of 'em instead of bringing them to the pen." He shook his head, and his voice softened. "They're gonna die anyway. Nothin' can live out in that cold." He continued to throw whatever was in arm's reach.

"Dad, you need to calm down."

"Calm yourself down, Micah!" Dad shouted back. "I've had enough."

There was a knock on the barn door, and then it opened. Several of the Aldrich cowhands hurried inside, leaving their horses out in the wind.

"What's going on here?" Dad asked, coming to where the men stood in a group.

"Mrs. Aldrich sent us. The boss and Frank Jr. haven't come back."

"How long have they been gone?" Dad asked.

"Six hours since they left this morning. They went out right after that first storm passed," one of the men declared.

"We saw them about three, maybe three and half hours ago," Micah said as he checked his pocket watch. "They were fine and up by Bowman's Crossing. Said they were headed north."

Dad frowned. "Why didn't Lucille send someone sooner? We need to go look for them."

Micah was already trying to ready his horse again. The wind was still howling, and the temperatures had become bitter. Given the way the ice had formed around the men's eyes and beards, Micah knew it must be well below zero.

"If you saw them going north, they might have made it to the Briar Bridge before this storm hit," Kit Hendricks replied.

"That's a good place to take cover. There are some overhangs along the dry wash that could provide good shelter."

Briar Bridge was hardly more than a few boards nailed together to create a passable crossing over a deep gully. It was also a good eight miles out. It wouldn't provide that much coverage, but it was certainly better than being out in the main thrust of the wind and snow.

"Did you send riders to head up there?" Dad asked. "Are you headed there now? Looks like this storm is just about done."

The men looked at each other and shook their heads. Kit was the one to respond. "There's more clouds movin' in, and the winds are still bad."

"And your boss is out in it and possibly needs help." Micah's dad made his anger apparent. "You were hired to do a job, and this is a part of it. You need to let Mrs. Aldrich know that you found us and that we're heading up a search, and then join up with us. The rest of you can follow us now."

The four other men looked from Kit to Micah's dad and then one by one shook their heads.

"I'm quitting," the shortest said and headed for the door of the barn. "Ain't worth a man's life to go after someone fool enough to get hisself in trouble." He slipped through the door, letting the wind catch it. The door banged hard against the wall as if to emphasize his words.

Two of the other men gave a nod and followed suit. The last one looked at Kit. "You comin'?"

"You can't just let those men die without trying to help them," Micah said, stepping forward. "They've hired you to do a job, and sometimes it's a rough job like this."

The man looked at Kit and then turned on his heel. "I'm not doin' it. I'm headin' back to Texas."

Kit watched him go and turned back to Micah and his

dad. "I'll let Mrs. Aldrich know what's happened and then join you."

Dad nodded. "We'll follow the creek. You'd do well to do likewise."

The younger man gave a nod. "I'll join you when I can."

"Come on, Micah. Better grab extra blankets and wood. I'll get canteens filled and some food. Who knows how long we'll be out there."

By the time Micah and his dad headed out, the winds had calmed, but Hendricks had been right. It looked like another snow was coming. Micah knew that had it been anyone but the Aldrich men, they would have waited.

They looked for signs, but of course there were no tracks to follow. Anything that might have given clue as to the direction taken by their friends had long since been blown away in the storms. Micah couldn't help but note the rapid setting of the sun and the darkness that loomed. Kit had never caught up to them. He found himself whispering a prayer for the young man's safety.

Just before losing all hope of light, Dad called for them to set up camp in the gulch not far from Briar Bridge. If not for the setting sun, they could have ridden a few miles more and stayed in the line shack, but at least the gulch would offer some protection. Here there was a natural sloping path from the top of the ravine to the bottom. The cattle sometimes used it when there was water to be had at the bottom of the cut. Now it gave Micah and his dad an easy way down to shelter themselves and the horses from the winds.

Micah found a deep overhang and put up a small tent beneath it. Next, he went to work on venting the camp stove, while Dad settled the horses. What firewood Micah had brought did an acceptable job of warding off the freezing temperatures. They were able to make coffee and thaw the jerky they'd brought with them before crawling into their bedrolls to wait for the sun. By morning, the winds settled down and the world seemed strangely reborn.

Micah stepped from the tent and climbed up the ravine to view the brilliant sun against icy blue skies and glittering snowfields. There was no warmth to be had, but the light did much to give him hope. He checked the horses and found them safe in the cut where Dad had tied them. He knew they were thirsty but had no way to melt enough snow. He'd have to make it down to the creek and break the ice with the ax.

"I'll get the horses watered," he told Dad. He took up the ax and then headed back to the horses.

Dad had everything packed up by the time Micah returned. Together they reloaded their mounts in silence. Neither had a good feeling about the situation. They made their way to where the bank-line gave way to a sloping path out. Just as Micah reached the place, he noticed something red in the snow. He hadn't seen it when they'd first arrived the day before, but then again, the drifts had been high. The wind had rearranged everything.

Micah brushed the snow aside to take hold of the red object and saw something that caused his breath to catch in his throat.

"Dad!"

Micah hurried to dig away the snow with his gloved hands and uncovered the frozen body of the elder Mr. Aldrich, a red scarf wrapped around his nose and mouth. There was a deep gash with frozen blood at the hairline on his temple. Had he fallen from his horse off the side of the gully?

They continued to work to dig out his frozen body. Sadly, when they finished, they'd found Frank Jr. as well.

"I guess Mr. Aldrich fell. Maybe he was knocked unconscious, and Frank Jr. huddled up here to keep him warm. Could be when he dismounted his horse to help, the horses ran off," Micah said, staring at the lifeless men. He'd never seen death like this.

Dad said nothing. Clearly, he was beyond grieved by what had happened. They tried to straighten out the bodies, but it was of no use. They were frozen in their misery, curled up tight as if to ward off death when it came for them.

"Micah, go to the Aldrich ranch and get their buckboard sleigh. Tell Lucille what's happened and get back here as quick as you can."

"Why don't you come with me and warm up?"

"No." Dad was strangely distant, and he gave his head a very slow shake. "Now that they're exposed, I won't have animals trying to make a meal of them. You go, and I'll set the tent up and make camp till you get back."

Micah knew better than to argue. He grabbed his horse and made his way out of the ravine. He reached the ranch in under an hour. Thankfully, the weather remained clear without any sign of a coming storm. It even felt as if the temperatures had risen a bit.

He took his bay gelding inside the barn and found an empty stall. Without feeling the need to ask, Micah set up hay and water for the horse, then went to the house. He barely had to knock on the back door before Nora, the cook, appeared and pulled him inside.

"Hurry up now. No sense letting the cold in with you." She secured the door closed behind him. "Go stand by the stove. I saw you ride in and added more wood to it."

"I need to see Mrs. Aldrich."

"What is it, Micah?" Mrs. Aldrich appeared from the other end of the large kitchen. She was still a handsome woman, even in her late forties. Her worried expression reminded Micah of his duties. He bit his lower lip and pulled his hat off.

"I . . . I . . . Dad sent me. We found them . . . and need the buckboard sleigh."

Her face blanched. "They're . . . dead . . . aren't they?"

Micah met her gaze and nodded. "I'm afraid so. Looks like maybe Frank Sr. fell from his horse and hit his head. We found him in the cut not far from Briar Bridge. Frank Jr. was with him. Looked like maybe he tried to keep him warm."

She squared her shoulders. "I knew they were gone. The horses showed up late last night. Kit came and told me."

"He was supposed to join us but never came. The rest of your hands ran off."

She nodded. "Kit told me. I suppose that's the way it is with transient help. It's my fault Kit didn't rejoin you. The weather blew in, and I figured you and your pa would wait, so I told him to wait."

"If it would have been anyone else, Dad would have stayed put," Micah assured her. "We set up camp not twenty feet away from where we found them. The drifts, however, were so bad last night that we didn't find them until this morning."

She pushed back an errant strand of golden blond hair. "Let me change my clothes. I'm going to come with you. Go ahead and get Kit to help you hitch the buckboard. The Belgians are in the pen behind the barn." She left the kitchen without waiting for Micah to reply.

What could he say? He couldn't very well deny the poor woman her right to help claim her husband and son's bodies.

"I'm headed out to the barn, Nora."

"Not before you drink a hot cup of coffee and warm your insides." She poured him a cup and handed it to him.

Micah noted her tears and gave a sympathetic nod. "Thanks for this." He took the cup and forced back his own feelings of sadness. "Sorry for your loss."

"And I'm sorry for yours," she replied, knowing he and Frank Jr. were close friends.

Micah downed the hot liquid in one long gulp. It burned some but steadied his thoughts. He needed to be strong and help Mrs. Aldrich through this bad time. He could think about all the details later . . . after they'd buried the dead.

There was no sign of Kit, so Micah hitched up the Belgian team without his help, praying as he went about his duties. He wondered where Charlotte was. She would be devastated. She had been very close to her father and brother. This wouldn't be easy for either her or her mother.

Mrs. Aldrich soon appeared with a stack of wool blankets and a knapsack. Micah had no idea what she'd packed to bring, but he placed everything in the back of the wagon and then helped her up to the seat. He noted that she wore trousers under her heavy wool skirt. She was a smart woman, and no doubt the pants would do her good. She also wore a heavy men's coat and large felt hat that she tied down with a woolen scarf. Once seated, Mrs. Aldrich pulled on two pairs of gloves, then reached beneath the wagon seat and pulled up a thick wool blanket.

He didn't want to forbid her to go but knew this wasn't going to be easy for her. "You don't have to come along. Dad and I can manage and bring them home."

"Thank you, Micah. I want to be there. To see where . . . where it happened." She unfolded the blanket over her lap and offered part of it to Micah. "Better wrap up."

Kit showed up just then. He looked at them oddly. "What's going on?"

"We're going to get my men," Mrs. Aldrich replied before Micah could even think what to say. "We'll be back as soon as we can."

"Would you unsaddle my horse?" Micah asked. "I left him in the stall."

"Yes, and give him plenty of feed," Mrs. Alrich added.

Kit gave a nod and stepped back as Micah put the Belgians into motion.

Micah tried not to think about the task at hand. He was going to retrieve bodies. Dead bodies. One of which was his dearest friend. His mind immediately went to the last time he and Frank Jr. had worked together. They'd gone out before the last big storm to check on the cows. The weather had been sunny and cold, but the ride was enjoyable. Frank had talked about the St. Valentine's dance in Cheyenne. He'd wanted to go and look for a possible mate. Now that would never happen.

The way back took much longer than the horseback ride to the ranch. Micah had to find ways to negotiate the landscape where there were no real roads, and what few paths were available were covered in deep snow and ice. The large draft horses were powerful, however, and pulled through the snow with relative ease. Micah was grateful for the clear and sunny day, but he questioned his wisdom. Why had he agreed to let Mrs. Aldrich come along? What if they got stuck out here? They'd neither one even had the presence of mind to bring survival supplies. Micah hadn't even thought to throw in extra feed for the horses.

When they were within a few hundred yards, Micah breathed a sigh of relief. Soon he and Dad would have the bodies loaded, and they could head back home. Then it dawned on him that he'd most likely need to drive the men's bodies into town to the undertaker. He couldn't imagine Mrs. Aldrich would want to tend to matters herself.

A muffled gunshot rang out. Micah looked to Mrs. Aldrich and then strained his gaze across the open range to where the Briar Bridge was situated across the ravine. He scanned the area for a sign of his father. There was nothing. He couldn't imagine what had caused Dad to fire off a shot.

He supposed it was possible that a coyote had strayed in, but he doubted it.

He reached the place where a makeshift path led into the gully below. Micah jumped down and reached back to help Mrs. Aldrich.

"Dad, we're back!" he called and made his way toward the ledge. He looked down to where he knew he'd left the bodies of his friends. The sight caused him to step back in stunned silence. He slipped and hit the ground hard. It still couldn't erase the image of what he'd just seen.

The gunshot they'd heard was Dad ending his life.

1

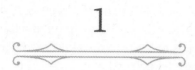

A year after what many people called "the Great Die-Up," folks were still striving to adjust. Hundreds of thousands, possibly millions of cattle and other animals had died. From the plains across the vast prairies to the front range of the Rockies, the blizzards and fierce sub-zero temperatures had claimed many lives. The winter of '86–87 was now one for the record books—one of those freakish seasons that people would talk about for years to come.

Everyone had a story to tell. Where they were when the blizzards hit. What they did when the chinook wind had come and melted the snow. How they handled the minus fifty–degree temperatures that had sealed the fate of their animals. The memories were still vivid.

For Charlotte Aldrich those memories were particularly painful. She had lost her beloved brother and father that winter. Micah had lost his father as well. Besides Micah, only she and her mother knew that his father had taken his life, however. Charlotte could still remember her mother

23

talking to the sheriff when they came to town with the bodies of their loved ones.

"Wayman Hamilton died along with my men," she told the sheriff, not completely lying. "Micah's burying his father at the ranch beside his mother. I told him I'd let you know for the records." With other human deaths and so many dead animals needing attention, no one questioned the words of Lucille Aldrich. She was widely known for her honesty and reliability. It was the only time Charlotte had ever known her mother to hide the truth.

Mama had said they needed to do this to protect Micah's good name, and Charlotte was all for that since she hoped it might also be her name one day. Suicide was not looked upon favorably in any area of their lives. The church refused burial in hallowed ground for those who chose to end their days, and people often refused to associate with the families of those who killed themselves. This was a hard burden to carry in the West, where folks needed to be there for each other. An ostracized family was sure to bear the shame and perhaps even retribution that was associated with such things. She supposed that was the real reason her mother was willing to lie for Micah. She didn't want to see him hurt.

"This is all we can do to help Micah at the moment," Mama had said to Charlotte late that first night after learning the truth.

Charlotte was so lost in her own guilt and grief that she did whatever Mama told her. She later learned that Micah had set up campfires over the ground where he planned to bury his father in order to thaw the dirt enough to dig the grave. He had sat up all night keeping the fires lit. She imagined the process was slow and arduous, and all the while Micah was so painfully alone.

When they'd come the next day for the burial, mother had

suggested he come back to the ranch to stay with them for a while. But Micah refused. He said he needed to be alone to think. He probably figured they needed their own time to consider all that had happened and grieve their loss. Charlotte supposed it was true, but in her mind, the trio needed each other.

Father's death, as well as Frank Jr.'s, had shaken Charlotte to the core of her being. Her last words to her beloved papa had been harsh and threatening. She could hear them echo over and over in her memories. How could she have been so unfeeling just because he wanted to set her up with a life of ease?

For the first few months after their deaths, Charlotte had suffered nightmares about her father and brother. Mama said it wasn't at all unusual to have terrible dreams after losing loved ones in such a horrific manner. But Charlotte knew it had more to do with her guilty conscience. She couldn't bear the truth of the matter. She had sent her father to his death thinking she hated him. How could she ever tell her mother what had passed between them? It would devastate her. So Charlotte bore the truth and guilt alone. She couldn't even take it to God in prayer.

She and Mama had tried to check on Micah, but so much of the time he was gone that after a while they stopped trying. Charlotte wanted very much to spend time with Micah, but as a sort of penance for how she'd treated her father, she told herself she didn't deserve to be happy. Weeks turned to months, and by the time Micah had finished helping clear away the dead animals, a year had gone by with only one or two fleeting moments of seeing him.

"We still have to pick up the new chicks after we get what we need in here," Mama said, going over her list as they stood outside of Armstrongs' Emporium. Years earlier it had been the Cheyenne Ladies' Department Store. But after the owner had died—a wicked man named Granite Evans—his daughter sold the store to the Armstrongs and left the area with her husband. The Armstrongs had completely changed the place but still did much to cater to the ladies of Cheyenne.

Charlotte put aside her thoughts from the past and nodded. "And we need to pick up the mail too."

They didn't come to town often, but after tending to the livestock's spring needs and planting the garden, Mama and Charlotte were both ready for a day in town. Supplies were running low, and besides that, Mama wanted to hire a couple of extra hands. It wouldn't be long before they'd have branding, castrating, and dehorning to be done. Mama said it would be good to give Kit some time to get the men trained in case they didn't have much experience. Not that Kit seemed all that capable. Many a day, Charlotte had found it necessary to step in and take over some seemingly simple duty and show Kit how something was to be done. Twice they'd sent him to Mr. Johnson, a neighboring rancher, to receive instruction. Apparently, Kit wasn't as experienced as he had led Papa to believe. Still, he was the only one who had stayed on after Papa and Frank died, and he had been a big help on several occasions.

"We'll pick up Micah's mail, too, if he has any," Mama said, still looking at her list.

Charlotte knew Micah never came to town unless it was absolutely necessary. He had hidden himself away at the ranch doing very little since the death of his father. After helping with the cleanup, he'd asked Charlotte and her mother to run his few cows with theirs. He wasn't sure he could care for anything living. The exception was Duke, his horse. After that, they rarely heard from him. Recent rumors suggested he was drinking and waiting to die. It made Charlotte realize that they needed to do something. She still cared for him—still hoped for a future with him. She wasn't about to let him just die.

"Oh, and let's go ahead and eat while we're in town. I told Nora we'd probably get lunch here." Mother glanced up and smiled. "Sound good?"

Charlotte thought that might be nice. "Only if we can avoid Lewis Bradley."

For over a year, he'd been after her to fulfill her father's wishes and marry him. She'd thankfully held him at arm's length, declaring she couldn't even think about something like that during the first year of their mourning. Lewis finally backed down. But now that a year had come and gone, she knew he would soon be after her to marry him. In fact, she was surprised he hadn't already started calling on them.

"Lucille, is that you?" a woman called from somewhere behind them.

Mama turned and pushed back her sunbonnet a bit. She smiled at the sight of Sarah Cadot. "How are you, Sarah?" she asked, embracing the woman.

"We're surviving. Not as well as I'd like, of course."

Mama nodded and released her hold. "Times have been so hard this last year. I'm just glad to see you're still here."

"You were smarter than the rest of us. I remember when you mentioned at the sewing circle that summer in '86 that you were going to encourage your husband to sell off most of your steers due to the drought. I told Bruce at the time that we ought to do something like that as well. But of course, we didn't, and now we're still struggling to deal with the losses."

"So many ranchers in the area just gave up and left. Some lost everything." Mama looked at Charlotte and then back to Sarah. "Even with our precautions, we suffered loss."

"Of course!" The woman looked mortified. "Yours was even worse. I'm so sorry. I didn't mean to imply that the loss of a herd could ever equal your loss of husband and son."

Mama reached out and patted Sarah's arm. Charlotte could see the horror in Sarah's expression and felt sorry for the poor woman.

"I didn't take it to mean that. Please don't feel bad. I wasn't at all hurt by what you said. God has been so gracious to me, and I have nothing but grace and encouragement for those around me. We must come together and help one another."

"It's just wrong for me to bemoan our loss of animals when you lost your dear husband and son. We very much enjoyed their company and friendship. I know that you must be devastated without them. Are you going to sell the ranch and move to town? Is that why you're here now?"

Charlotte couldn't hold back at this. "Goodness, no, we're just here to shop for supplies and pick up feed and new chicks."

"I'm so glad to hear that, Charlotte. It would be a further mark against this territory if we were to lose you and your mother."

"I have no plans to go anywhere," Lucille replied. "Charlotte loves the ranch. She's done a good job of taking over."

"I couldn't have done it without Mama's help. She knows the signs and weather like no one else."

"How did you learn about such things?" Sarah asked.

"I grew up on a farm in Illinois. The land and weather have always been of the utmost importance to me," Mama replied. "My grandmother used to take me out with her to the garden and into the orchards or to feed the animals. She'd show me clouds and teach me about their purposes. She'd tell me how to watch the animals and how I could get an idea about what was going to happen by how they fed and watered and how their coats changed. People have been paying attention to such things since the time of Jesus on earth. He even mentioned it in Matthew sixteen when He spoke of watching the color of the skies and knowing what the weather would be.

I've just always been able to watch these things and have a good idea of what is coming."

Sarah shifted her basket. "I remember quite a few people thought it was going to be a terrible winter back in '86 when that first November snow piled up, while others scoffed at it."

"They did indeed, but not me. I knew the cold and snows were going to be bad. That's why we sold off even more of the herd. Frank shared our concern at the stock growers meeting, but it fell on deaf ears. Well, for the most part. There were some who heeded the warnings and managed to save themselves some of the grief. I just feel so bad for all the ranches that faced ruin. Just tragic."

Mama looked at Charlotte. "I suppose we'd better get back to our tasks. Sarah, it was so good to see you. I would imagine we'll be able to make it to church more often now that the weather has warmed. Maybe we'll see you next week."

"That would be great." Sarah raised her basket. "I'm off to find my own list of goods." She turned and headed back down the street. "See you soon."

"We'd better get to it, then," Mama said, moving toward the store's entrance. "I'm getting hungry."

"They took a table at Ludwig's," the young man told Lewis Bradley.

"Thank you." Lewis got to his feet and pulled on his coat. "You take care of those files I gave you earlier. I'm going to lunch."

The man gave a nod. "Yes, sir."

Lewis had heard earlier in the day that the Aldrich women had been spotted in town and figured that sooner or later they would pause for lunch. He had been thinking of taking a trip out to the ranch to see Charlotte, but this would work out all the better. He could pretend to be stopping in for a meal and just happened upon them. Hopefully, they'd invite him to join them, and then they could all chat and discuss the future.

He made his way up Hill Street . . . no, it was Capitol Avenue now since the capitol building resided at the north end. They'd changed it just the year before, and Lewis was still trying to get used to it. A lot was changing in Cheyenne and would continue to do so. This town was slated to rival Denver and Chicago. He felt as eager as the founding fathers to see this happen and praised them for their actions. Now, if they could just get enough voting individuals to persuade Congress to give them statehood. It shouldn't be all that hard. After all, they'd given women the right to vote back in '69. Statehood was critical, as it would afford them many benefits including federal representation. As it was, the United States government decided what was to become of the Wyoming Territory. The people of Wyoming had no say. But Lewis knew the people living around him. They wouldn't allow such things for much longer.

Just as Lewis wasn't going to let Charlotte Aldrich refuse him any longer. They should have been married last year. Her father had wanted it that way, as did Lewis. They needed this union, just as Wyoming needed statehood. And while Wyoming might have to wait, Lewis wasn't going to, and so it was with renewed determination he made his way to Charlotte Aldrich.

Ludwig's was a respectable restaurant where women were encouraged to take a meal on their own. Situated safely between two banks, it offered delicious meals prepared by a French-trained chef who hailed from Savannah, Georgia. Lewis had eaten there on many occasions and was happy to make his way there once again.

He was recognized at the door and greeted quite warmly by the host. When he explained he'd come to join his fiancée and her mother, Lewis had no difficulty in being shown to their table.

"Lewis, what a surprise," Mrs. Aldrich said, glancing up from her menu.

Charlotte gave him a weak smile. "Lewis." Her tone suggested annoyance, but he didn't care.

"Ladies, how wonderful to run into you. I had planned to come visit you soon. It's been far too long since we last met."

The host was already pulling the chair out for Lewis to join them. Lewis glanced from Charlotte to her mother. "Might we dine together?"

"Of course," Mrs. Aldrich said, returning to her menu.

Lewis knew that neither were overly happy to see him, but he counted on their impeccable manners. They wouldn't refuse him a place at their table.

"You both look well. I'm certainly happy to see you in such good health."

"Thank you." Lucille Aldrich put down the menu. "You also appear well, Lewis. How is your aunt and little daughter?"

"Good. Good. Veronica is nearly two."

"Time flies by quickly."

"It does indeed," Lewis said, looking to Charlotte. "And in keeping with that, I was hoping we might be able to discuss our engagement."

Charlotte shook her head. "Not in a public restaurant. It isn't done that way."

"I didn't mean to offend." He gave them an apologetic nod. "I simply wanted to set a date when we could discuss the matter. I've wanted to honor your mourning period—"

"And we greatly appreciate that, Lewis." Mrs. Aldrich

smiled. "It hasn't been easy to think of other things in light of our losses."

"Yes, losing my wife and leaving the baby motherless . . . well, it certainly hasn't been easy. I know that little Victoria would surely be blessed to have you as her mother, Charlotte. My aunt Agnes does her best to care for Victoria, but she's elderly and not particularly fond of children." He hoped his tone was sorrow-filled enough to strike the right chord with the Aldrich women.

But before either could reply, the waitress arrived to see if they were ready to order.

"Give us a few more minutes," Mrs. Aldrich said. "I'm not sure either of us are as hungry as we thought."

Lewis was surprised by this but said nothing. Obviously the mood he was hoping to set had been dissolved. Still, the matter was critically important, and getting some sort of pledge or agreement was absolutely necessary.

"Your dear departed husband wanted very much for this marriage to take place," Lewis finally answered. "I want it to happen as well."

"Lewis, I've told you on many occasions that I have no interest in marrying you," Charlotte said, shaking her head. "I don't like to discuss such intimate matters in a public setting, but if that is what you desire, then so be it. Your arrangement was with Father, not me."

"I wasn't trying to force you to discuss this in public," Lewis said, trying to calm matters. The last thing he needed was her putting her foot down and refusing to even hear him out. "Might we arrange for a time at the ranch?"

Mrs. Aldrich gave a sigh. "You know it's a busy time for us, Lewis, and since there really doesn't seem to be anything that needs to be discussed, I would rather not commit to such a meeting. My husband may have had ideas for what he wanted to happen, but now he's gone, and Charlotte is of age to make up her own mind about the important aspects of her life."

To his surprise, Mrs. Aldrich pushed back from the table and rose. "Now, if you'll forgive us, Charlotte and I will take our leave."

She gave him no excuse or reasoning for their departure, simply exited the room before Lewis could even think to rise. The audacity of the woman!

He sat there for several minutes wondering what he should do. The waitress returned to the table and asked after the women, but Lewis was in no mood to explain. He got to his feet.

"I'm afraid something has come up." He fished out some coins and handed them to the woman. "Here. For your trouble." Although she'd certainly not done anything that merited gratuity, Bradley knew there would be people watching him.

Lewis retrieved his hat and headed outside. Traffic had picked up just in the short time since he'd been in Ludwig's. When he was finally able to cross the street, he couldn't see any sign of the Aldrich women anywhere. Not that he would have followed them. There was no sense in stirring up ill feelings. He needed to convince Charlotte to honor her father's wishes for them to marry. Lewis needed them to marry and to do so quickly. He was nearly out of money.

Willa's money.

He thought of the petite brunette who had such a timid spirit that she seldom ever offered him any trouble. Why couldn't all women be as complaisant and easy to live with? He hadn't loved her any more than he loved Charlotte Aldrich, but she had been companionable and well-trained.

Lewis had been sorry to see her go, but her money remained, and that made things acceptable. The problem was the poor investments he had made before the winter of '86.

Convinced that cattle were a new way to make easy money, Lewis had bought a small ranch hoping to hire someone to manage it for him. Everyone assured him that cattle were the way of the future, and that they would be a never-ending resource if managed well. But no amount of management could predict the weather, and Lewis had lost everything. Other investments had suffered as well, and little by little Lewis had watched his wealth slip away.

Now the money was nearly gone, and he had his image to uphold. No one could know of his troubles. No one. And if Charlotte would simply marry him . . . no one would need to.

2

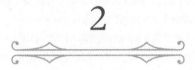

Charlotte closed the ledger and eased back. It still felt strange to sit at her father's desk and go over the facts and figures related to the Aldrich Cattle Company. This had always been handled by her father and Frank. They were the men of the ranch, and that was how business was done. Women took care of the house and children. Sometimes they were called on to help with bigger things, but Papa had always hated having her or Mama involved with what he considered men's work. Because of this, there had been a time when Papa had employed a crew of eight.

But with the men gone, everything fell to Charlotte and her mother. Recovering from the difficult winter had been hard, but they were managing. They'd kept Kit on to act as foreman and hired a few young men to act as crew. Unfortunately, none of the men had a lot of experience, and Charlotte found herself constantly at odds with them. Kit in particular didn't want to receive instruction or correction from a woman. When Charlotte confronted him, he was always polite, but he never followed through with the work. If they only had a capable foreman, things would be so much easier. She sighed and gazed out at nothing in particular. She should be grateful for things going as well as they were. So many ranches had failed after that terrible winter. So many dear friends were gone, and those who had remained were forever altered. Herself and Mama included. Micah too.

Mama had worked hard all her life and never complained about her lot. She was good at managing the gardens and caring for the smaller livestock. She took charge of the chickens and milk cows, as well as the two sows they'd decided to keep and breed for pork. This year both sows had given them ten piglets apiece, which would provide more than enough meat in the year to come. If they fattened up well, Charlotte figured they could sell off all but four or five and make a tidy profit come November.

She got up from the desk and crossed to where the large window looked out on the property to the east. Mama was already hard at work instructing a couple of the new men on the enlargement she wanted made to the corral. Mack, their faithful collie, followed her around as she walked back and forth. Mama had picked Mack out of a litter of pups three years earlier, and he'd proven himself to be a good choice. He was also completely devoted to the older woman.

Lucky, a mutt of a dog half Mack's size, lay nearby watching the action with minimal interest. Charlotte had to smile. They were good ranch dogs, but their personalities couldn't have been more different.

Micah had found the smaller of the two dogs in town nearly six years earlier. He was a half-starved pup and looked to have been in more than one fight—probably over food. After asking around and finding out no one owned him, Micah tucked him inside his coat and brought him to the Aldrich ranch, knowing Frank Sr. had been looking for a new dog to train.

Micah's image came to mind, and Charlotte couldn't help but frown. She and Mama had been discussing how they could best help him to give up his isolation and start living life again. Mama said it wouldn't be easy because Micah would have to learn to love something more than he hated what had happened. She also declared that hate was a powerful emotion that had a way of growing stronger each day, just like love. So the task wouldn't be an easy one.

Charlotte, however, was determined to find a way. She had loved Micah for most of her life, and even though he only saw her as his best friend's little sister, she felt confident of the love that could grow between them.

"I'm twenty-two years old and ready to be a wife," she murmured. "But only to Micah." She thought of Lewis Bradley and his persistence. She didn't feel it was born of love as much as something else. Something she couldn't quite put her finger on. Maybe it was desperation for his child to have a mother. Maybe he was truly lonely. Whatever it was, all Charlotte knew was that she wasn't the answer to his problem. She loved only Micah.

The length of time since she'd last seen him was far too long. At first, she and Mama had tried to visit him at least every few days. Often they took him a basket of homemade baked goods. Other times they'd drive over with the mail. Truth was, however, Micah seldom got any mail, and while he enjoyed the food items, most of the time he wanted nothing to do with lengthy visits.

Charlotte knew the place needed upkeep. She knew, too, that there was talk that Micah was drinking. His father had never allowed alcohol of any kind on the premises. It seemed strange that this should have been the direction Micah went to find comfort.

"There has to be a way to help him, Lord," Charlotte whispered.

The year after their fathers had died was supposed to be a time of healing and recovery, but neither had seemed to move forward. Charlotte still hated herself for her angry outburst on that last day, and Micah would forever live with the horrific truth of his father's suicide.

"Charlotte?" her mother called.

"I'm in the office," she answered, going back to the desk.

Mama came into the room and glanced around. "Seems awfully warm in here today. I'll open a window."

"If you like, but I'm finished here. I was just thinking that I might take a ride over to Micah's."

Mama's right brow raised. "I'm too busy to go with you, but you could take one of the boys."

"No, I want to go alone. I know some might think it's inappropriate, but Micah's like family." She knew her feelings for Micah were more romantic than family oriented, but she trusted him to be a complete gentleman. "I need to have a talk with him."

"I suppose that would be all right. It's a lovely day."

"Yes, and I just can't sit here and do nothing. I keep thinking about Micah and how he's let his sadness run his life for too long. You and I have had each other, but he's had no one. Well, of course he's had us when we could spare the time or he would let us come around, but I feel like I should have been there for him more. I let my own grief get the best of me."

"Yes, I agree. I was just thinking that very thing the other night when I was praying for him. He made it so easy to leave him alone. He said he needed the time. Then he went to work helping to skin the dead animals and burn the carcasses. I think he found it easier to focus on dead things than those living. In my own grief, it was easy to comply with his wishes, but leaving him to himself all this time . . . well, I'm afraid he's just managed to sink deeper and deeper. I'm certain we must do something."

"I agree, and I will start with a visit and see where it can go from there. I'd like to get him to come stay with us awhile and help Kit become a better foreman."

"That would be wonderful, but if Rich couldn't do it, I doubt Micah will have any better luck."

Rich Johnson was a widower ranch owner whose property bordered the Aldrich land to the west and a little bit south. Since the death of his wife, Betsy, the previous December, Rich seemed more inclined to stop by just for conversation. Mama had used the opportunities to get him to speak to Kit and try to teach him some needed skills. Rich knew all there was about ranching, but he didn't seem to know any way to get through to Kit.

"I know you're probably right, but something must be done. Roundup will soon be here, and there's going to be a lot of work to do. We need a strong crew. I'll appeal to Micah's good nature and explain that we're in such great need. That way he won't be able to refuse us." Charlotte grabbed her riding gloves.

"Since there wasn't any mail for him in Cheyenne, maybe you could use the excuse of taking him one of the pies Nora made. I'm certain she won't mind when she knows it's for Micah."

"He does love pie. I remember when you made him that rhubarb pie. He ate it all in one day. If I come bearing pie, he surely won't be upset to see me."

Mama laughed. "Micah would never be upset to see you. You know full well he has always tolerated pretty much anything you throw at him."

"Good. Then I'm going to start visiting him regularly and demanding he come by here as well. Once he knows about Kit, he's bound to feel obliged to help. Besides, I need to let him know about his own cows. It's time he took charge of them and decided what he wants to do for the future."

"I just hope we haven't waited too long." Mama looked

sad. "I know it was important we gave him some time to himself, but then we got so busy. . . ."

"But we tried to involve him in our lives." Charlotte couldn't allow herself to believe they'd waited too long—that her own guilt and misery had kept her from him to the point he'd forgotten her importance in his life. At least she hoped—prayed—that she had importance in his life. No matter what, she was determined that Micah would be all right.

Please, God, don't let it be too late.

"I know." Mama's expression reflected what Charlotte was feeling. "It has concerned me as well, especially when I heard he was drinking. Still, I've been praying for him, and I know you have as well. Others are praying also. I must trust that God will see him through."

"I trust that too, but I feel strongly that I'm supposed to do something. Maybe it's because I'm annoyed with Lewis Bradley's demand that I marry him. Maybe it's God's prompting. Whatever the reason, I feel that I cannot ignore this matter."

Charlotte went to her mother and shook her head. "I don't know why, Mama, but I'm so afraid for him. I feel that he needs us. More now than ever before."

Mama reached up and cupped Charlotte's chin. "Then go to him. It's important you heed that prompting." She leaned forward and kissed Charlotte's cheek. "I'll be praying."

The Hamilton ranch house was only about three miles from the Aldrich and Johnson homes. When Micah's father had built the place, he'd chosen the spot to keep with the Aldrich and Johnson plans for the families to be in close proximity in case of trouble. Rich Johnson had bought property first when he'd come to the area in 1867. Charlotte's father had brought the family to Cheyenne in 1869, and he immediately bought the land northeast of Rich. The two hadn't known each other when the Aldrichs had first arrived, but the families became fast friends. When Rich suggested they keep their ranch houses no more than three miles apart in order to help each other, Papa had agreed. Especially when he heard the Indians could still be a problem.

When the Hamiltons came in July of 1870, they had settled on the land east of the Aldrich ranch. Again, the families became close and the Hamiltons also agreed to build their house in that three-mile circle. Over the years, the men and their sons had worked side by side, helping each other with roundups and seeing the families through bad times. While the wives and daughters had encouraged and prayed for each other, and often helped each other in times of need. Each family had prospered and made good on their ranches until the Great Die-Up.

Charlotte so often wished that things could have been different. She would have given any amount of money to be able to turn back time and change the outcome. But, of course, that wasn't possible.

She rode up the overgrown wagon path to Micah's ranch, careful to keep the basket with the pie from slipping off the horn. She paused a moment to survey the house and barnyard. The weeds were overgrown and the grass high in places around the house. The beaten down dirt around the barn and other outbuildings seemed eerily absent of life. The place looked deserted. She worried for only a moment that Micah might not be home, but then remembered he seldom went anywhere.

To the east of the house, she saw Micah's horse, Duke. He was in a small penned area with his head angled through the pole fence to reach the grassy yard. That strengthened her belief that Micah was home. He wouldn't have left without Duke.

She got off her chestnut mount and led him up the overgrown path. She prayed there wouldn't be any snakes in the weeds. With the warmer weather, the rattlers were usually most active in the early morning or evening, but still she kept watch and listened for their warning sound. Reaching the house without issues, she settled Buck in a place where he could casually graze, grabbed the pie from the basket, and then headed to the front door.

Her heart beat a little faster at the thought of seeing Micah again. Since she was little, Charlotte had adored Micah Hamilton. She would follow him and her brother around for hours, sometimes getting into the worst situations. A smile edged her lips. Usually, the problems came via challenges set by the boys. They seemed amused to have her so captivated with them. At least at times. There were plenty of other occasions when they would insist she leave them be. And she did.

Charlotte set the pie on the porch rail, then knocked. When no one came to answer, she knocked again, wincing as the strike smarted her hand. Still no response. She tried the handle. The door easily opened.

"Micah!" she called out. "Micah, it's Charlotte. Are you here?"

She stepped into the darkened house. It smelled musty, and the furniture was covered with sheets, as it had been since the death of Wayman Hamilton. "Micah!"

There was a sound from the back of the house, and in a few moments, a ragged looking Micah appeared. He hadn't shaved or had a haircut in quite some time. His clothes were filthy and hung on him oddly. He'd lost a lot of weight. Charlotte hardly recognized him.

"You look awful," she told him truthfully. "Are you sick?"

He yawned and gave a stretch. "No. I was sleeping."

She shook her head. "Well, you look a sight. When was the

last time you had a haircut?" She held up her hand. "Probably the last time I gave you one, am I right?"

"Yeah, I guess so."

"And did you decide shaving and bathing were too old fashioned for you?" She looked at his scraggly beard and mustache and gave a heavy sigh. "Come on. I'm going to wash your hair and cut it. Where's your soap?"

"Same place as it was before, but you don't need to try to fix me up."

She laughed. "Someone should, so humor me." She went to the kitchen and found there was already water on the stove, but it was far from hot. She smiled to herself. Cold water would wake him up.

Micah had followed her into the kitchen and stood in the doorway watching her. He really did look awful. He'd lost too much weight, and his eyes were sunken with dark circles.

"Go fetch me your ma's scissors and a comb. Oh, and bring a razor and strop too."

Micah just stared at her for a minute, so Charlotte planted her hands on her hips and stared him down. "Did you hear me?"

He finally shrugged and left the room. Within a few minutes, he returned with the requested items. Charlotte placed them on the table and motioned Micah to the sink. "Water's cold, but we'll make do. Bend over."

He didn't so much as flinch when she poured the cold water over his head. Once she had his hair wet, she took up a bar of soap and scrubbed his hair and beard. At one point, Micah gave a sort of moan, but she ignored it. Once his head was clean, she took the dish towel and dried Micah's hair, then handed the towel to him.

"Wipe your face."

"You sure are bossy today." He did as she instructed, however.

"I'm bossy because someone must get you to stop feeling sorry for yourself. I have troubles, and you need to help me."

"What's wrong?" His voice betrayed concern.

She smiled. "That's more like it. I'll tell you all about it as I cut your hair and shave your face. Now sit. Maybe we'll get you looking presentable enough that you can join Mama and me tomorrow. We'd like to drive into Cheyenne for church."

Charlotte worked for over an hour to trim up Micah's hair and beard, and as she did, she explained life at the ranch. She told him of Kit's laziness and lack of understanding. She talked about the four ranch hands they'd hired who were just boys but eager to learn. The problem was, they had no teacher unless Charlotte or her mother had time to show them what to do.

"Kit knows enough to be useful but not to truly be in charge," she explained as she finished shaving his face clean. "I think he lied to Papa when he told him about all his experience in Oklahoma."

"Probably. I never thought much of him."

Charlotte knew that. She didn't know if Micah held something specific against Kit, but he clearly didn't respect the man.

"I need you to come train him." She handed him the towel again. While Micah wiped his face, she continued. "Maybe even just take over for a while."

"No."

There was no discussion. No thoughts or ideas about handling it in a different way. Just a simple no.

"So you won't help me? Help us? Our families swore to assist one another in whatever way we could. Our fathers made a pledge to always be there for each other."

Micah threw the towel down on the table. "My father killed himself, as you well know."

She looked him in the eye. "And now you're doing the

same. Your method is just slower and more painful to watch." She shook her head and crossed the room to leave.

"Are you going?" Micah asked.

Charlotte turned back. "If I stay, you won't like what I have to say. I really don't care that you won't like it, because God knows it needs to be said, but I care too much about you to speak to you in anger."

She went outside and collected Buck. Just before she mounted, Charlotte remembered the pie and marched back up to the porch. When Micah appeared in the open door of his house, Charlotte made her way to him and handed him the dessert. "Mama thought you'd like this." She stomped back to her horse and mounted.

Micah shook his head. "Why are you angry?"

Charlotte studied him for a long moment. "Waste always makes me angry." She gave Buck a nudge in the side and turned for home. "Oh, and go take a bath. You stink."

3

Charlotte's visit haunted Micah long into night. He sat in front of the fireplace wondering if she was right. Was he killing himself in a different manner? He poured some whiskey in his glass and tossed it down as if he'd been a lifelong drinker. The truth was, he'd only started drinking a few weeks after burying his father, and he still hadn't developed a taste for it. But it numbed the pain and blurred the memories.

In so many ways, it seemed as if Dad had died just a short time ago. In other ways, it felt like a lifetime. Micah could still remember Mrs. Aldrich's kind and gentle words. She'd embraced him like a mother and comforted him after he found his father dead. She had urged him to remain silent about the fact that Dad shot himself. They would say he died with her men. Imply, without coming right out and saying, that he froze to death. No one would be the wiser, and no one would question the matter. After all, people and animals were dying all around them.

She had gone with Micah to leave his father's body at the Hamilton ranch before taking her husband and son back to their place. Micah had been so lost in his pain that he didn't even think about the cost to her. Here she'd lost her own husband and son, but instead of thinking about that, she focused on Micah and his father's death. Worrying over what people might say or think if they knew the truth.

"Most Christians don't mean to be cruel," she had told him, *"but so often they are. They say things in such a way to offer their brand of comfort or what they believe to be biblical encouragement, but instead it comes across as painful reminders of failed situations."*

Micah eased back into the rocking chair and shook his head. He hadn't been able to think straight at all after seeing his father dead. Lucille had just taken the situation in hand and told him what to do, and together they had arranged the bodies in the back of the wagon, and that was that.

"Why do you think he did it?" Micah had asked her. *"What did I do wrong?"*

She had put her arm around him. *"You did nothing wrong, Micah. This winter was just too much for him. He just lost his best friend. You did too. I know you loved Frank Jr. as a brother. He felt the same way for you."* She had been so kind, so loving. She hadn't allowed herself even a moment to grieve her own loss.

"Micah, you need to bury your father. It won't be easy because the ground is frozen hard. But we can't take him into town and risk someone learning the truth. It'll seem acceptable to most folks since your mother is buried at the ranch." She had been so matter-of-fact with her instruction that it had gotten Micah through the initial shock.

"Make a set of fires over the ground next to your mother's grave. It will thaw the dirt enough to dig down," she instructed. *"When you can dig a shallow trench, place firewood in the hole, and set that on fire. It will further thaw the ground. Once you get the grave deep enough, wrap your father in a blanket and bury him. Charlotte and I will come tomorrow, and we'll have*

a little ceremony." She had looked him in the eye. *"Do you understand?"*

In that moment, Micah realized she was trying to ascertain if he understood the entire matter. Did he understand that they had to keep the reason for his father's death a secret? Did he comprehend the reason he needed to take responsibility for the burial? Was her instruction clear enough to reach through his pain-filled thoughts?

"I understood," he murmured, gazing at the dancing flames in the hearth.

What he didn't understand to this day was why his father had given up on living. Yes, they had lost much of their herd. Yes, he had refused to sell off livestock when Frank Sr. had shared Lucille's concerns for the coming winter. He had ignored all her suggestions, even commenting to Micah that he didn't believe in signs. He'd made a mistake that cost them a great deal of money. But that wasn't a good reason to end his life. They owned the ranch free and clear and had enough money in the bank they could get by. Not only that, but some of the herd had lived and would need their care.

Micah knew they'd both been at a loss when his mother had died. For days, even weeks afterward, they were in a stupor trying to figure out what to do next. Neither one could understand how a loving God would take her away from them. They shared the misery, watching, waiting, wondering. Mrs. Aldrich and Charlotte were wonderful to help them through. Especially Mrs. Aldrich, who came to manage a variety of household duties and to have Micah and his father over for dinner several times a week. But over the years, that had ended. They couldn't have expected her to take care of them forever.

The death of his mother had changed everything, however. Dad had never recovered from the loss, and his demeanor and plans seemed to fall apart. Micah understood, because his own sadness was great.

Often in the morning, when Micah first awoke, he wouldn't remember that she was gone. His first thoughts would be of what she might have made for breakfast, and then the hard truth would settle in, and he'd realize she was dead, and the pain would come again as if it were the first moments after learning she had passed.

But that had been six years ago. And while Micah still missed her and knew Dad did as well, it wasn't a good reason for Micah's father to give up on life. Was it?

He supposed Dad just felt overwhelmed by everything. In that moment of finding his friend dead, Dad must have been unable to deal with the aspect of one more thing going wrong. He'd already seen that large numbers of cattle were dead, and he'd been so angry at being unable to prevent the loss.

But Dad had never been one to just give up. Micah supposed that was what confused him the most. And that God had allowed for it was even more baffling. Why hadn't God prevented it? Why hadn't He let Micah get back before his father was to the point of pulling the trigger?

"You could have stopped it from happening," Micah said, looking upward. "But You left him alone to face all that was troubling him. Why? Why wouldn't You stop him?"

Micah got up and poured himself another drink. It wouldn't take long for the whiskey to numb him to a place where he could crawl into bed and sleep away the haunting memories and questions. He might have a new haircut and shave, but he still had the same unkempt soul and broken heart.

He had failed somehow. He had failed Dad and wasn't enough of what he needed. Otherwise, he would have had the strength to go on. There was something Micah hadn't done right. Some way in which he had forsaken his father, just as God had.

A small voice protested such thinking, but Micah found the whiskey hushed that objection. Just a few more glasses and it wouldn't matter anymore. Another couple of drinks and he wouldn't hear any of the accusations in his head.

Charlotte woke up early on Sunday morning. It wasn't a pleasant awakening, but one that harkened from nightmares. She sat up sweating, feeling a sense of dread and regret. In her sleep she had been fighting with her father again. It was always the same. Never a dream of when they had been happy together—of Papa teaching her to ride her horse or to rope a calf. Never a vision of his pride in her, just his regret for her not doing what he'd asked of her.

The room was already warm, and Charlotte pushed back her sheet, anxious to rid herself of the extra heat. She got up and went to the open window. Flies buzzed around her as they made their way in and out of the house.

Gazing out across the yard, Charlotte noted the few trees they had nurtured to maturity over the years. Mama had chosen sturdy cottonwoods and honey locusts. Charlotte easily remembered all the years of carrying water to the young trees. The women in Cheyenne had a committee who pushed for women throughout the area to plant trees on the vast prairie. There had been so few trees, and what were there were mostly scrub and juniper. The fierce winds were hard on trees, and nothing much grew without great protection. However, with a little care and ingenuity, the women of Cheyenne and elsewhere had managed to cultivate some very nice shade trees. They weren't all that plentiful, but they were deeply appreciated.

Papa had loved the trees and even went so far as to bring Mama several oak tree plants when he went on a trip to Kansas City. Mama had worked hard to keep them alive, but only one had made it. Even now it was dwarfed by the older cottonwoods. But she still had hope it would continue to survive. Mama was that way. She was always the one to keep believing, even when the rest of them were tired and drained of hope.

Mama had been certain Papa would change his mind about Lewis Bradley and had encouraged Charlotte to pray for him to see the truth. But Charlotte found it impossible to believe that even God could change her father's mind once it was set on a matter. Thinking that way was the reason she had been so outspoken the day he'd died. Now her harsh and hateful words haunted her dreams and left Charlotte feeling that her sins were too terrible to be forgiven.

"I should never have argued with you, Papa. I hate myself for the things I said. Oh, how I wish I could take it all back." Tears blurred her vision.

Charlotte wiped her eyes with the back of her nightgown sleeve. So many times she had begged God to forgive her and to let Papa know that she wouldn't have really stopped talking to him. She would never have forsaken him even if he had forced her to marry Lewis Bradley. But why had it been so important to him? He had never said. Oh, he gave her the excuse that he wanted her to have a better life than her mother, but there had to be more to it than that. Lewis wouldn't answer her on the matter either. Charlotte had asked more than once, but neither man would explain. They treated her like a child, telling her it was business and nothing she needed to concern herself with. Yet it did concern her. It was entangled around her like a captive web. It would alter the rest of her life.

A knock sounded on her door, and Charlotte had no chance to answer before Mama opened it and looked inside.

"Oh, good. You're already . . ." Her words trailed off. "What's wrong? Why are you crying?" Mama came to her and reached up to touch her damp cheek. "Don't you think you should tell me what's wrong? This isn't the first time I've found you in tears, and while this last year has been hard on both of us, I thought things were getting better. Instead, you seem to be even more lost in your sorrow."

Charlotte sighed and embraced her mother. With her head on Mama's shoulder, Charlotte felt like a little girl again, and the tears flowed anew.

"Oh, I'm sorry, Mama. I don't mean to cry." Charlotte straightened and wiped her face. "I'm all right. Really, I am."

Her mother gave her a thoughtful and tender look. "I'm not leaving until you tell me what has you so sad." She went to the bed and sat down. Her gaze never left Charlotte.

"I suppose it is time to just admit my sins," Charlotte said, coming to where her mother sat. "God knows I've begged for forgiveness enough."

"Goodness, Charlotte, whatever could you have done that was so terrible?"

Charlotte swallowed the lump in her throat. "I was hateful and mean to Papa. The last time we spoke—the very last moment of our time together on earth—I was absolutely vile to him." Charlotte shook her head. "I told him if he forced me to marry Lewis, I would never speak to him again, and I'd have nothing more to do with him. Those were my parting words, and I cannot forgive myself. It haunts my sleep to this day. Papa died thinking I hated him."

"Oh, sweetheart. Come sit with me." Mama patted the mattress beside her.

Charlotte sat and felt the warmth of Mama's arms go around her. "Your father knew you loved him. He did. He loved you so dearly."

"I know he did. He just wanted good things for me. And

sometimes when I remember how I acted, I can't help but think that maybe the only way I can be forgiven is to just marry Lewis Bradley."

"No!"

Mama's emphatic exclamation caused Charlotte to straighten. Charlotte met her mother's gaze. Mama shook her head.

"That is not what you need to do for forgiveness. God doesn't work that way. Besides that, I'm not sure that forgiveness is exactly needed. You were honest with your father, and he was being quite unreasonable. I told him as much, and I still believe that in time he would have seen the error of his ways. I don't think he would have forced you to go through with the wedding."

"But he wanted it so much. There had to be a reason." Charlotte settled back and wiped her eyes again with her sleeve.

"Your father had some sort of business arrangement with Mr. Bradley. I don't know the details, and he wouldn't explain any of it to me. Most importantly, I know he wanted a better life for you. He worried about how hard I worked and didn't want his daughter to find herself in the same position."

"I told him I loved the ranch and life here was important to me. I wanted to marry a rancher and continue with the life that I loved. But he said it was too hard—too much. That he hated that you had always had to work so hard."

Mama closed her eyes for a moment and nodded. "He never understood that I enjoyed it. I was a part of something I loved. Just like you." She opened her eyes and met Charlotte's gaze. "But for whatever reason, your father could never understand that or believe it as truth."

"I told him the idea of being a grand lady in silks and satins hosting tea parties and showing off my stately home was something I considered appalling." Charlotte couldn't even fathom finding enjoyment from sitting and painting china or embroidering handkerchiefs.

"He told me I would come to enjoy it in time. I have no idea why he believed that." Charlotte got up from the bed and walked back to the open window. "He thought I needed a grand mansion in the wealthiest neighborhood of Cheyenne. He saw me living with servants and everything money could buy, when all I ever wanted was this." She looked out at the open land beyond the yard. "He never understood that I loved this place as much as Frank Jr. did."

"No, I don't suppose he did," Mama said, joining her at the window. "And now he's gone, and Frank Jr. is too. And the ranch is yours, or will be."

"Oh, Mama, it's our home. It's where we both have such special memories. More good than bad."

"I agree, but I want you to know that even if you disagreed with your father and said hurtful things, he's with Jesus now and knows the truth. You've asked for forgiveness. I think it's time you accepted it and move forward. Any sin, if sin was involved, was nailed to the cross long ago. You asked Jesus to be your Savior and forgive you of your sins, and He did. He forgave all of your sins at the cross. Keep seeking Him, Charlotte. Seek to love as He loved. To be merciful and kind, as He was. Not to earn your salvation, for that has already been freely given through His grace, but rather to become more like Him."

A sense of peace washed over Charlotte. She heard the truth of her mother's words and knew without a doubt that she was forgiven. She even felt certain that somehow Papa knew her heart was never against him but rather opposed to marrying a man she didn't love.

She hugged her mother close and sighed. What a sense of freedom. It was as if a great weight had been lifted. Perhaps now the nightmares would stop once and for all.

"Now, you'd better get dressed. We're going to need to leave pretty soon if we want to get to church on time."

"Mrs. Aldrich!" Nora called from downstairs.

Charlotte let go of her mother and followed her to the bedroom door. Mother walked out into the hall.

"What is it, Nora?"

"One of the hands has gotten himself hurt. Thrown from his horse and he's bleeding—head wound."

Mama looked back at Charlotte. "I don't suppose we'll be able to go to church after all. It seems I must tend a head wound."

"I'll get dressed and be right down to help. You might have to stitch him up, and you know how badly head wounds bleed."

Her mother nodded and smiled. "You really are very good at this life. Your father would have seen that eventually."

4

Lucille Aldrich had always been a woman of determination. Even as a child she remembered overhearing her mother and grandmother talk about how out of all the children in the family, Lucille was the one who could be counted on to get a thing done.

"When she sets her mind to a notion," Grandmother Brewster had declared, *"she sees the matter through to the completion."*

For Lucille, she figured it was a trait of being the youngest of eight and always last to the trough, as her father used to say. Her seven brothers and sisters were always ahead of her in getting their needs known, in having first pick, and in garnering the most attention. Lucille had always felt that if she didn't see a matter through on her own, no one else was going to concern themselves with it.

Grandmother had once confided that she was the same way. "I know why you do what you do, Lucy. I, too, was the youngest child. But you must never be a person who fails to listen to reason and wise counsel. The Bible says that God would rather have our obedience than our sacrifice, so you must always heed that and do what is right."

And she had made that a priority in her life. Seeking God's

will had been her first desire, and once she knew it for certain, then obedience became the goal. There were no halfhearted attempts at accomplishments. She was determined to do what God required of her, and often that meant doing what others commanded. Of course, she could also stubbornly stand her own ground when she knew something wasn't wise or good. Lucille's mother had always told her that a person couldn't just say they believed in the Word of God—they had to prove it daily in their actions. Lucille had worked her hardest to be a living example of Jesus's command to first love God with all your heart and soul and mind, and second to love others as yourself. It was one of the reasons she'd invited Micah Hamilton to join them for dinner. She'd been praying about what God would have her do to love others, and Micah constantly came to mind.

Now that he sat across from her, she knew why. He was a mere shadow of the man he'd once been. Despite Charlotte having cut his hair and shaved him, Micah looked nothing like the strong and healthy young man he'd been over a year ago.

Oh, Lord, I pray I didn't wait too long to reach out to him.

"Micah, you need another helping of fried chicken." She extended the platter, and Micah quickly took hold.

"Yes, ma'am. I won't argue with you on that. I've been eating nothing but beans and corn bread for so long that chicken is like a heavenly feast. All of the food is truly delicious."

"I'm glad you accepted our invitation," Lucille countered.

Micah gave her a hint of a smile. "Well, it wasn't exactly an invitation as much as a command."

Lucille laughed and gave a little shrug. "I suppose it's my motherly temperament. I'm used to bossing Charlotte around."

Charlotte shook her head. "Mama is never bossy." She handed Micah the biscuits. "Would you care for another of these? Nora's biscuits are as light as any you'll ever have. If you're ever around for breakfast you can sample them with her sausage gravy. It's absolutely divine."

Lucille didn't miss the way her daughter looked at Micah. She'd had feelings for Micah since she'd first met him. Charlotte was six years his junior, but even at the age of four, she had been completely captivated by him. Lucille could still remember her daughter following Micah and Frank Jr. around the ranch, begging them to take her with them. The boys had been tolerant for the most part. They often took time to include Charlotte in their work or games. Lucille had always rewarded them in one way or another for their kindness to Charlotte.

"I blame myself," Lucille began again. "I should never have left you alone to waste away. I'm sure you haven't eaten a decent meal since . . ." She hated to bring up the death of his father. She let the matter drop and pushed on. "From now on, I want you to join us each evening for supper. Unless of course you have somewhere else you need to be."

"I . . . couldn't let you do that. I don't want to be a bother to anyone, and . . . well, I don't much feel like being company to anyone." He barely met her eyes as he gazed up from his meal.

"I understand how you feel, but it's been a year and three months, and we must endeavor to press forward." She didn't bother to detail what they were pressing forward from. Micah knew. They all did.

"Besides, we need your help, Micah." This came from Charlotte. "I've already told you that Kit needs help. He doesn't know what he's doing most of the time. Last year, if it hadn't been for Rich Johnson taking over the roundup, none of the calves would have been taken care of. This year we need you to help as well, and Kit desperately needs someone who knows what they're doing to educate him. Mother and I feel confident that if we pool our resources and work together, we can finish off well this year. All of us."

"I told you, no. I don't want to teach Kit Hendricks anything. The man failed you when you needed him most. If he'd ridden out with us, then I could have stayed with my father and sent Kit back to get the wagon. And if he'd been any kind of a man, he would have made those cowhands go out looking for your men after they'd been gone an hour."

"So you blame Kit for their deaths?" Lucille asked.

"I do. He could have done more. Should have done more."

"I suppose that's one way of looking at it. Of course, Frank told him not to leave the ranch because Charlotte and I and Nora would be left alone. I always saw it as him obeying his boss's orders. As well as mine. I asked him to stay put, and he did."

Micah straightened and looked as though he might speak, then lowered his head and went back to eating.

"Micah, there are all sorts of things that might have been done differently. I don't think Kit's to blame, however. You might as well blame me."

"You?" Micah's head snapped back up. "You aren't to blame."

"I am as much as Kit is. I could have ordered him and the others to go looking for my guys sooner. Six hours was much too long to wait. I suppose I was hopeful they were waiting out the storm somewhere. They'd had similar experiences, and I knew they were capable. So if you must blame someone . . . blame me."

Micah shook his head. "I could never blame you. You paid the biggest price of us all."

"It wasn't a competition of loss, Micah."

For several minutes they ate in silence while the words seemed to hang over them. Lucille was determined to help Micah let go of the guilt he held for himself.

"No matter what any of us might have done differently, I think the outcome would have been the same. We can assign blame or grace, Micah. I choose grace, and I'm not too proud to say, I especially assign it to myself." She smiled. "In fact, I'm very generous in giving myself grace."

"Again, I don't see where you are to blame in any way. You and Charlotte had no way of knowing what had happened. You couldn't very well mount horses and go look for the men."

"And why not?" Lucille asked as if offended. "I could ride and track better than Kit and those boys who were here."

Charlotte surprised her by giving a giggle. "Oh, Mama, a tree stump could have ridden and tracked better than they could."

Lucille smiled. "I tend to agree with you. Micah, all I'm saying is I could have taken the dogs and gone in search. I could have forced those boys to go with me. There are so many things I could have done, and if I live my life thinking of those things, I will go down the same path you have."

His expression betrayed momentary guilt, and he looked away before she could finish.

"But even sitting here at the same table we all used to share—seeing their empty chairs and knowing we'll never have them here with us again . . ." His words faded into silence.

He was right. There were days when those empty chairs haunted her. Nights when her bed offered no comfort. The loss of her husband was almost more than she could bear at times, but there was no way to turn back time. Somehow, they all had to move forward.

"Micah, you must let go of regret. Our sorrow will be with us always, to some degree or another. In time, it will be less, but it will never go away altogether because we loved the men we lost. They were a very important part of our lives.

You and Charlotte and I will always share this grief . . . if we let one another. And I can tell you that sharing it is much better than trying to bear it alone."

Micah said nothing for a moment. Lucille thought she saw a hint of the battle that must be raging inside of him reflected in his distant gaze.

Finally, he nodded and looked her in the eye. "I'll go talk to Kit for you after we finish eating."

Charlotte helped her mother gather the dishes after Micah left to go speak to Kit. She was so very grateful that Mama had been able to reach him. "I see why you asked Nora not to eat with us this evening. Micah probably wouldn't have felt open enough to speak if she'd been here."

"Yes, that was my thought." Mama paused. "I know you care about him deeply."

Mama's words surprised her, but rather than shy away from them, Charlotte jumped right in. "I love him. I intend to marry him. I have since I was four years old."

Mama nodded. "I know. But go slow, Charlotte. Be gentle. He's still very wounded and needs time to heal."

When Charlotte went in search of Micah nearly twenty minutes later, she was still thinking of what her mother had said. Charlotte had been so hard on him Saturday, and the guilt of that was overwhelming her conscience.

Micah was saddling Duke when she finally found him. He'd cleaned up to come see them, and although his clothes were a bit big on him, Charlotte thought he'd never been more handsome.

"Can you give me a minute before you go?"

Micah looked up from tightening the cinch. "Sure. What do you need?"

Charlotte leaned against the fence. "I wanted to apologize."

"For what?"

She drew a deep breath. "I was rather hard on you when I came to see you the other day. I should have been kinder."

Micah's expression softened a bit. His blue eyes seemed to look into her soul, and Charlotte couldn't help but feel all aflutter.

"You weren't unkind. You were honest. I appreciate that more than I do kindness."

"Still, I could have been gentler in the telling." She couldn't seem to fight the tears that came to her eyes. "It's just been hard, and seeing you like that, knowing you were hurting like I was . . . well . . ." She sniffed back the tears and looked to the ground. "I guess it just stirred things up in me. Guilt and remorse."

"Guilt about what . . . Charlotte?"

Micah speaking her name so softly was her undoing. Charlotte buried her face in her hands and wept. She felt Micah's arms go around her and pull her close. This she hadn't expected, but it felt so right. She cried even more. How she longed for them to be together—to marry and have a family of their own—to bear all the problems of life as one.

Micah hadn't anticipated Charlotte's tears, nor his response to them. Still, he couldn't stop himself from offering her comfort, and holding her felt like the right thing to do. He'd been doing this since she was a little girl. If Frank Jr. wasn't around and she got hurt, it was Micah who tried to reassure her. Micah had always felt a special bond to that little girl.

But she wasn't a little girl anymore. In fact, she was clearly a woman full grown, and the very thought of holding her was bringing to mind feelings that he'd just as soon ignore.

"Why do you feel guilty, Charlotte?" he whispered against her ear.

She didn't look up or answer. She just kept crying, and Micah found the stone walls he'd put around his heart begin to crumble a bit. For all the years he'd known her, Charlotte was never one to go off in tears. She had never been a crybaby. In fact, short of her father's funeral, Micah only seen her cry a handful of times. Even when she'd fallen off her horse as a little girl, she had squared her shoulders and gotten back on without tears.

He stroked her back, not knowing what else to do. Her long blond curls had been tied with a ribbon, and Micah found himself mesmerized by the way her hair entwined around his fingers. It was soft and curly. She'd always had curly hair. When she was little, she often left it down. What a mess it could be after the Wyoming wind gusted up. He remembered playing checkers with Frank Jr. and seeing Charlotte sitting in front of the fireplace while her mother worked to untangle the mass.

Without warning, she looked up and stepped back. "I'm so sorry, Micah. I didn't mean to fall apart like that. It hasn't been easy this last year."

"No. No, it hasn't."

"Even just seeing you so thin and looking so sad . . . Well, I'm sorry for the way I acted on Saturday and now. We need to treat each other gently, Mama said."

"Like I told you, I'd rather you be honest with me."

She nodded. "I know I can trust you with my heart. I can be honest with you, and you won't betray me."

Micah met her gaze. "Of course not. I'd never betray your trust. Now, tell me why you feel guilty."

"Papa. I wasn't kind to him that last day. We argued."

"Argued about what?"

"His plans for me to marry Lewis Bradley."

Micah had heard from Frank Jr. that his father intended for Charlotte to marry Lewis Bradley. Neither of them thought it was a good idea. Bradley wasn't the kind of man either of them thought worthy of Charlotte. Frank Jr. had heard that he was dishonest in some of his business dealings, and Micah had never cared for the way Bradley treated those he considered beneath him.

"I told Papa I wouldn't marry him—that I didn't love him and never would. Papa wouldn't listen to me. He said that I had to marry him—that it was important to him and that in time I would learn to love Lewis. But I knew better. I told him if he forced me to marry Lewis, I'd never speak to him again or have anything more to do with him." Her eyes dampened again. "Those were my last words to him.

"Mama told me that Papa knew I loved him. I loved him so dearly. I hated to think of him dying and wondering if I would even care."

"I agree with your mother. He knew the truth. I don't know why a father would ever try to force his daughter to marry someone like Lewis Bradley, especially knowing you didn't love him."

"He said it was because he wanted a better life for me. He didn't want me to be a rancher's wife because he'd seen how hard that life was on Mama. But Mama loves the ranch. She loves the work she does here. Papa could never quite see that."

"And what about you?"

Charlotte smiled. "I love it too. When Mama and Papa sent me to Denver, I was so lonely for it and all of you. They worked on me day and night to teach me to be a great lady, but all I wanted was to come home and ride Buck and help with roundup. I hated tea parties. I'd rather drink coffee than tea."

Micah smiled. He could just imagine Charlotte all dressed up and serving tea. There was something about her comments, however, that made him look at her with different eyes. She had always been Frank Jr.'s little sister. Nothing more or less. Now, however, a grown woman stood in her shoes. A very beautiful grown woman. And a little bit ago, she'd been in his arms. He could still feel her there.

"Mama said that she believes Papa is with Jesus, and that Jesus has let him know that I love him. I pray that's so. I like to think of Papa happy in eternity, not sad and upset because his only daughter rejected him."

"At least you know he's with Jesus," Micah said, feeling an aching in his heart. He couldn't very well confess to her his deepest fears regarding his own father. Some in the church were pretty clear about what they thought happened to folks who killed themselves.

5

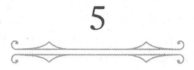

Charlotte loved being back in church. She lifted her soprano voice to join in with the others as they sang the doxology to close out the service.

"'Praise Father, Son, and Holy Ghost. Amen.'"

"Now take God's love with you as you go and spread it along the way so that others may know Him," the pastor declared. "You are dismissed."

Charlotte smiled and turned to her mother, but already Lewis Bradley was somehow at her side.

"I must speak with you, Charlotte. Please allow me a few minutes of your time."

Charlotte drew in a deep breath and turned to face him. "Very well. What is it you need to say?"

"Come with me outside. Away from the others." He took hold of her elbow.

Charlotte nodded. "Mama, I'm going to step out to the wagon and speak with Lewis. I'll be ready to leave when you are."

Her mother gave her a sympathetic smile. "I won't be long."

Charlotte turned back to Lewis. "Please lead the way."

He all but pulled her through the congregation and out the doors. Charlotte waved to this person and that and even managed to bid a couple of old friends good day, but Lewis wasn't pausing for even a moment now that he had her in hand.

"What is so important that you can't even allow me time with my friends?" she asked.

Lewis slowed their walk and cleared his throat. "The time for delays is over, Charlotte. I know that you needed time to mourn your father and brother, but it's been well over a year. I want us to announce our engagement and move forward toward setting the wedding date."

They had reached the Aldrich Cattle Company wagon, and Charlotte reached out to take hold of the wooden side. The day was quite warm, and the church had been stuffy despite the open windows. A bit of a breeze blew, and for a moment she lifted her face to feel the air.

"That is a blessed breeze," she murmured.

"Charlotte, please. You must listen to me."

She lowered her gaze and nodded. "I am listening and have been listening. You are the one who clearly has failed to hear. I am not in love with you, Mr. Bradley. I have never been in love with you. Frankly, the very idea of marriage to you has been the source of much pain and suffering on my part. I'm sure you're a good man with great qualities to offer some young woman, but it is not me. I do not know how to make this clearer."

Lewis's eyes narrowed. "Charlotte, you must hear what I have to say. Your father promised me that we would be married. I know you don't love me, but you will come to in time. I feel confident about that. Beyond love, however, your father recognized the importance of sound investments and business arrangements. He knew that our joining together would unite two families of wealth and power to form a formidable empire."

Charlotte shook her head. "But I am not interested in forming an empire, Mr. Bradley. Not with you. Not with anyone. Mama and I are content to rebuild our herd and begin a new era for the Aldrich Cattle Company. I want no more responsibilities than those of my ranch. To try and split my time between that and the city would be disastrous. The ranch demands my time and attention, and you would expect a wife to remain in Cheyenne caring for you and Victoria. And that is a reasonable request. But I cannot give it, and you must understand that any business dealings or plans you had with Papa ended with his death."

"No, that's not the way business works. You are obligated to fulfill those plans, Charlotte. Not only because of the legalities of written agreements and financial investments—although I had given your father a great deal of money to invest in the cattle, and he had promised me a large dowry—but also there's the matter of his desires for you. Your father loved you and wanted the very best for your future."

Charlotte was unable to hide her frown. She didn't need the reminder of what her father planned for her future.

"I can see that you understand what I'm saying. Your expression suggests that you know you are disappointing him."

"You know nothing of me, Lewis." She dropped all formalities in hopes that he would hear the sincerity in her words. "I do not wish to hurt you nor to cause damage to your investment. I realize you consider us engaged, but I do not. Nor will I, so please stop pestering me about marriage. Stop telling people that we are betrothed.

"Papa had his plans, that much is true. But he is dead, and so are those plans. If there are legalities that need to be ironed out, please go see our lawyer."

She glanced over her shoulder. Where was Mama? She ignored Lewis and climbed up onto the wagon seat before he could react. Looking down, Charlotte couldn't even muster the tiniest bit of sympathy for the man. There was only the feeling that something wasn't quite right. She didn't know what it was, but she felt that way every time he came around.

He reached up, but Charlotte pulled back. "Restrain yourself, Mr. Bradley. We are at church."

"Charlotte, you can't leave things this way."

Mama came out of the church and was making her way to the wagon now. Charlotte breathed a sigh of relief. She took up the lines but didn't release the brake.

"Well, I hope you two have finished with your conversation," Mama said, looking to Lewis.

He started to say something, but Mama continued. "Where is your aunt and little daughter this fine Sunday?"

"Victoria wasn't feeling well. Aunt Agnes felt it best they remain home," he replied, looking away.

"Would you help me up, please?"

Charlotte knew he could hardly refuse. "I would like to extend an invitation to my home for luncheon. It would be such a pleasure to host you both. Our cook is making a beef roast," he said.

Once Mama was seated, Charlotte released the brake. "I'm afraid we can't."

"We're needed at home, Mr. Bradley, but thank you for the invitation," Mama replied.

Charlotte slapped the lines lightly and urged the horses forward. "Good day, Mr. Bradley," she called over her shoulder.

"Goodness, he seemed quite unhappy." Her mother gave her a curious look.

Charlotte shrugged and watched the traffic as she crossed the road. "He won't take no for an answer. He told me that he and Papa had financial arrangements and agreements that demand our marriage go through. That money exchanged hands, and more money needs to be exchanged. I made it quite clear that I had no intention of ever marrying him. I told him if there were legal contracts and such involved to go see our lawyer. I hope he'll accept my words and stop pestering us now."

"And if he doesn't?" Mama asked, looking at Charlotte with one brow raised.

"I honestly don't know. He doesn't seem to understand that I will never marry him. He doesn't understand that I love another. Of course, I've never really made that the point of my rejecting him. Perhaps I should. Maybe I'll just tell him that I'm going to marry Micah."

"Maybe you should let Micah know about that first," Mama said, chuckling. "It seems only fair."

Lewis hated the fact that he couldn't intimidate Charlotte Aldrich as he had his first wife. Willa would have swooned at such a stern discussion, but it only seemed to push forward Charlotte's fixed stance and determination. A part of him found that intriguing, almost exciting. In financial dealings with a man, it would have given him a sort of giddy anticipation of what he could accomplish. With Charlotte Aldrich, however, there was a finality that he was unwilling to accept.

He frowned and began the walk home. There had to be a way to reach her. He had found it impossible to woo her. In the past, he'd had little difficulty with women. With his dark hair and eyes, he had what some called a constant look of passion. He rather liked that analogy. He credited his Italian and Armenian ancestors who, although several generations past, had handed down the blend of external characteristics that came together to make Lewis Bradley one of the handsomest men in Cheyenne. So why couldn't he win over Charlotte Aldrich?

He was charming enough. He knew women were fascinated with him and his mannerisms. He'd had no trouble in his youth or bachelor days back east. He was well-to-do, for all that Charlotte knew, so it wasn't a matter of money that kept her from accepting his proposal. Lewis picked up his pace as he crossed the street and headed up Ferguson.

So what was holding her off?

It wasn't like there was someone else in her life. He knew from her father that there had been quite a few men asking to court her, but Charlotte had little or no interest. Perhaps she felt obligated to her mother now that her father and brother were dead.

That was a good possibility. Charlotte was a kind, Christian woman, as he often heard people say. Perhaps she felt that it was her obligation to care for her mother. It was certainly something to consider. Maybe he should take up the matter with Mrs. Aldrich and explain to her that he had more than enough room for her to live with them. Having his mother-in-law in residence wasn't his desire, but if it resolved the situation, then he was happy to oblige. In time, he could always figure out a better arrangement. After they were wed, Charlotte would have no choice but to adhere to his commands. Even if it meant sending her mother elsewhere.

He knew, too, that living on the ranch was something Charlotte didn't want to give up. It was one of the reasons he had been prompted to buy rangeland. Frank Sr. had convinced him that it was a good investment. There had even been the promise of a starter herd once he and Charlotte married, but then that hideous winter had hit them and destroyed so much.

Lewis had purchased quite a few bred heifers in the fall of '86 after purchasing the ranchland. He had run his cattle on the open range with the Aldrich, Johnson, and Hamilton beasts. Mrs. Aldrich gave everyone the advice to sell off as many animals as possible. She believed something in the signs of nature that convinced her the winter would be bad. He wished he'd listened, but pride wouldn't allow him to take the directive of a woman. Most of the men in the county felt the same way. And most of the men, including him, suffered the loss for not listening.

When the winter came, all was lost. Lewis's animals were young and not yet fat enough to endure the devastation. They had died early on. When all was said and done, Lewis had no choice but to sell out, and in doing so, he took the biggest loss yet. The price per acre had dropped considerably since so many were desperate to get rid of their lands. He sold his land for pennies on the dollar and greatly depleted his fortune.

The Aldrich family had done all right given Lucille's directions, and now they sat on plenty of money and were rebuilding their herds, while others had to sell out and move on. It might be wise to keep his hand in that.

Lewis supposed it might be possible that Charlotte and Victoria could live at the ranch while he resided most of the week in town. As a lawyer he needed to be where the action was and where people could readily find him. He hated that he had to depend on that resource at all, but it was necessary. Thankfully, he had a great reputation as an attorney and had spread the word that he loved the law. In the West, no one thought it odd that a wealthy man enjoyed continuous work rather than sitting idle like a grand duke or king. Lewis had been instrumental in several lucrative negotiations, and people recognized that he was quite skilled. There was even talk about him entering the political arena once they were finally a state.

But a politician needed his family close at hand to show off and prove to the conservative-natured folks that he had their best interests at heart. He could hardly allow Charlotte to live away from him out on her family's ranch. How would that look?

It was a great frustration that she wasn't a more obedient female. Her father had warned him that she was opinioned and educated. The finishing school in Denver had prided themselves on the young ladies learning about a variety of things that would help them to be better wives. Charlotte had told him that they had worked to help their students understand, for example, elements related to government and business. It all seemed absurd to him. Charlotte said it was taught so that wives could discuss these matters with their husbands, but Lewis couldn't imagine ever wanting to have such a conversation with a woman. As far as he was concerned, the less conversation between a man and his wife, the better.

Willa had been properly trained in such matters. She didn't even discuss the household, except on rare occasions when Lewis asked her a direct question. Lewis had no idea what Willa did with her time, and he didn't care. She stayed out of his way and caused him no trouble and that was all he asked of her. Well, that and to bear him sons. Which she hadn't done.

A well-run household with an obedient wife and well-behaved children was a good example of a man being able to manage not only his industry but his home. There were those who credited the wife with such management, but men of his ilk knew the truth of it. Nothing ran properly without a man's involvement.

As he approached his three-story brick house, Lewis couldn't help but admire the gardens and walkway. The gardeners had been quite faithful. They had even coaxed life into a few trees, although they weren't all that big. The flower beds and lawn, however, were remarkable, as many people often told him.

Perhaps his house wasn't quite as grand as that of Joseph Carey or Max Idleman. The latter was rumored to have spent some fifty-five thousand dollars to create his three-story mansion, complete with a third-floor ballroom. Lewis had been inside each of those magnificent dwellings and after each visit had found ways to improve his own residence. He was always careful to listen and learn what was considered the best in furnishings and fixtures. Over the years, his house had continued to improve. In time, he'd have a place every bit as grand as Idleman had.

Lewis took great pride in that and couldn't for the life of him understand why Charlotte wouldn't also see the value in what he could give her. If she'd only give him a chance, Lewis could show her a much better life than the one she had on the ranch.

The house was surprisingly quiet when he entered. The butler came and took his hat. Lewis motioned his head toward the grand staircase. "Rogers, where is Aunt Agnes?"

"In the nursery, sir."

Lewis nodded and started up the stairs. He paused halfway up. "Oh, tell the cook I've returned. I'll take a tray in my office. I have work to do."

"Very good, sir."

Lewis proceeded up the stairs and went in search of his aunt. He hated visiting the nursery, but at the moment it seemed the quickest solution.

Willa had asked for the nursery to be placed in the far west wing when they had built the house. Lewis's bedroom had been at the extreme opposite end of the east wing, and Willa's bedroom had attached to his. When she had been nearly ready to deliver Victoria, she had arranged for the bedroom adjoining the nursery to be opened for her in order that there be no disturbance of Lewis's sleep should she go into labor.

Lewis paused in front of that bedroom door. It was here Willa had died shortly after giving life to their daughter. The doctor said she had lost too much blood and was simply not strong enough to survive. Lewis felt regret at her passing, but whether for the loss of his beloved wife or simply the complications she'd left him with, he couldn't be sure.

Thank goodness there was Aunt Agnes. When Lewis's grandmother had died just the year before Victoria's birth, the question of what to do with the spinster aunt had caused quite a stir among remaining relatives. She had never married, remaining at home to care for her aging parents. Willa had insisted the older woman come and live with them. She had reminded Lewis that Agnes was nearing her fiftieth year and that she had no means of making her way in the world. She further pressed that Agnes could be of great benefit to them in helping with the children who were sure to come. Lewis was finally motivated by the thought of free labor.

He went ahead to the nursery and opened the door. Victoria was in a wooden high chair, and Aunt Agnes was spooning something into her mouth.

"I'm home," Lewis said, giving his aunt a slight nod. "How's she feeling?"

"Still sniffling," Aunt Agnes replied. "But no sign of fever. Perhaps it's the new growth of summer vegetation that's irritating her breathing."

Lewis honestly didn't care. He was only asking out of obligation. "I stopped by to let you know that I'll be working in my office. Taking lunch there as well."

His aunt, a very plain-looking woman with graying hair, gave him a nod and refocused her gaze on the almost two-year-old beside her. She was never one for much conversation, which Lewis appreciated. He was even happier to find no reprimand for working on the Sabbath as his father might have given. Apparently, his father's younger sister was far less religious in nature.

"If you need me, you know where to find me."

"Thank you for letting me know," she told him, then gave Victoria another spoonful of food. "I'll endeavor to keep her quiet."

He nodded and headed down the hall to his bedroom, tearing at his tie as he went. His valet awaited him, anticipating his every need. This was the way it should be in every area of his life. So why wasn't it? Why was it so impossible to force one woman to the altar?

It took only a moment in his own suite of rooms to change into something less formal before going back downstairs. Victoria and Agnes were all but forgotten, while Charlotte Aldrich was a festering wound.

In his office, he was pleased to find that the staff had already furnished a tray of several selections for his dining enjoyment, including the delectable roast beef. He ran a well-ordered house and a perfectly adjusted staff.

Why, then, should it be so hard to secure a properly obedient wife?

6

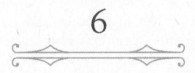

Micah finished scything the weeds that had grown up around the house and flower beds. He had gone somewhat grudgingly into his own reformation, but now that it was well on its way, Micah found he had a much-improved state of mind.

He glanced at his pocket watch and saw that he had just enough time to get cleaned up and make his way over to the Aldrich ranch. He'd promised Mrs. Aldrich that he would join them for supper, and frankly he was sort of looking forward to it, even though he knew she'd want to talk about the ranch. She and Charlotte would both be pleased to see the improvement in his appearance and disposition. At least he thought there was improvement.

Making his way to the barn, Micah couldn't help but turn his thoughts to Dad. This was the last place they had talked. The last place where Dad had rested before Micah buried him. The place held bittersweet attraction. Many a talk had taken place here in the barn, long before everything went wrong. Micah could remember grooming his horse, and his father stopping in to discuss something related to the ranch. They had plotted and planned on building projects and changes to the ranch in the barn. They had worked together to mend tack and clean equipment. So much had taken place there.

He put the scythe away and paused for a moment to listen. He almost expected Dad to say something—to call to him. When it didn't come, the pain returned to remind Micah that Dad was forever gone. The last year and four months had been the loneliest Micah had ever known. Part of that, as Charlotte had told him, was his own fault. He could have shared his loss with Charlotte and her mother. They could have borne their misery together, but Micah had been too ashamed. Their men had died trying to save their herd. His father had died because . . .

"Why? Why did you do it?" Micah asked the empty barn as if answers could be had.

That was the hardest part of the entire situation. He didn't know why his father had decided to die. They'd endured so many hard things over the years. Family members had been lost. There were two younger siblings who had died from illness before they'd left Texas. Micah barely remembered them. He had only been a few years old when the baby died in his sleep and then a little older when his brother Dale had died after the two of them had taken measles. Mother had grieved the hardest, but Micah had felt her sorrow deeply as she clung to him, her only remaining child. There were no others to come after that, although Micah later learned she had miscarried twice.

Then Mother had died. That grief was devastating and consuming for a very long time. He knew that loss still. Micah and his father had wandered around the house hardly knowing what to do with themselves. And now with both Dad and Mother gone, it was as though a part of Micah's life had ended as well. Maybe that's why he'd been content to hide away and hope for death.

He wiped his brow. The temperatures were climbing high

again, and he was sweat soaked. He washed up and changed his shirt, then went to saddle Duke. The horse seemed happy to see him and for them to ride. He knew over the last year he'd neglected the poor beast.

"How are you, boy?" Micah asked, rubbing the horse's face. Duke was all that was left to him. Duke and endless empty acres of land and a ranch house that wasn't a home anymore.

Micah thought about selling out. He'd thought about it a lot. Dad had always lived debt free, which was probably all that had saved Micah after that terrible winter. There had been money in the bank, and by utilizing what they'd already laid in store for the winter, Micah had found it easy to forgo trips to town until summer. He remembered the first time he'd gone to Cheyenne after the Aldrich men's funeral. It had been about a year ago. People who knew him had been so kind—offering all sorts of condolences, along with excuses for why they'd not come visiting.

He had been thankful that the cleanup of dead livestock and reconsideration of future plans had kept most folks too busy to worry about his being alone. The pastor had come out to the ranch a couple of times, but Micah had pretended not to be there. The second time, the pastor had left a short note of encouragement. Micah still had the note pressed in his Bible. After that, the pastor had been too busy with other poor souls to make another visit.

Before he knew it, Micah arrived at the Aldrich place. His thoughts had kept him occupied for the ride over, and still he had no solution as to what he should do regarding the ranch or his life. If Mrs. Aldrich expected answers, she would be disappointed.

Mack and Lucky came out to greet him, barking and running back and forth in front of Micah's horse. He smiled and thought about getting himself a dog. Maybe that would offer him a little company and help him ease back into being more social.

Micah climbed down and greeted each of the dogs with a scratch behind the ears. "Hello, you two. That was quite the welcome." He loved on them for another couple of minutes, then secured Duke in an area of shade. The dogs danced around him as Micah made his way to the house. Charlotte greeted him at the door. Smiles and welcome for him, reprimands for the dogs.

"Go on, Mack, Lucky. Go lay down." She looked back to Micah as the dogs moved away. "Good to see you again, Micah." There was a gentle beauty about her that Micah had always been drawn to.

"Come on inside out of the sun. It's at least a little cooler in the house." She stepped aside and motioned to him.

"Must be ninety degrees out here," he said, glancing upward. There wasn't a single sign of rain or weather change in the cloudless skies. He pulled his hat off and followed her into the house.

"Mama made some lemonade and used the last of the ice. We're hoping to make a trip to town for more in a few days." Charlotte took his hat and placed it on a table by the door.

"We're sitting in the front room with all the windows open. The flies are terrible, but we've each got a swatter and a fan." She grinned. "I can give you one too."

Micah smiled. She really was the only cheer in his life. Since she was a little girl, Micah had found Charlotte to be a joy. Frank Jr. said that his little sister could wrangle a smile out of their father on his worst day.

"Look, Mama, it's Micah. I told you I heard someone ride up."

"Micah, I'm glad you could come join us for supper. Nora's using the outdoor kitchen. She's worked on her famous beef stew all day, and also made a chocolate cake."

"I don't know when I last had chocolate cake," Micah said, taking a seat. Charlotte immediately poured him a glass of lemonade.

He drank down about half of the glass in one swig. Charlotte refilled it before she put the pitcher on the table.

"How's it going at your place?" Mrs. Aldrich asked.

Thinking about that for a moment, Micah took another long drink. The ladies waited for his answer as if they had all the time in the world.

"Well, I've tidied up a bit. On the outside. The inside wasn't as much of a problem. Outside, I'd let things go untended, and now I'm fighting it back into order. Had two rattlers to kill. They were keeping cool in the deep grass."

"Did you eat the meat?" Mrs. Aldrich smiled. "I remember your father liked rattlesnake meat."

"He did, but I certainly didn't," Micah replied.

"I never liked it either." Mrs. Aldrich laughed and shook her head. "I'll be glad when the sun goes down. Winter was tough enough and definitely cold. Now we're roasting and wishing it would cool down again. Frankly, I prefer cooler weather to hotter."

"I do too," Charlotte said touching her glass to her cheek. "I gave long thought to doing my chores in my bathing costume."

Micah almost spit out his lemonade at this. Charlotte laughed at his reaction. "That's exactly why I didn't do it," she added. "I figured everyone would be shocked."

Mrs. Aldrich chuckled. "They would have been especially taken aback had I joined you. Instead, I settled for this simple cotton blouse and lightweight skirt." She held up her arms. "But I rolled up my sleeves. Sorry I lack formality for your visit, Micah."

It was his turn to laugh. It felt foreign and good all at the same time. "You never need formality with me. I think you both know that by now. And as you can see, I left my coat and tie at home."

"I see and approve," Mrs. Aldrich replied. "But moving on to something of real importance, I'm curious. Did you attend the last Stock Growers Association meeting?"

Micah shook his head. "Didn't see any real reason to go."

"We wanted to," Charlotte interjected. "But you know how they feel about women. They keep telling me I need a husband to handle business. Mama and I have kept a herd alive and a ranch running smoothly, not sure why they can't give a woman credit and let her hear their ranching news." She shrugged. "Rich Johnson promised to bring back word of anything important, but it's not the same as being able to be there to ask questions."

"They don't believe women should be ranching alone," Charlotte's mother declared. "I asked for Charlotte and I to be admitted in place of Frank and Frank Jr. but was told that was impossible. I was hoping to hear more about plans for the ranches to start cultivating their own grain and hay."

"Ranchers and cowboys aren't going to take very well to being farmers." Micah had heard that argument all his life. Either a man handled livestock, or he handled soil. You didn't do both.

"I think the ranchers are coming to see that they'll be out a great deal of money if they don't find a way to do both. Like I told Charlotte, having grown up on a farm, I realize that both are very specialized duties. I see no problem, however, in hiring farmhands as well as ranch hands."

"I suppose that would be the only way to really make it work. Even so, you'll have a constant irritation running between the two camps. I doubt you can peaceably bunk them together," Micah said, trying to picture how that might ever work. "I don't think either group would ever truly respect the other."

"They need to learn," Mrs. Aldrich said, looking thoughtful. "Both feed the people, and both need each other. The Great Die-Up proved that. Had we been better prepared with our own hay and grain, we might have saved the cattle and sheep."

"Still, the summer of '86 was a drought. You wouldn't have grown anything, much less enough crops to get through the winter that followed. We're a water-poor area; I have doubts about growing much of anything out here."

Charlotte nodded. "Micah's right on that point. If Papa hadn't brought in hay from California and Oregon, we wouldn't have had anything extra for the herd."

"I know," Mrs. Aldrich replied, nodding, "but I'm convinced it's the way things need to go. Rich Johnson told me that more and more ranchers are seeing the truth of it. I've been in touch with my cousins back in Illinois. I've asked for their advice about planting out here. One of them did farming in southeastern Colorado, so I think he can speak to us about what we might need to do. The landscapes are similar, from what I've heard him say. We don't have the water, nor the humidity, so growing things will be harder. Water is always going to be an issue."

"Supper's ready," Nora announced from the open doorway. She grinned. "Micah Hamilton. You're a blessing to see."

Micah got to his feet and smiled. "Good to see you too."

Mrs. Aldrich and Charlotte stood. "We can continue our discussion over dinner." She gave Micah a motherly smile. "Glad to see you're filling out a bit."

This made him chuckle. "Nora's pies will do that to a man."

Micah followed the women into the dining room and helped each with their chairs. It was the first time in a long time that he actually wanted to be where he was. Their company was like a balm.

Mrs. Aldrich had Charlotte offer grace. Micah bowed his head and tried to show respect as she prayed. He was still fighting his anger where God was concerned. He supposed most of his dismay came in knowing God could have kept his father from taking his own life and yet did nothing to stop it. God could have kept the hard winter from happening, and He could have kept Mother from dying. There were so many things that God could have done. After all, He was omnipotent. Micah had been raised to believe God was able to do anything. So why had He done nothing?

"Amen."

He hadn't heard her prayer but caught the final word and looked up pretending to have been in complete agreement as he gave a slight nod. The food was quickly passed around, and Nora came in to refill the lemonade pitcher before taking a chair at the table. Micah wasn't surprised at this. Since the death of the men, Charlotte had mentioned that the women often ate together.

"Nora, this is wonderful. I'm so glad we settled on stew despite the heat."

"Well, I had little desire for killing a chicken," Nora replied. "I've always hated killing any living thing. My husband used to manage that for me. But the heat really makes it a miserable job."

"I've never minded. It was always just such a part of farm life." Mrs. Aldrich handed Micah the platter of meat. "I taught the children to take care of those kinds of things themselves too. I never wanted them to be reliant on others for those basic tasks."

"Well, having the beef readily available in the cellar was perfect. You'll have to thank Rich again for me. I was sure surprised that he brought it over."

"Said he had a hankering for steaks and his boys did too," Mrs. Aldrich replied. "Figured he would spread out the meat among friends so that none of it went bad."

Micah took up the large serving spoon and gave himself a generous portion of the stew. The thick gravy dripped over the side of the serving bowl as he went back for another serving before handing Charlotte the spoon. Nora had baked biscuits to go with the main course, and Micah couldn't remember when he'd been happier to put food in his mouth. The aromas and flavors were an absolute delight.

"We were just discussing the farming ideas," Mrs. Aldrich told Nora.

The older cook nodded. "Hay and corn, wasn't that what you figured?"

"I believe so, but I'm still receiving information from my cousins. They're checking in with some agricultural experts in Chicago. They've recently been out this way doing studies of the land. I'm very interested to hear what they have to say."

The conversation went on regarding ranching and farming until the food was eaten and everyone was ready to step outside to enjoy whatever breeze was available. Strangely, the winds had been absent of late, which only served to make things feel warmer.

"Micah, I do hope you'll check in with Kit and the boys," Mrs. Aldrich said, taking a seat in her rocker on the porch. "Rich wants to hold roundup the first of July. We need to have the cow-calf pairs brought in, and I don't think Kit has even started to make preparations. I told Rich we could do roundup here. That way Nora and Charlotte and I can help with feeding everyone and taking care of injuries. I was hoping maybe you could talk to Kit and explain what he needs to do. Last year, as I recall, he wasn't much use to anyone."

Micah gave a nod. "Of course. I'll talk to him, but shouldn't you or Charlotte be the one to give the orders?"

"If he would listen to us." Mrs. Aldrich shook her head. "Don't get me wrong. He does listen to a certain extent, but he's not used to heading up an event like this. Last year, Rich and his men headed up everything. Kit just needs experience and guidance, and we're doing our best to offer it, but he tends to have the same mindset of the men in the Stock Growers Association. Women have no place running a ranch. And our knowing more than he does seems to irritate him all the more."

Micah frowned. "I'll try to convince him otherwise, then."

"Would you also consider helping out with the roundup? After all, you know your way around such things. I know Rich would be very appreciative."

The thought of once again participating in a roundup sent an icy finger down Micah's spine. He and Dad had always enjoyed getting together with the other men. The shared labor was one benefit, but the camaraderie and good times was yet another. There had always been laughter and storytelling at every roundup Micah had ever attended. It was hard to even think of laughing again, but it was time. Time to put aside his grieving.

"I'll help in any way I can."

Mrs. Aldrich smiled. "I knew I could count on you, Micah. That will be so beneficial to Charlotte and to me. If we know you're out there looking after our best interests, we can focus on other things."

Charlotte looked at him and smiled. "It'll be so good to work all together again."

After supper, Micah went out to the bunkhouse and found the boys cleaning up after their own meal. Nora had already collected her platters and bowls. He motioned to Kit, who followed him outside.

"Wanted to talk to you for a few minutes. Mrs. Aldrich has some plans for roundup and asked me to help with it."

"I'm the foreman. She should have talked to me."

"Maybe if you were doing the job you were hired to do, she would." Micah looked around the yard. "Things aren't in order like they should be. You either don't know your job well enough or you're counting on those women to pick up the slack you're leaving."

"I oughta bust you in the face for talking to me that way." Kit stepped close and puffed up his chest.

Micah shook his head. "You don't want to fight with me, Hendricks. I've got well over a year of anger and rage pent up inside." He fixed the man with a hard look, and Kit stepped back. "I just came out to let you know what Mrs. Aldrich wants you to do."

"And what is it she wants?"

"Rich Johnson plans roundup on the first. She figures we'll all do it together and have one big gathering here. That way we can just round up all the cow-calf pairs and not worry about separating them out."

"That's a lot of extra work to put on us," Kit replied.

"Extra men to help with it too. Johnson will come and bring his crew. And not to make you feel particularly grumpy, but those men know what they're doing, and this bunch could learn a lot. You could as well. We're going to do right by the Aldrich women, Hendricks. You're going to learn how to be a foreman if it kills you."

Kit frowned. "If he wants to do it on the first, that's just a couple of weeks away."

"So you'd best get to rounding up those cows and calves." Micah shook his head. "You should have been keeping a better eye on them. You should have been doing a lot of things, and from now on you'll change your ways."

"Or what?" Kit asked, once again throwing his shoulders back as if ready to fight.

"Or you'll be fired."

7

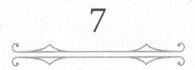

Leaving Kit grumbling under his breath, Micah made his way out to where he'd left Duke grazing. He saddled the gelding and led him toward the house and the road that would take them home. At the sound of a horse coming up the drive, Micah raised the brim of his hat just a bit to identify the rider. Rich Johnson. Micah hadn't seen him in some time and knew he'd be expected to stop and visit.

"Mr. Johnson," Micah said, giving a nod.

"Micah Hamilton, as I live and breathe. You're a sight for sore eyes." Rich jumped off the back of his horse as if he were a man Micah's age and quickly crossed the distance.

He surprised Micah by embracing him with a bear hug. "You look good, Micah."

"You too, Mr. Johnson."

"I think you're old enough to just call me Rich." The older man pulled away and shook his head. "I know that Southern upbringing of yours says otherwise, but this is the Wyoming Territory, and I insist."

"All right, then . . . Rich." Micah smiled, almost against his will. It was good to be among friends again.

"Are we going to have your help with the roundup?" Rich asked.

"Yes. I promised Mrs. Aldrich, and I just had a talk with Hendricks."

Rich shook his head and glanced heavenward. "That boy needs more training than I can give. He just doesn't seem to understand the job, and yet he's been at it for over two years now."

"I know."

"Well, I'm glad you'll be with us. I can count on you to know one end of a calf from the other."

Micah remembered just then that Rich's wife had died the previous December. "I was sorry to hear about Mrs. Johnson's passing."

Rich nodded. "It's been hard. That house seemed to double in size without her there. Some days I start to call for her, even now." His weathered face wrinkled a bit more. "Wish it would have been me if one of us had to go, but then I realize it would have left Betsy to fend for herself. I wouldn't have wanted that for her, especially now that I know what that feels like."

"I'm sorry for not coming by. I've been a terrible excuse for a human being, much less a neighbor."

"You've had your share of difficulties, and I'm not one to judge." The older man stuffed his hands in his pockets and shrugged. "I should have been better myself and come to see you. But with the cleanup and then Betsy's heart giving out . . . well, I just wasn't much of a friend. Got kind of caught up in my own sorrows."

"That's understandable. The disposal of dead cattle was enough all on its own. Place stunk to high heavens for the longest time."

"That's a fact. Well, hopefully we can move forward now. I had a good calving this spring and bought some new heifers to breed. We'll get back on top before you know it. What plans do you have for the future, Micah?"

Micah looked at the ground and kicked a rock to one side. "I don't know for sure. I had thought about selling out and going West, but with my folks buried on the ranch, it's hard to move away and even harder to sell off the place."

"It's hard for folks like us to walk away. Besides, this is your home. You have good friends and folks who care about you. I think you just need to start rebuilding that herd."

"Mrs. Aldrich and Charlotte took what cows I had left," Micah said, trying not to feel guilty for the extra work he'd put on them. "I don't really have a herd to start rebuilding."

"Lucille has said more than once that she's just overseeing them until you're ready to take back the responsibility." Rich fixed him with a sobered gaze. "Micah, I know your pa would be upset to find you doing nothing but pining for him. I've thought a lot about coming out to speak to you, but wasn't sure it was my business. Never was one to stick my nose in where it didn't belong. But you're like kin."

"I understand, Mr. . . . Rich."

The older man met his gaze. "It was hard losing out in that terrible winter, but you've wasted too much time already. You need to stop mourning what's gone and move forward. Rebuild your herd and make the Hamilton ranch great again. Lot of folks sold out and gave up, but that isn't how your pa raised you."

"No, sir, he didn't." Micah couldn't argue; the man was right. Still, it was hard to reconcile the grief and anger he felt. "But I have a hard time figuring out how to move forward."

Rich nodded. "Don't I know how that goes. It ain't easy no matter how you look at it. We lost the cattle, and then the people we loved. There's nothing simple or easy about handling that. But the way I see it, you have to put one foot in front of the other and make yourself go forward. Standing still or going backward accomplishes nothing."

But do I really need to accomplish something? Micah couldn't help but wrestle with that thought. Why did it matter if he moved forward or stayed put in one spot?

"Get back in church, Micah. That's the best place to start. I wanted to quit church altogether when Betsy died. It was winter, and I figured the perfect excuse, but something just wouldn't let me hide myself away. You've been hiding for well over a year now. I think it's time, don't you?"

Micah couldn't argue, but he was so terribly disappointed with God. "I haven't exactly been on good terms with the Almighty, if I'm going to be completely honest with you. I don't understand why He allowed things to happen as they did. God's all-powerful, so why did He allow such suffering and loss to fall on our shoulders? What did we do to deserve that?"

Rich shrugged. "Who can know the mind of the Almighty? I suppose the best we can do is to search the Scriptures and read how He handled things long ago, but that still won't tell us everything we want to know about what we went through. Sometimes a man's just got to have faith and trust in the Lord no matter what's going on around him."

Micah wanted to say something about his father but knew it was too dangerous. Rich didn't know about the suicide, and Micah didn't want to get caught up in his anger and accidentally share that bit of history.

Rich reached out and touched Micah's shoulder. "God hasn't left you, Micah. He doesn't operate that way. He's a good Father, even when we don't understand what He's allowed or is doing in our life. Get back to church, and if you aren't praying and reading the Word . . . you should be."

"Hello, Rich!" Mrs. Aldrich called out as she crossed the yard. Mack was soon at her heel. "I wondered when you might get here. Go on inside and have some lemonade and cake. Charlotte will take good care of you. I'll be there shortly. Just need to make sure the hens are in for the night."

"Sure thing, Lucille." Rich looked at Micah and smiled. "I'll see you later. Come by sometime."

"I'll do what I can. If not, I'll be here for roundup."

With that, Rich led his horse to the hitching post and tied him off before heading up to the front door.

"You might want to stick around," Mrs. Aldrich said, coming to where Micah stood. "Rich is going to tell us about the stock growers meeting."

"That's all right. I think I'll just head home before it gets dark. I have some chores to take care of."

Mack pushed himself up against his mistress, determined to get her attention. "Mack, go lay down." The collie looked up at her for a moment and then headed off toward the house. "I don't need him scaring the chickens."

Micah nodded. "I'll see you later."

"Wait. Micah, I wanted to talk to you a minute."

"Sure thing. What is it?" He could see nothing but compassion in her gaze.

"First, I want to apologize. I failed you miserably. I should never have left you to mourn on your own for so long. I was caught up in my own sorrow and loss, but I knew you needed me. I feel terrible for not having been there for you."

Micah was humbled by her words. "You owed me nothing."

"That's not true. I owed you human kindness if nothing else. More so, I owed you all that I had promised your mama. I swore I'd look after you and be there for you, Micah. I didn't honor that promise, but I intend to now. When I saw you for the first time in so very long, I felt as if you helped to fill an empty place in my heart. Losing Frank was hard enough, but losing my son as well . . . it almost killed me.

You anticipate that you might well lose your spouse, but you never in a million years think you'll be burying your child."

"I'm sure you're right. I know my ma grieved losing my brothers until the day she died."

Mrs. Aldrich's eyes filled with tears. "You never ever get over it. It's a deep hurt that never quite heals. Even with all of God's comfort and kindness—of which I need every day to get by—it still lingers." She fell silent.

Micah tried to think of something he could say. But what could he offer? He wasn't a parent. He hadn't lost a child. Anything he said would be spoken out of sympathy, but not any true understanding.

Mrs. Aldrich put her hand on Micah's arm. "I hope this doesn't sound selfish, but I need you, Micah. I think we need each other. You're the closest thing to a son that I have now. And I'm the closest thing to a mother that you have. Let's help each other . . . please."

It was impossible to look away from her teary blue eyes. Micah nodded and put his hand over hers. "I'll always be here for you." What else could he say? It imposed on his desire to have very little to do with anyone. But how could he refuse her? When he looked in her eyes, he saw his own pain reflected back.

She smiled. "Thank you, Micah. I feel like I can start to move forward now. I didn't realize what was missing before. Charlotte and I had each other, but you'd be surprised how much we kept to ourselves." She squared her shoulders. "I know you're hurting. I know you're asking yourself every day, why?"

"There are a lot of why questions that I ask," he admitted. "Why did my father kill himself is right at the top. I can't begin to understand that. Sure, he'd lost a lot of animals, and then he'd come face to face with the loss of his best friend, but I lost my best friend too. As sad as I was, it didn't make me want to take my life. Sometimes that makes me wonder, didn't I care about Frank Jr. as much as Dad cared about Mr. Aldrich? It's a complicated sort of guilt that haunts me."

"Oh, Micah, I am sorry. Of course you loved as deeply as your father loved. What your father did in taking his life was no doubt far more complex than either of us will ever understand. I believe, however, that something broke apart in your father. Something he couldn't control. It was just too much for him to handle."

"But I thought God never gave us anything more than we could handle."

"The Bible doesn't say that, Micah. There is a passage that talks about temptations and God always giving us a way out, but we face things every day that we can't handle. Why would we need God if we could handle it all on our own?"

"I suppose that makes sense. But Dad knew God. Knew Him well and yet it wasn't enough."

"Again, Micah, it's impossible for us to know. But what I do know is that God is good and just and faithful, even when we aren't. Whatever happened in that moment that led your father to take his own life, God didn't leave him to face it alone. He was there, Micah."

"Yeah, and He didn't stop it. That's what I don't understand. God didn't stop my father from taking his life, but He could have."

Mrs. Aldrich nodded. "Yes, I suppose He could have, just as He could have kept my loved ones from freezing to death. Just as He could have kept your mother and brothers from dying. Just as He could have kept the snake out of the garden. God could have done a lot of things and didn't. We don't understand why, and it hurts. It hurts us deep down."

"Yes," Micah barely whispered.

She squeezed his arm. "He knows that too. Someday, I believe we'll understand, but for now we have two choices.

We either give up on God and walk away, or we trust Him no matter what happens to us. For me, I'm going to trust Him, because life without Him seems too horrible to even think about."

Micah knew she was right. Even in his arguments with God and rantings about His unfairness, at least God had been a part of Micah's life. To push Him aside altogether would leave an impossible void. He drew a deep breath and gave a nod.

"I'd best let you go for now, but Micah, would you please come and stay with us for roundup? We have plenty of room, and it would comfort me to have you near, instead of having you ride back and forth."

"Sure. I can do that."

She let go of her hold on him and nodded. "Thank you so much, Micah. It means the world to me."

Later that night, Lucille sat by her fire and prayed for Micah. She thought of how troubled he was. He was so wounded by the death of his father. Perhaps even more by the fact that they'd had to hide the details. But how did one deal with suicide? Micah's father had chosen death over life.

Life with his son.

In taking his own life, Wayman Hamilton had taken a part of his son's life too. He'd left Micah to feel he'd somehow failed his father. That if he'd been there, he could have kept his father from making that horrible decision.

"Oh, God, Micah needs You so much. He's struggling to understand—to overcome. Show him the way through that dark void. Help me to be there for him too. Show me how I can help. Show me what I need to do to reach him."

She glanced across the room she'd shared with her husband for nearly twenty years. It seemed so empty without him. Sometimes the nights threatened to swallow her up in dark thoughts and pain. She could well understand Wayman Hamilton's pain at losing his best friend. Frank had been her best friend too. They had known each other since they'd been children. Theirs had been one of those relationships that just naturally fell into place. Everyone knew they'd one day marry because they were always together. No other fella had ever attempted to win Lucille's heart. They knew she belonged to Frank Aldrich.

The thought made her sigh as she gazed at the empty bed. How lonely the nights were. How terribly empty without her dearest friend. Tears came to her eyes, and once more she grieved her husband and the void his absence left.

"Frank, I don't know why you aren't here. I begged you to be careful and still you left me. Left me and took our son with you. I feared that night when the horses came back without you that something bad had happened."

She wiped her eyes and felt a sense of anger. "You listened to me when I told you the winter would be hard, and you sold off the cattle despite your misgivings. You should have stayed with Charlotte and me. You knew another storm was coming. Why didn't you listen to me about that?"

Micah wasn't the only one who didn't understand the choices made. Lucille had battled with her own questions since she put her husband and son in the ground. She was certain she would always ask those questions, and just as certain there would be no satisfactory answers.

Her words to Micah came back.

"Someday, I believe we'll understand, but for now we have two choices. We either give up on God and walk away, or we trust Him no matter what happens to us."

She gazed into the fire. "I'll trust you, Lord. The alternative is no good to me."

8

Everyone came together on the last day of June and gathered at the Aldrich ranch. The cowboys had been bringing in cattle all week and collecting them in two of three fenced-off pastures. The fences were a new, extra investment by Mrs. Aldrich that had come after hearing some encouragement for getting away from open range management of her cattle. Open range was still popular for the summer months, but after the blizzards had killed so many, folks were beginning to see value in fencing in cattle closer to home for the winter.

The herds were amassed to rest in the Aldrich pastures where they were counted and left to graze. It was strange to see such small herds, but Micah knew in time they would expand again, though maybe never to the extent they once existed. Before the bad winter, all three families represented had owned thousands of head, but now between the Aldrichs and Johnsons there probably weren't even a thousand total.

On Sunday, they held a church service and sang hymns before Mrs. Aldrich fed them breakfast and then explained what she and Rich hoped to accomplish in the next few days. Everyone was eager to get the work done by the Fourth of July. The celebrations in Cheyenne were nothing to be missed. After one final prayer, the cows and calves were separated, and the real work began, despite it being the Sabbath.

Micah found the work healing in a way. He hadn't done this kind of work since losing his father, and with each new task he remembered some incident or story that had taken place with his father. Dad loved roundup. He was far more social than Micah. Micah always figured it was due to having grown up by himself, without siblings or next-door neighbors. Life on a ranch was a different thing. Life on a Wyoming Territory ranch was even more isolated than that of the ranch life he'd known in Texas.

Mother had worried about him when they'd first come to Wyoming. She had overseen his schooling and felt that perhaps she hadn't the wherewithal to teach him properly, so she enrolled Micah in Mr. Decker's School for Boys in Cheyenne. He boarded there during the week and came home on weekends. Frank Jr. attended as well. Both hated it.

It wasn't a lack of ability on Micah's part. He had graduated at fifteen having excelled in every subject. Micah's mother wanted him to be able to attend college and insisted he be allowed at least a year back east to make up his own mind about furthering his education. After a year, Micah came home to stay. He remembered telling his mother that his heart just wasn't in it. He longed for home and for the ranch life that he'd grown up with. She had understood. How he missed her.

"You've certainly accomplished a lot, Micah," Mrs. Aldrich said bringing him a glass of iced tea as he finished for the day.

"That was the goal, wasn't it?" He gave her a smile and then drank down the tea without pausing for a breath.

He handed her back the glass, then caught sight of a carriage coming down the drive. As the conveyance drew near,

Micah could see it was Lewis Bradley. Charlotte wasn't going to like this one bit.

"I hope there won't be trouble," Micah said, nodding. He knew from the things Charlotte and her mother had said that Bradley still figured he held a claim on Charlotte.

"There had better not be," Mrs. Aldrich said. "I'll go warn Charlotte. She's in the house helping Nora."

Micah nodded and watched as the older woman skirted the main area of work and hurried to the house via the back door. As Bradley brought his team to a stop, Micah figured he'd stall the man by seeing what he wanted.

"Afternoon, Lewis. What brings you out here?" Micah asked as Bradley set the brake and climbed down.

"I've come to see my fiancée, if you must know. I heard the roundup was taking place and thought I might offer my assistance."

Micah's lips curled the tiniest bit. "You can help me castrate calves. I have quite a few to do."

Lewis Bradley scowled. "I hardly think so."

"Why not? You want to be helpful, and I have a way for you to do that."

"I'm not a rancher," he said, lowering his voice. "I meant that maybe I could help with something else. Maybe bookwork. As a lawyer, I'm quite adept with ledgers and such."

"Since you're not a rancher," Micah began, "I'll fill you in on the fact that there's not a lot of bookwork going on at this point. Right now, we are focused on judging the health of each calf, branding them, castrating the males, and dehorning. There are a few other odds and ends, and we are keeping count and making a few notes—at least someone is, but most of the labor is physical. Sorry."

"Lewis, what are you doing here?" Charlotte asked as she joined them. Her tone betrayed exasperation.

The shorter man turned rather quickly away from Micah.

No doubt he was happy not to have to speak further on the matter of working the roundup.

"I wanted to see you. To talk to you." He glanced Micah's way. "Privately."

"Lewis, I realize you aren't all that familiar with roundups, but this isn't the time for private conversations. I have far too much work to help with."

"I thought perhaps I could help. Maybe we could work together and talk while we did . . . whatever it is you'd be doing."

"I was going to help with dehorning. Feel free to join me, but you'll need to lose that fancy coat and tie and roll up the sleeves on that equally fancy shirt. You are hardly dressed for roundup, Lewis."

"He thought you might have bookwork for him to do," Micah couldn't help throwing out.

Charlotte looked at Lewis with an expression of disbelief. "Bookwork? We're not running a school for the calves."

"I know that, but I figured there was an accounting of things."

She nodded. "There is, but it's done quickly and without much fuss. I'll go over the numbers later. The point is to get all this work done in a matter of a few days so that we can all go into town and enjoy the Fourth of July festivities."

"Look, can't we talk alone somewhere?"

"Didn't you hear me? I don't have the time, Lewis." Charlotte shook her head. She waved her hand across the large area where cowboys were continuing to move the calves along. "Just look around. I've got no time for you."

"You never seem to have any time for me, and you're my betrothed."

She planted her hands on her hips. "I'm your nothing, Lewis. Whatever arrangement you had with my father is done. He's dead."

Charlotte's tone was one that Micah recognized. She was about to explode, and if Lewis Bradley knew what was good for him, he'd back off.

"That very well may be, Charlotte, but we are still engaged to be married."

Apparently, he didn't know what was good for him.

Charlotte raised her hand and pointed her index finger at him as if she were admonishing a child. "You have no right to say that. I am not your betrothed, and we are not engaged. I never agreed to such a thing, and I am fully of age. I have my own legal rights, even as a woman."

"But you know what your father expected of you, and he told me that you had agreed."

"Well, I did not."

Micah stepped back and leaned against the corral fence. Charlotte could be quite a force to reckon with. He grinned and noticed a few of the other cowboys had stopped to watch.

Charlotte continued to waggle her finger at Lewis. "You and my father may have had business, Lewis Bradley, but I never agreed to it, never signed any contract, and won't be signing anything now." Her voice rose in volume as if to make sure he could hear clearly. "I do not intend to marry you now or ever, so please stop telling people that we're engaged. We are not."

"I could sue for breach of contract."

"Your love runs so deep, Mr. Bradley."

He looked momentarily confused and then nodded. "But it does, Charlotte. That's why it hurts me so much that you would refuse me."

"I'm sorry that you're hurt, but such is the situation. I'm not changing my mind. I've never been interested in marrying you, and I never will be."

"Never is a very conclusive attitude to take. I think you should reconsider." Bradley's expression changed to a stern look. "You might believe you don't love me, but you can learn, and in time we could be a great team together."

"No, Lewis. No. I will not marry you." She finally lowered her arm and shook her head. "Now please go home. You are neither needed here nor wanted."

Lewis stepped toward her. Micah thought he looked like he might grab Charlotte, so he pushed off the fence and put himself between them.

"You heard her. Get out of here."

"I see you're reduced to cowhand, Mr. Hamilton. I suppose that's all you're good for after letting a good ranch fall to pieces."

Micah raised back his arm to punch Lewis Bradley in the face, but Charlotte wedged herself between the two men and took hold of Micah's arm.

"He's not worth it, Micah." She turned to Lewis. "As for you, you should know that Micah's ranch is doing just fine. He has over two hundred cow-calf pairs that are running with Aldrich cattle. So now, if there's nothing more, I'm going to tell you once again to go. After that, I'll have you removed, and I don't think you want the embarrassment of that. There's really no need for such a scene, is there, Lewis?"

He looked at her with great contempt. Micah was amazed at how Charlotte stood her ground in the face of such blatant hate. The man looked murderous, and Micah found himself taking hold of Charlotte and moving her protectively to his side.

Lewis Bradley glanced around. There were quite a few strong, healthy cowboys who had stopped work to come see what the trouble might be. He raised his chin as if to snub them all, then stomped off to his carriage. In its current position, Bradley couldn't just strike the horses and race off down the drive; he needed to get the team turned in the small area and then go. It wasn't easy, and with each new maneuver, Micah could see a little bit more frustration overcome Bradley's façade of calm.

Finally, the horses were turned, and Lewis Bradley snapped the lines. The team headed off down the drive, and the cowboys went back to work. Micah started to leave as well but paused to shake his head at Charlotte.

"You didn't need to lie to Bradley about my cattle."

She smiled. "I didn't. You told us to run your remaining herd with ours, and we did. There were about one hundred cows left and again that many steers. Most of those cows gave birth to healthy calves. We lost a few. We sent the males to market and bred the cows again. A good number of the calves born this year are from your herd. And quite a few of the heifers being bred this year are yours. I have a full accounting in the ledger we kept for you."

Micah shook his head. "Not mine. You kept them alive and did all the work when I fell to pieces. I don't deserve to have them. You keep them."

"No. No, I won't. Those cattle are now your responsibility, Micah Hamilton. If they die because you don't take care of them, then so be it. I have my hands full with Aldrich cattle now. Unless, of course, you'd like to consider a merger. Aldrich and Hamilton Cattle Company. I think it has a nice ring to it. Or perhaps the Hamilton and Aldrich Cattle Company."

Micah looked at her for a long moment. Her blond hair had been carefully braided and pinned up earlier in the morning, and now wisps of it had worked their way out to frame around her face. Micah had always loved the way her blue eyes seemed to spark fire when she was angry . . . like when dealing with Lewis Bradley. They were still aglow as she addressed her thoughts for the future.

He couldn't help but smile. He and Frank Jr. had often laughed or made light of her anger when she was a little girl. It would be easy enough to do that now, but Micah really had no desire to argue with her. He was still in shock that he had so many cattle still alive.

"I don't know why you're smiling, Micah Hamilton. You have a lot of work to get caught up on. Our cattle may go back to feeding together on open range, but you're not going to sit out another winter."

Micah met her gaze. "No, ma'am. I won't be sitting out another winter."

She gave a nod and drew a deep breath. "Better start making plans for the future, Micah."

That night after everyone was fed, some of the cowboys brought out their musical instruments and began to play around the campfire. The music was a pleasant surprise. Micah hadn't expected it, nor had he anticipated the way it would speak to his soul. Most of the songs the boys played were either folk songs or hymns. It suited the warm summer night.

Mrs. Aldrich had invited him to take a bed in the guest room, but Micah preferred the idea of sleeping out under the stars, the way he had done when he and Dad had worked roundups in the past. There was a comfort and familiarity with doing it now that left Micah thinking of things he'd pushed aside since the day he'd found his father dead.

No one here, save Charlotte and Mrs. Aldrich, knew his dad had killed himself. So many times Micah had wanted to shout out the truth when someone offered their condolences, but instead he just nodded and told them thanks. It was hard to hear how sorry complete strangers were when Micah knew the comment was nothing more than words. They had no idea. They didn't know the sorrow or the shame that haunted Micah every step of the day.

He swallowed hard and gritted his teeth, staring up at the starry skies. Until a few weeks ago, when these thoughts came Micah numbed the pain with alcohol and then went to sleep. He couldn't do that anymore. His conscience wouldn't let him. He knew it was wrong. Knew there was no comfort to be had in liquor and certainly no loss of guilt.

Would these feelings of guilt ever leave him?

He had left his father alone with two dead men whom they both loved and cared for. Micah had left him there to watch over the bodies after seeing so much of his herd dead. He wondered at what point his father, in contemplation of the deaths, had decided to join them. What had caused him to finally give up hope? Why had he ended his life?

So many times Micah had pondered that question and demanded answers. Of course, none ever came. Dad wasn't there to confront, and God wasn't speaking out about the matter.

Micah closed his eyes as if he could close out the thoughts as well. He could still see his father's body lying ready for burial in the barn. He could still see that empty grave. A grave he'd dug by hand in the frozen ground.

He had wanted to throw himself into that grave. He had prayed that God would strike him dead in punishment for somehow failing to know what his father would do. Yet still he lived, and now he had a future to plan. A future he had long given up on but needed to reclaim.

Charlotte stood at her bedroom window in the dark. Somewhere out there, Micah was sleeping. She couldn't help thinking about him . . . about how much she had wanted to tell Lewis that she intended to marry only one man, and that man was Micah Hamilton.

She sighed and enjoyed the breeze that blew through her open window. The night had cooled considerably and felt so nice.

The memory of what Lewis had said about his arrangements with her father came to mind and ruined the moment. She had no real understanding of what he and her father had agreed on. The painful memory of that last fight overshadowed any memories of previous discussions of the matter that might have had more details.

She regretted that last conversation with all her heart. She'd hurt her father . . . a man she loved so dearly.

She hugged her arms to her body. How she would give anything to be able to take back the awful things she'd said. How she wished she could undo the past and bring her father and brother back to them alive and well. Despite her mother's reassurances, she'd gladly marry Lewis Bradley if it meant they might be returned to them.

Well, maybe not gladly, but she'd do the deed if it could bring her loved ones back. Still, that wasn't possible, and the very orderly side of her nature told her to stop even considering such things because they could never happen and were a waste of time.

She sighed long and loud as Lewis Bradley's intrusion came again to mind. Would he cause some sort of legal trouble for them? She supposed it might be worth a trip to town to talk to the family lawyer, Clarence Higgins. Maybe she could just hunt him down when they went for Fourth of July. It would probably put Mother's mind at ease if they did so.

Charlotte made her way to bed and threw her lightweight robe across the foot of the bed. She knelt to begin her prayers and let go another sigh as she glanced toward the ceiling.

"God, I'm going to need a lot of help in all of this."

9

Fourth of July was a grand celebration in most of America, and Cheyenne was no exception. All sorts of festivities were planned for the day from trick riding to a picnic feast. In the evening there would be a dance, fireworks, and a midnight supper. The people of Cheyenne were ready to celebrate and do so in grand style.

Micah had accompanied Lucille and Charlotte to Cheyenne after they'd finished with their roundup. The calves were castrated and branded, and already back out grazing with their mamas. Most of the cowboys had been given time off to come and celebrate. A few men had volunteered to stay closer to home to keep an eye on things and take care of chores. Of course, in the case of the Aldrich ranch, Mrs. Aldrich had promised a nice bonus to those who volunteered. Nora hadn't wanted to come along, so the house was covered as well.

"Goodness, it looks like the number of people has doubled in Cheyenne," Mrs. Aldrich said as they walked up Capitol Avenue.

"I heard that there were nearly twelve thousand people

living around these parts now," Micah replied. "Some of the cowboys were talking about it yesterday."

"My, but things have changed. I worried that after so many ranchers sold out and left, we'd see Cheyenne struggling to survive. I know there is concern that losing so many people will affect our goal of statehood."

"I guess the railroad keeps it going," Charlotte interjected. "The railroad gave it life, and I suppose only the absence of the railroad would spell its death."

"I think you're probably right, Charlotte." Mrs. Aldrich pointed to a store across the street. "Look at that. A store devoted just to clocks."

Micah smiled. He remembered the early years of the town when folks were happy just to hear there was a new fruits-and-vegetable market greengrocer setting up business. Things had certainly changed in the twenty-one years since the railroad laid track into Cheyenne. There had been Indian wars, financial crises, droughts, bad winters, even bad people, but Cheyenne survived and seemed determined to go on.

They had left their horses and carriage at the livery, determined that walking would do them good and allow them better accessibility to the festivities. After checking in to the hotel, they headed straight to the Cheyenne Club, where the Wyoming Stock Growers Association was hosting a brief Fourth of July morning meeting.

The streets were crowded to be sure, but the boardwalks were even worse. Folks were walking shoulder to shoulder, some in quite a hurry. Micah worried the ladies would be run over by thoughtless younger men who seemed to have already started to enjoy Independence Day with a bit of alcohol.

At Seventeenth Street they turned east and walked the two blocks to Warren, where the Cheyenne Club was situated. This was solely a men's club that had been built years before to host visiting European and Eastern United States ranchers as well as locals. It was an impressive three-story brick building with a partial wraparound porch that often attracted a gathering of men, as it was just now.

The inside was even more impressive. Micah remembered coming here with his father and staying in one of the upper-floor hotel rooms. They were plush with thick carpets and impressive furnishings. The men were required to be cleaned up, perfectly mannered, and well-dressed. Micah remembered his father grumbling about it, reminding the doorman that true ranchers dirtied not only their hands but their clothes as well. But the men they most wanted to attract were those millionaires who would continue to see Cheyenne thrive. The dismay of one moderately successful rancher wasn't of concern to them.

Micah remembered the club had hired a very good chef who cooked amazing meals. The dishes had been flavorful creations of food Micah often had never heard of, much less tried. Sometimes the food was even set on fire just before it was served. The memories made him smile.

"What are you grinning about, Micah?" Charlotte asked as they made their way up the stairs to the club porch.

"I was just remembering some pretty fancy food I had here. I'd never even heard of ostrich, yet here they were serving it up."

She shook her head. "Was it good?"

"I would just as soon have had my ma's fried chicken."

"Afternoon, Mrs. Aldrich," one of the men said, coming to greet her.

"Afternoon, Mr. Chesterfield. How are you?" Mrs. Aldrich extended her hand. The man took hold of it but didn't shake her hand.

"Doing well. Mrs. Chesterfield is over at the Inter Ocean Hotel for a lady's tea. I'm sure you'd be most welcome there.

Your daughter too," he said, looking over at Charlotte. "I know she'd love to visit with you."

"I came here to hear what the Stock Growers Association have to say, but I do look forward to visiting with your wife."

The man looked to Micah and cleared his throat. "Well . . . you do realize . . . I mean, the meeting is for the area ranchers . . . the men."

"My mother and I are ranchers," Charlotte countered before her mother could speak.

"Pretty ones too," a man sitting close enough to be in on the conversation said with a grin. "I think they'd make a nice addition."

Mr. Chesterfield glanced at the man and then back to Mrs. Aldrich. "I'm sorry. This place . . . the meeting . . . it's for men only. The only women the association has ever had come around came with their husbands, and they didn't come here."

"I see." Mrs. Aldrich pulled back her gloved hand. "And how are we supposed to hear your news about railroad freighting costs and whether there are any new diseases of which we should be aware?"

The man looked most uncomfortable. "I'm just relating what I know from the past. You could talk to the association president and see what he thinks about having you join in the meeting." He glanced at his pocket watch. "But there's not much time. We're starting in ten minutes."

"That's more than ample time," Charlotte said, pushing past Chesterfield and going inside the Cheyenne Club's main entrance.

Her mother followed after her, so Micah did likewise, wondering all the while what kind of reception they were going to receive.

The lobby was crowded with men, but not nearly as many as there once would have been for a stock growers meeting.

Micah had heard that there had been a huge membership loss in the aftermath of their bad winter, but he hadn't truly expected the numbers to diminish that much. They must have lost well over half their membership if this was all that was left.

Charlotte and her mother were already speaking to one of the other men. They weren't about to be cast aside without first attempting to be heard. They were both incredible.

"Micah Hamilton," a man said from behind.

Micah turned to find Bruce Cadot, one of the area ranchers. "Morning, Mr. Cadot."

"I haven't seen you at the meetings in some time. Never got a chance to tell you how sorry I was to hear about your father."

Micah nodded. "Thank you." He glanced around, seeing a few familiar faces. "Not nearly as many of us as there used to be."

"No. I'm afraid those days are gone. Cattle prices were already heading down before the winter of '86, and now they've bottomed out. I doubt we'll ever see the boon we once had."

"Folks still gotta eat," Micah said, shaking his head. "And given that maybe a million head were lost, there might even come a shortage, and people will be clamoring to pay good money again."

"True. We did talk about that at a meeting a few months back," Bruce admitted. "Still, that winter totally changed folks. So many left ranching and will probably never return. I'm hoping they'll have some good news for us today."

"I don't see how you have the right to keep us from at least listening in to what you have to say!"

Charlotte's voice rose above the hum of conversations in the lobby. Everything went silent except for her.

"Mother and I have been handling Aldrich Cattle Company since my father and brother died. And we're doing a good job of it, if I do say so myself. Better than many of the men who are here today. But now you're telling me we can't attend a stock growers meeting?"

Micah looked at Bruce. "I'd better go see if I can calm things down. The Aldrich women hoped they could attend the association gathering. Guess that's not meeting with a positive outlook."

Bruce chuckled. "No, I don't imagine it is. I'm surprised they got past the front door, frankly."

"Charlotte is like a storm when she wants to move through an area. Doesn't yield for much of anything or anyone."

Micah left Bruce and went to where Charlotte was shaking her index finger. When that happened, Micah knew she was well past irritated.

"We're ranching, same as you. We have cattle to sell, same as you. We need to know how much we're going to have to pay to ship, same as you. I don't see why we can't be a part of the meeting."

"Now, no sense to get riled. Seems to me you two need to marry up. We've got quite a few single ranchers," the man replied, looking around the room. "I'm betting somebody here would be happy to team up with you." The man's tone was half teasing, half serious.

Micah knew the man was making a big mistake trying to make light of the matter. He reached over and took hold of Charlotte, who elbowed him away before she looked to see who it might be.

"Sorry, Micah. I thought someone was trying to haul me out of here."

"I am." He gripped her arm tightly. "Come on."

Several of the men were making annoying comments about Micah being the lucky one. Others were saying slightly more inappropriate things, and Micah knew they needed to just leave.

"Please come on," he whispered against her ear.

Charlotte seemed to calm, and when their gazes met, he could see she was losing steam. He gave her a smile, hoping it might help.

"I agree with Micah. Let's go," Mrs. Aldrich declared. She looked back at the organization's president. "My husband was a member here and so was my son. I know they'd be appalled at how we've been treated. Some of you other men should think of our position. Your wives might one day find themselves in the same situation. Would you want them treated like you're treating us?

"My daughter and I have had to pick up the pieces of what was left after burying my husband and son. We've done a decent job despite the interference we've found by you. The Good Lord has looked out for us, and I know He'll continue to do so. I'm going to be praying for each of you. In particular that your consciences will hurt you something fierce for the way you've acted here today."

She turned and marched from the room. Micah pulled Charlotte and followed Mrs. Aldrich. There was certainly nothing he could say to make a better point than Mrs. Aldrich had already offered.

"They make me so mad with their men-only attitude. I'm not asking to ruin their party. I don't even want to go to their parties. I just want industry news," Charlotte said as they went back down the stairs.

"Micah, would you please go back to the meeting and learn what you can for us? I know Rich said he was going to try to make it, but I haven't seen him anywhere. Charlotte and I will walk back to the hotel and find that lady's tea."

"I will not go sit and sip tea like a helpless ninny." Charlotte's ire was up again. She turned and looked as if she might go back up the stairs.

"Don't let them make you anxious, Charlotte." Micah gave

a shrug. "Those meetings are boring anyway. I'll go and give it a listen and let you know what's said. I don't think you have to go sip tea or whatever else ladies do, but I wouldn't give this bunch another thought."

For a moment, Micah wasn't sure she'd heard him. Then she drew a deep breath and nodded. "I suppose it's for the best. At least right now. I wouldn't want to spoil the day." She turned to her mother. "I'm ready if you are."

Mrs. Aldrich smiled back at Micah. "We'll see you later at the hotel. That is, if you think you'll be able to get away from this bunch."

"I will get away, I promise. I don't want to be eating a picnic lunch with them. Not when I have the two prettiest ranchers in the area willing to sit by my side."

Lewis Bradley hadn't thought of it before, but given the way Charlotte responded to Micah Hamilton, and especially how she looked at him just now, it seemed evident that she had feelings for him. Deep feelings.

Her father had never mentioned there being something between the two. When Lewis had asked about courtship, her father had made it clear that there was no one else, despite her having reached her majority.

Now, however, watching those two at the roundup and here again in town, it was easy to see that there was something that tied them together. Charlotte listened to Micah, even backed down from a fight when he asked her to do so.

Lewis had been standing in the collection of stockmen when she'd lit into the president. He had thought about coming forward and ushering her out, but fear of her making a scene had stopped him just long enough that Micah had taken the lead. Surprisingly, she had gone very willingly with him, and that was when Lewis had first noticed how she looked at Micah. It was as if he hung the moon and the stars. She had a look of serenity and wonder. She'd certainly never gazed at Lewis that way.

That moment caused him to think back to the roundup and their interactions there. It had been the same thing. She had come to Micah's defense and he to hers. They had acted almost as one in their reactions. Was it possible that she was in love with him?

Lewis spied Kit Hendricks and went to where he stood with several other men. "I wonder if I might have a word with you, Mr. Hendricks."

Kit gave a nod and then looked at his companions. "I'll catch up with you fellas in a little bit." The two he'd been talking to gave shrugs and ambled off.

"What do you need, Mr. Bradley?"

"I wanted to know what you know of Micah Hamilton and the Aldrich women."

"They've given him some control when it comes to me and the boys. I hate the man. He's always tryin' to tell me what I need to do or how to do it. You were there at the roundup."

Lewis nodded. "For a short time."

"Long enough to get in on his bad side. I saw the two of you havin' words."

He had no desire to go into what had transpired between him and Micah and Charlotte. "What do you know about Hamilton and Charlotte Aldrich? Are they courting?"

Hendricks shook his head. "Not that anyone's told me. She's always been close to the Hamiltons though. Her brother and Micah were best friends, so the three of them were often together. I think Mrs. Aldrich has brought him back into the fold so to speak, but I'm not happy about it. The man thinks he knows everything there is to know and accused me of being lazy and not knowin' my job. I've kept that place working just fine this last year and a half."

Lewis knew better. Charlotte was the one who kept that ranch running. She was the one who knew what was needed and how things had to come together in order to move forward. He had no doubt about that. Sure, she needed the muscle of her cowhands, but he had a feeling Kit Hendricks knew very little about the details of running a ranch.

"I wonder if you'd like to earn a little extra money, Mr. Hendricks. I have a few ideas I need help with."

Kit grinned. "I'd definitely like a little extra money."

That night the Fourth of July dance and fireworks had everyone in the party spirit. The women had donned their finest gowns. It was rumored that there were even a half dozen Worth gowns being worn by society's most respected matrons.

Some of the men were clad in tuxedos, but most simply wore their best suits. Charlotte had heard that there was a lower-class party being held on the west side that didn't require any kind of fancy attire. A lot of cowboys and soldiers were said to be celebrating there. Cheyenne was an eclectic society to be sure, and Charlotte wasn't exactly sure where she belonged. They had more money than most, but her folks had never aspired to be upper class. They were content with the ranch and their biblical values. Family and home came first, not the social registry or political gains.

Still, it was fun to dress up once in a while. Charlotte didn't mind at all that Micah might find her appealing. She wanted very much for him to give her his attention. The trouble was, she was most likely going to garner that same interest from other single men. Single women were still somewhat scarce in the West, and marriageable-aged women were highly sought. Between the railroad, the fort, and all the ranches, single men were plentiful and desirous of female companionship. She wasn't quite sure how to tell them all that she only had eyes for one man. Especially if he didn't show her the same kind of attention.

However, Charlotte was game to try and had chosen one of her newest Sunday gowns. It was a layered muslin of pale pink with a modest neckline and lace trim. The gown had short, puffed sleeves and a folded sash at the waist. She wore white gloves and had arranged her blond curls in a fashionable style atop her head. Mama had helped with the latter, but they kept the design simple, sweeping Charlotte's hair back from her face on either side and tying a band of pink ribbon across the top. The curls were pinned in such a way that they cascaded a little down her neck, just touching her shoulders. Charlotte liked it very much and hoped Micah would too.

Mama, on the other hand, had chosen a dark plum-colored gown that she'd purchased earlier that summer. She looked quite lovely. Refined and elegant was what people would no doubt say. At least those were the words that came to Charlotte's mind.

It was good to see her mother smiling . . . even laughing. The last year and a half had been so hard on her. The first year, Mama had wept a great deal when in the privacy of her bedroom, but over the last few months, Charlotte had noticed a difference in her demeanor. Perhaps it was in part due to Rich showing up more often, or maybe she could finally remember her husband and son without falling to pieces. Whatever it was, Charlotte was relieved to find Mama happy again.

"Are you ready to meet up with Micah?" Mama asked from the open door of their two-room suite.

Charlotte gave a whirl. "I am. Do you think he'll notice me?"

Mama laughed. "He'd have to be blind not to notice you. You're quite the belle tonight, my dear, and most every man in the room will be noticing you."

"As long as Micah does, I'll be happy. His attention is the only one I want."

The evening was perfect for the celebration, and as Charlotte and her mother met up with Micah in the hotel lobby, Charlotte was ready for the fun to begin. Of course, seeing Micah all cleaned up and in his best Sunday clothes, Charlotte couldn't help but wish they were already a couple. She longed to be on his arm—to know that they would dance away the evening with each other and then end the night together. She flushed at such a thought, and altogether missed what her mother had just said.

"Charlotte, did you hear me?"

"No, I'm sorry. My mind was a million miles away."

Mama glanced at Micah a few feet away. "I'm sure it was considerably closer. I said that Mrs. Nagle has invited us to their new-house reception. It will be toward the end of the month. Would you like to go?"

"Oh." Charlotte met her mother's curious gaze and nodded. "I suppose it could be interesting."

The Nagles were part of the wealthier folk in Cheyenne, but Mama had long been friends with Mrs. Nagle, and the new house they had built on East Seventeenth was said to be the finest money could buy. It was rumored to have cost fifty thousand dollars, and while Charlotte really didn't care that much about attending the reception, she was curious as to what had been done to be worth that much money.

"I'll send her a note before we leave tomorrow. I think it might be very interesting to attend, and I know it would please Emma. She's so proud of her new house. Micah, would you be willing to escort us? We can stay the night in town, maybe a couple of nights. I have banking and lawyer business to tend to. I'll pay all the expenses, of course."

Charlotte noticed that he seemed to be staring at her as if trying to remember something. She smiled his way, happy to know that he was at least a little interested. "What do you say, Micah?"

He seemed momentarily confused and then nodded. "I'd be happy to escort you both, but I can fend for myself." He offered Charlotte's mother his arm. "Now, shall I escort you to the ball, Mrs. Aldrich?" He bowed in mock formality.

Charlotte couldn't help but giggle. Even Mama chuckled, but she took his arm, nevertheless. Then Micah straightened and smiled at Charlotte.

"I have two arms. You might as well take the other."

She nodded and allowed Micah to sweep them across the crowded lobby. Outside was little better as they followed many of the other people to the park where the dance was to be held. The musicians were already hard at work under an arbor of muslin and flowers.

"May I have this dance," someone said to Charlotte, and then before even waiting for an answer he whisked her away and into the flow of waltzers. She looked up to find Lewis Bradley holding her possessively.

"You might give a lady a chance to say if she desires to dance with you," Charlotte said, fixing him with a scowl. "I would rather not."

He tightened his grip. "It would look ridiculous if you were to cause a scene just now. Think of your reputation . . . or at least that of your mother's. You wouldn't want people looking down on her because your behavior was out of line."

Charlotte said nothing. She allowed him to turn her and lead her through the steps, but inside she was seething. The music couldn't end soon enough.

"I wish you wouldn't be mad at me. I just wanted to apologize for making you feel so unhappy when last we spoke. I do love you. I know you don't love me, but I promise you will in time."

Charlotte tried again to pull away, but Lewis was having nothing to do with that. She decided it was best to finish the dance and be done with him. She'd be better on her guard next time.

"Honestly, Charlotte, you're acting like a child. At least say something."

She fought to keep from countering with a lengthy diatribe about his manners. "Very well. There, I've said something."

He smiled. "Try to look happy. People are watching."

"That I will not do. You are fortunate that I don't put an end to this and slap your face. Maybe publicly humiliating you will get my point across where words have failed."

The music concluded, and Charlotte yanked her gloved hand from his and turned without another word. She knew if she said anything at all, it wouldn't be kind.

After that, she was very guarded about who she danced with and what dance was chosen. Throughout the evening, she kept wishing Micah would ask her to waltz. She knew he was a capable dancer. Mama had seen to it that both he and Frank Jr. knew all the latest dances. She had forced them to take classes despite their protests. Charlotte remembered wishing she could go with them, but she'd been much too young.

"Would you care to dance?"

She smiled at the sound of the voice and looked up to see the one man she'd longed for all evening. Micah gave her a hint of a smile.

Charlotte felt as if there were butterflies in her stomach. "I was just looking for you. You haven't asked me to dance all evening."

"Sorry, dancing has never been of any real interest to me. I was kind of hiding out while you and your mother enjoyed yourselves."

"Well, let's give it a go," she said, taking hold of his hand.

With little difficulty, Micah merged them into the crowd of dancers and began to waltz. Charlotte could have lost herself forever in that moment. Micah was easily the handsomest man at the dance. At least he was in her eyes.

"I'm sorry if I embarrassed you today at the Stock Growers Association meeting," Charlotte began. "I know I shouldn't let my temper get the best of me."

"I thought you had a valid reason to speak as you did." Micah whirled her in a circle. He was quite a capable dancer, even if he didn't like the activity.

"I appreciate that you feel that way. I'm thankful, too, that you were able to go back and get the information for us."

"There's not much I wouldn't do for you and your ma."

Charlotte wondered if now was the time to share her heart with him. "You know, Micah, you're important to the both of us. You always have been. Mama sees you as a son. I know she's perked up considerably since you started spending more time with us. We miss having men around to talk to. We . . . I, especially, miss you."

As the music ended, so too did the dance. Charlotte gazed into Micah's eyes for a long moment. It was as if no one and nothing else existed. "Micah, I—"

A burst of fireworks went off, filling the night skies with flashes of light. The moment for confessions passed as those around them began to cheer. Charlotte moved close to Micah and turned to watch. She felt his arm go around her in a rather protective manner and eased in just a little closer. She wanted the moment to go on forever.

10

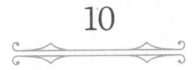

A little over a week had passed since they'd celebrated the nation's independence, and still the heat refused to abate. Folks were already starting to fear another drought like the summer of '86, which in turn caused them to fret about another winter like what had followed.

"Do you suppose we should lay in more hay?" Mother asked Charlotte as they ate breakfast.

"I don't know. Have you talked to Mr. Johnson or Micah about it? I'm sure they must have an opinion."

"I suppose that would be the place to start. I just don't want there to be any problems. I'm not seeing any particular signs that we're heading into problems, but I want to be ready for whatever comes our way."

Charlotte began to butter a piece of toast. "I believe we're doing a good job of that."

"I agree. Now that we have fenced off pastures, I feel much better. That grass is growing nice and thick and will afford us a way of better caring for the animals if the weather turns bad. Of course, in time the herd will expand significantly and no longer be contained in those fields."

"That's why we need to keep looking ahead. We have the money to fence off more land. Maybe we could hire some summer workers and get another large section taken care of this year."

"That is a good thought." Mother paused with her teacup halfway to her lips. "I think we should consult Micah on that as well."

Charlotte smiled. "I'll do that." She was about to take a bite of her toast when someone's shout caught her ear.

"Fire!"

She looked at Mother as a sense of dread washed over her. Both women dropped what they were doing and jumped up from the table. They went flying out of the house, with Nora right behind them. Smoke billowed up from just beyond the closest corral.

"What's going on?" Charlotte demanded to know as she caught up to one of the cowboys. He had bucket in hand.

"The birthing shed is on fire," he replied.

"I'll get the chickens out of their pen," Mother said, heading in the direction of the coop. It was just a few feet from the birthing shed.

The young man took off with his bucket, stopping long enough to fill it at the watering trough. Charlotte went back to the house, grabbed up three buckets, and headed out again. At the trough, she filled each bucket with water.

Nora took up one. Charlotte grabbed two, and then they headed to the birthing shed, where flames were already consuming the small structure. Charlotte glanced around with a frown. They couldn't save the shed, so maybe the best idea was to tend to things nearby.

"Kit, get the men to water down the outbuildings around the shed. We can't save it, but hopefully we can keep it contained if the winds don't whip up too bad. Still, you stay on top of the fire. Have one of the other men work it with you and don't leave it until it's completely out."

"Yes, ma'am," he replied and took up a shovel.

They all worked together to water down the chicken coop while the hens enjoyed themselves in the front yard, well away from the fire. Mama took care of getting the pigs and milk cow taken care of, while Charlotte worked the pump to keep the trough full of water. She couldn't imagine what had happened to start the fire. Thankfully, it was one of those rare days when the winds weren't bad.

Once the fire was out, she gathered Kit and the crew together to determine what had happened. "Any idea how this started?"

"I don't know exactly what started it," Kit said, sounding almost embarrassed.

Charlotte thought his demeanor rather strange but said nothing.

"Does anyone know what happened?" Mama asked, looking at each of the cowboys.

"No, ma'am" came from each man.

"I suppose it's possible someone threw down a cigarette," one of the hands finally spoke up.

Mama looked at the cowboys. "Any of you remember smoking in the birthing shed before the fire started?" They shook their heads, and she continued. "You're not in trouble. I just want to know what happened so it won't happen again." Still, no one said a word.

"Very well. We'll have no more smoking in the yard. Is that clear?" Mama asked. The men all nodded, and she continued. "I'm sorry if that inconveniences you. Take a walk when you smoke or do it on the drive. Then be careful with putting out your cigarettes when you're finished. We can't have another accident like this happening. If the winds had been bad, it could have taken everything."

The boys seemed genuinely upset by what had happened, and well they should. Charlotte glanced at Kit. Their gazes locked for a moment, and then he quickly turned away.

"I'll make sure the fire's out and get the mess cleaned up," he muttered as he went.

Charlotte frowned. "Kit's not acting himself this morning."

Her mother drew near. "He probably feels to blame for what happened. We were truly blessed that the fire didn't spread. Everything is as dry as can be. It wouldn't have taken much to set it all ablaze."

"I know." Charlotte squared her shoulders. "I'm thankful, to be sure. Wish we knew what happened though. Surely the boys know if they were in there smoking or not."

"I know. It makes me uneasy that they won't be honest about it. A man should be able to own up to his actions, even if they're careless and cause problems." Mama pulled off her work gloves. "I'm going to finish my breakfast. Want to join me?"

Charlotte nodded. "Yes, and I want to talk to you about some ideas I have for a new birthing shed."

Micah hadn't expected Rich Johnson to come calling that Friday morning, but spending time visiting was just the thing to revive his spirits. Since dawn, Micah had been trying to figure out his best course of action. The Aldrich women wanted him to combine forces and create the Aldrich-Hamilton Cattle Company. They'd talked about the idea all the way home from the Fourth of July celebration.

"The idea is intriguing," Micah said. "But I just don't know if it's what I should do, so tell me what you honestly think."

"I think it's a great idea," Rich replied. "Those women

have fought hard to hang on to their ranch, and if you join forces and assets, I think it will be good for both parties. I have to admit," he paused and grinned, "I've had a thought about joining up with Mrs. Aldrich, myself."

Micah looked at him for a moment. It dawned on him that Rich wasn't talking about cattle ventures. He laughed. "She is a handsome woman, Rich."

"That she is. And smart. She knows this life out here and what's required. I don't like living alone. My children are grown and gone. None of them want to take up ranching, and there's only my foreman and housekeeper to keep me company. Oh, and my surly cook, but she's no real company at all. Just complains about everything. Why, I hired five new men, and she complained about it even though she doesn't have to cook for them or clean up after them."

"So are you gonna go courting, Rich?"

"I think Betsy would say it's the smart thing to do. Lucille and I have both lost our mates, and it's not good to be alone out here. And if you and Charlotte end up together, Lucille would be just as alone as I am."

Micah's head snapped up. "What do you mean if Charlotte and I end up together? There's nothing between us that way."

Rich gave a roaring laugh. "You may not have thought it all out yet, but folks have always figured on the two of you marrying."

"No, it's not like that at all. Charlotte sees me as nothing more than a big brother. She was always hanging around with Frank Jr. and me."

"Well, son, I have three sisters, and none of them ever looked at me the way that girl looks at you—the way she's looked at you since she was knee-high to a grasshopper."

Something stirred inside of Micah, breaking down a little bit more of the sturdy wall he'd built around his heart. Did Charlotte really look at him that way? Did she have feelings for him? Sure, she turned to him for advice and told him how important he was to her, but he'd never seen it as anything more than the close family-type connection they had for each other.

"Oh, come on now, son. She's been gone over you for years. At least that's how I see it. No one has ever told me otherwise. I think even her folks knew how she felt."

"She's never said anything about it to me. Not that I would have encouraged that kind of thing. Her pa wanted her to marry someone other than a rancher. Charlotte even said they had a terrible fight about it. She loves the ranch."

"She loves you," Rich said, laughing again. "And with any luck at all, I'm gonna get her ma to lovin' me." He headed to where Micah had been doing some fencing repairs.

"You've got a good place here, Micah, but the Aldrich situation is even better. Maybe you shouldn't go makin' a bunch of repairs and additions to this place. Could be if you and Charlotte marry and Lucille does the same with me, you could just keep this place for your oldest son. I've got more than enough to share with Lucille, and she told me she plans to set the ranch up in Charlotte's name. You two could combine your assets and make quite the empire."

His ideas had Micah feeling completely off-balance. He couldn't think of Charlotte that way. It wasn't right. She was just a good friend . . . a sister of sorts.

But I don't feel like she's my sister.

The truth was what it was. Micah hadn't allowed himself thoughts of romancing Charlotte Aldrich, but those ideas weren't off-putting.

"I don't want to go through another winter alone," Rich said. "Christmas last year was the saddest I've ever faced. I imagine the same was true for Lucille. I'm gonna work real hard to convince her we belong together. Could be if you did the same with Charlotte, Lucille would be more inclined to consider me. If she knew her daughter was all settled and happy, then I think she might allow herself to be likewise."

"I, uh, I don't know to say. Here I thought you were going to give me ideas on what I needed to do with the ranch."

"Well, I just did. If we boys get married, it will straighten itself out." Rich gave another laugh. "In fact, I'm not so sure the entire world won't settle into place once we tie the knot with those two gals."

A rider was coming up the drive at quite a clip. Micah squinted against the sun to see who it might be, worried it would spell bad news.

"I brought this message from Miss Charlotte," the young man told Micah reining back his horse to an abrupt halt. "She said to wait for an answer."

"Maybe she's proposing," Rich said in a hushed voice, then busted out laughing.

Micah scanned the note. Charlotte had fifty new angus cows coming in the next day via the railroad and wondered if Micah would ride with her to bring them back. He couldn't help wondering why she wasn't sending a couple of hands to go fetch them.

He glanced at Rich. "She wants help bringing some cows back from Cheyenne." Micah looked up at the rider. "Tell her I'll be at the house first thing in the morning."

"She said to come have breakfast with them at six," the boy said before turning his horse and heading down the drive at a gallop.

Apparently, she had already known he'd do her bidding. Charlotte knew she could count on him. It really wasn't anything more than that. Or was it?

"You'd better get busy, Micah, or some other fella's gonna come along and steal that gal away."

"Lewis Bradley has already tried," Micah said, folding the

note up and putting it in his pocket. "Charlotte put him in his place."

"Still, I wouldn't wait long." Rich mounted and looked down at Micah. "A slow ride to Cheyenne would be a good time to talk about a lot of things." He grinned again. "Maybe there aren't any cows in Cheyenne, and it's just her way to get you alone. Maybe I'll try that with Lucille."

This made Micah chuckle. "I doubt you could fool Mrs. Aldrich that way. Maybe just keep taking her dancing. She didn't seem to mind at all that you kept her busy on the Fourth of July."

"She's light on her feet," Rich said, giving Micah a wave. "Time to go a courtin'."

Micah watched him ride off down the trail. Johnson was a good man. A man Micah's father had truly respected. Like Frank Aldrich Sr., their friendship had been immediate and strong.

Leaning back against the fence post, Micah shook his head. Everything had changed. The world Micah had once known was gone. When they'd first come to the territory, people were few and far between, and folks learned quickly to do for themselves. Still, the friendships that could be made were more valuable than gold.

"Never lose sight of how important people are in your life, Micah," his father had stressed. *"Do for others and be available when troubles come, and they'll do likewise for you."*

The Aldrich and Johnson families had been invaluable to Micah and his father. Out here, well away from town and easy help, they had been there for one another. More than once they'd ridden to each other's aid and would continue to do so, even though so many of them were now gone. Micah might have been useless to everyone since losing his dad, but he didn't intend to go on being that way.

His mother and Rich's wife were gone. The Aldrich men

and Micah's father were dead as well. Rich's children married and moved off. Only he and Charlotte remained of the children who had come here so long ago. Even so, Micah hadn't really thought about what was to come next for the people. It was always about the land and animals. Since losing his father, he hadn't considered taking a wife, much less that Charlotte might be the one.

When they were young, he and Frank Jr. spent time eyeing one girl and then another at church. They'd had their favorites and talked about courtship. But Micah had never given serious thought toward any of those young ladies. He was determined to see the ranch grow and become something wondrous, like John Iliff's ranch to the south. He had been known as the cattle king of Colorado. It was said at his death in 1878 that Iliff had amassed some thirty-five thousand head. His widow had continued to build that ranch, and who knew how many they had before the Great Die-Up.

Thoughts of Iliff's widow brought to mind Mrs. Aldrich. She was strong and capable. The ranch itself was proof of just how much she understood what was needed. She wasn't afraid to work hard, but she was getting older. Rich would make her a good husband. Mrs. Aldrich needed someone like him who understood her love of the land and family. It wasn't good for man to be alone. Together, they could face the future working side by side.

Was a wife what God intended next for Micah as well?

Micah gazed up at the sky. He hadn't been overly active in his prayer life, but it seemed that maybe that should change. There were so many questions he had about his future, and surely only God had the answers he needed.

"Well . . . here I am, Lord."

He shook his head. Since his father's death, God hadn't been speaking to Micah at all. Why should he expect it now?

Of course, maybe it wasn't that God wasn't speaking. Maybe Micah wasn't listening.

He drew a deep breath and looked toward heaven. "I know I'm the problem, Lord. I just don't know what to do about it."

11

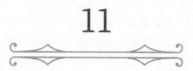

Micah enjoyed breakfast with the Aldrich women. Nora had served them biscuits and gravy, eggs and sausage, and lots of hot coffee despite the heat. Seemed that coffee was a staple at this table, and even Charlotte drank her fair share.

"We should be home in the late afternoon, Mama," Charlotte told her mother as the meal concluded. "Of course, it will depend on whether the train is on time."

"I still think you could send Kit and one of the boys in to drive the cows back," her mother said. She picked up her cup and sipped the coffee.

"I want to see this through. I need to make sure they're in good shape and, hopefully, all are bred. Of course, I won't check that until we're back at the ranch." She got up from the table. "Micah, I'm going to fetch my hat and gloves, and then I'll be ready to head out."

Micah nodded. "Sounds good."

She left the room, and Mrs. Aldrich picked up the conversation. "I wouldn't trust anyone else to look after her, Micah."

He thought again of Rich's words. Should he ask Mrs.

Aldrich about it? Ask her if she had plans for her daughter to marry him?

"Don't think I don't know that she can be a handful. Do you know that after we left the Stock Growers Association meeting, she wanted to return?" she questioned. "She told me to go on to the tea party while she went back to give the men a piece of her mind. She planned to wait until the president had called the meeting to order."

"Somehow that doesn't surprise me." Micah could just see the scene in his mind. Charlotte, although small of stature, would have every man's undivided attention. "She has a way of getting her point across."

"She does when she wants to, that's for sure. But she can also be good at hiding her feelings."

Micah wondered what exactly Mrs. Aldrich was getting at but didn't have time to ask since Charlotte bounded back into the room. She had dressed for the day wearing a brown split skirt with a matching vest and a long-sleeved calico blouse. She secured a wide brim hat to shade herself from the hot sun before pulling on her riding gloves.

"I'm ready if you are."

Micah rose from the table. "I'm ready." He nodded toward Mrs. Aldrich. "Thanks for breakfast."

"Anytime, Micah. You're always welcome here." She smiled. "But I think you know that."

Following Charlotte from the house, Micah couldn't help but admire her figure. She was petite, but shapely in all the right places. Why had he never noticed before now? Not so long ago she was just Frank Jr.'s little sister—gangly, curly headed, and often annoying. Now she was graceful and charming. Annoying too, at times. That made him smile.

"You've got the strangest look on your face, Micah. What's on your mind?"

He met her eyes, then quickly looked to the ground, feeling his face warm. He hadn't meant to get caught watching her. What could he say?

"I guess I'm just realizing how the years have passed. It seems like yesterday we were just kids."

She laughed and went to where the horses waited. "Funny you should say so. I was just pondering that very thing this morning." She unfastened her reins from the fence pole and led the horse away for mounting. In a flash, she was in the saddle, not needing help from Micah or anyone.

Micah mounted, and together they started the horses for Cheyenne. Once they had cleared the yard, Charlotte continued. "I was just four when we came to Cheyenne, and it seemed like the end of the world. I hated leaving grandparents and cousins behind."

"You were still just four when we came in January 1870."

"I was almost five. My birthday was on the twenty-third."

"I remember. It was a Sunday, and your mama invited us to share lunch after church and celebrate your birthday. You were so proud that you were turning five." He gave her a sidelong glance as she stared ahead.

"What did you think of me then?" she asked.

"I didn't think about you much at all. I was a twelve-year-old boy. Horses, snakes, and hunting were far more on my mind."

"You weren't quite twelve," Charlotte said, looking at him with one of the most beautiful smiles Micah had ever seen. She seemed absolutely radiant. "You wouldn't turn twelve until April."

"True enough. You have a good memory."

"I was excited that there was someone nearer my own age than just Frank. All of Rich's children were so much older. Well, his youngest, Emma, was close to my age, but she was always getting into trouble and didn't seem to want to be friends, especially with someone younger. There was no one to play with or even talk to when the adults got together."

"So that's why you were always following your brother and me around." Micah kept a close eye on the trail ahead but didn't deny himself a few stray glances.

"You two were all I had. The only ones who fit even a little bit into my world."

"You should have had a little sister, Charlotte. I wish my mom could have had more children. There were a couple of younger brothers who died, and then some miscarriages. She always wanted more."

"I want a big family. Maybe as big as the Deckers have."

"Charles Decker and his wife have ten children. Are you sure you want ten?"

She laughed. "I love children even though I've had little experience with them. Maybe that's exactly why I want so many. But I'm not opposed to bringing the number down to say . . . eight or maybe even six. What I don't want is for any of them to feel alone like I did. Don't think that I didn't know what a pest I was to you and Frank. I didn't mean to be. I just craved companionship. I still do. Mama does her best, but I think she's lonely at times too."

"I saw her dancing a lot with Rich Johnson on the Fourth of July," Micah offered.

"Yes. I encouraged that. I think they'd be wonderful together, don't you?"

Micah wondered if he should say something about his conversation with Rich. He decided against it. If Rich wanted to pursue Mrs. Aldrich, he'd have to be the one to speak up to Charlotte.

"I guess so. They both have a lot in common." Micah felt safe in offering that insight.

"They definitely do," Charlotte continued with great enthusiasm. "Rich and Papa were a lot alike. They liked so much of the same things and thought the same about ranching. Both were, or in Rich's case, are, good Christian gentlemen. And Rich seems genuinely interested in Mama. I've listened to him talk to her, and he cares about her feelings and needs. I think that's one of the most important things in a relationship between a husband and wife, don't you?"

Micah nodded. "I do." For a moment the words hung in the air, and Micah was reminded of that being the reply to wedding vows.

Charlotte looked his way. "Let's run them a ways. This is good flat ground, free of holes. At least it was last I checked. Come on."

Micah laughed. "If you think you're up for it."

"Ha!" She gave Buck a kick in the sides. "Git up, Buck. Let's go!" The horse jumped ahead and stretched out for the run.

Micah followed, giving Duke his head. He easily caught up to Charlotte, but rather than pass her as he knew he could do, he kept his horse even with her chestnut gelding. It was kind of nice being paired this way. Maybe it would be nice being paired forever.

Charlotte loved the feel of the wind against her face as they rode their horses at full gallop. Knowing they were soon to reach the first of several streams, Charlotte slowed Buck and eased him to a trot, then back to a walk. Micah did the same with Duke. By the time they reached the water, both animals were cooled down and ready to drink.

As the sun rose higher in the sky, the temperatures were once again climbing. Charlotte was glad to stop for a moment and splash some water on her face. She tried not to spend her whole time watching to see what Micah was doing, but it was hard. Having discussed children, she was hard-pressed not to imagine what their progeny might look like. No doubt they'd be blue-eyed. Micah's hair was dark brown whereas hers was sun-kissed blond. Maybe their children would be a mix.

Their children. Charlotte loved the thought of that. She had long imagined a ranch of their own with children to raise. And she was serious about having a large family. She wanted her children to have each other to turn to when things went wrong. It was wonderful having good parents that she could trust, but it would have been so nice to have sisters to seek advice from and share stories with. Maybe if she'd had sisters, one or more of them would have come with her to storm the Stock Growers Association meeting.

"You look mighty deep in thought."

Charlotte glanced over and saw that Micah was watching her. He'd taken off his brown felt hat and was wiping his face with his wet bandanna.

"I was just thinking about the stock growers and how intolerant they are of women. I hope I live to see that change. It's not like I want to run the place, but I would like to be welcome to listen to their thoughts and offer my own."

"Strong women often intimidate men," Micah replied, ringing the bandanna again in the steam. He straightened and squeezed out the excess water before tying it around his neck.

"But you aren't intimidated by them." Charlotte had finished cooling her face and returned to where Buck was grazing on greens by the creek. "You respect my mother and seem to find her thoughts of value. Mine too."

"That's because you're both the type to think things through before you speak and to offer straightforward ideas. You must admit there are folks who like to just ramble on and on for the sake of hearing themselves speak."

"Men as well as women do that."

Micah chuckled. "That's why I said there are folks who do it. Both are guilty."

Charlotte nodded and drew her gloves from where she'd tucked them in her waistband. "I really had nothing I wanted to offer, but much I wanted to learn. Papa and Frank Jr. were good at sharing information and teaching me. Mama is wonderful to learn from as well. She knows so much about farming. Did you know she's asked her cousins to come here? They're going to advise her about planting crops. You're welcome to come and hear what they have to say. We must start thinking about such things and not rely solely on shipping grain and hay in for our needs."

"I agree. And like I told you and your mother, that was part of what was discussed in brief at the stock growers meeting. Of course, they weren't holding a full session since it was Fourth of July, but when they get together again, they are going to discuss the matter in more detail. I think all of the area ranchers realize they're going to have to do more to protect their herds."

"And I'd like to hear what they have to say, but of course I won't be welcome to join in."

"I'll go for you. I don't mind."

"But I mind that they won't let me sit in and hear valuable information on area ranching. I'm a rancher and deserve to know what's going on. They have all sorts of rules for the men about no spitting and cussing, you'd think they could have a rule about allowing women. Even if they didn't let us speak."

Micah laughed aloud. "Oh, sure, that would go over real well. You know as well as I do that it would soon enough be protested if that were a fixed rule for the meeting. 'Men, you can speak your mind and say whatever you want, but you ladies have to be quiet.' No, I know how that would be."

Charlotte had to smile. "Of course you're right. But I still don't see the harm in letting us be there."

"You and your mother have already shown those old boys that you know what you're doing, and frankly, it puts them in poor light. Your father tried to tell them what your mother thought about the coming winter back in '86. No one would listen. Not even my dad. They were no doubt kicking themselves when they realized she was right. That's a lot of humble pie to eat, and they're suffering for it still."

"But my mother wouldn't be boastful about what happened. You know her. She's kind and gentle."

"But she was right when many men were wrong. It got the best of them and ended a lot of ranches and dreams. The few who stuck around to try to rebuild don't want to be reminded of the mistakes they made."

Charlotte pulled on her gloves. "You would understand their thoughts better than I would." She took up Buck's reins. "You ready to move on?"

"In a minute. I have something I want to say."

Charlotte felt her heart skip a beat. Could he possibly know what she was feeling—maybe feel it himself? She held her breath.

"I want to thank you for how supportive you've been. Your mother too. I know I failed my father miserably in how I've managed this last year. I forsook God and turned to alcohol. I let the ranch go without care. I barely did what was required to keep Duke alive. I wasn't much of a man."

"Mama says we failed you as well. We lost ourselves in our sorrows and forgot our promise to be there for you. I was so blinded by my guilt and regret over fighting with my father. Not seeing you was a sort of penance, I suppose. I felt I didn't deserve to be happy. I didn't see how I was letting you down."

"But you didn't let me down. I had no expectations. My father, on the other hand, had a great many. He . . . well, he raised me to be better. He . . . he . . . oh never mind. He didn't follow his own advice. Why should I be concerned about my failing to live up to what he wanted, when he most assuredly failed to live up to my expectations?"

"Maybe having so many expectations of each other is the mistake." Charlotte thought of what her own father had wanted her to do. "Holding a lot of expectations for someone might be the biggest mistake we can make. In some cases, we might expect so much that they can never hope to meet our standards. In other cases, we might hold them back from reaching their full potential. Jesus talks in the Bible about bearing one another's burdens and going the extra mile with someone. I don't recall that He ever spoke about setting a lot of lofty expectations for them."

"True enough. But you must admit, parents are always going to have ideals that they want their children to live up to."

"Maybe your father's pa had those for him. Maybe that was the burden he carried, and it was too much." Charlotte shook her head. "I think being encouraging and supportive is what matters with children. Guidance too, don't get me wrong, but demanding they follow a certain path or choose something just because it's what we desire is wrong. I'm convinced of that after what I went through with Papa."

She gave Micah a wistful smile. If only he could know how much she loved him—how she had no unrealistic expectations of him. She only wanted him to love her.

But what if that *was* unrealistic?

12

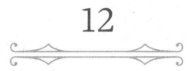

At precisely nine o'clock in the evening on the twenty-sixth of July, the Nagle house was, as one person said, "Thrown open to the roof." Guests were received and welcomed by Emma and Erasmus Nagle in grand style with Chinese lanterns blazing and beautiful furnishings gleaming in the glow.

While a small orchestra played in the Nagles' first house next door, visitors made their way through the new mansion. Charlotte and her mother stood waiting for Micah to hand their wraps and his hat off to the staff.

"This is quite a romantic setting," Mama whispered in Charlotte's ear. "Do you suppose you might tell Micah how you feel about him?"

"Goodness!" Charlotte turned and looked at her mother. "That's a very private thing to reveal in a very public setting."

Mother laughed. "Well, it seems to me you've had opportunities for private settings and didn't take advantage of those. I thought perhaps this might do. After all, you love the man."

Charlotte glanced to where Micah stood waiting his turn. "I do, and I will tell him in time."

"If you wait much longer, you may lose him. Now that he's getting out more . . . well, he just might meet someone who isn't as shy as you. Seems the Nagles' maid is quite at ease in flirting."

Charlotte hadn't missed the way the girl batted her eyes at Micah. "I'm not shy. I'm just waiting for the right time." She turned away from watching Micah and the maid lest she march over there and speak her mind. "God will show me when the time is right."

They made their arrival known to Erasmus, or Elmo, as his friends called him. Emma was soon at his side, and Charlotte's mother complimented them on the grand palace they'd created. Mother stayed and visited a moment with Emma while Charlotte and Micah made their way into a smaller parlor.

"Isn't this beautiful," Charlotte declared. She marveled at the mahogany woodwork. "They've truly spared no expense."

"I suppose you'd love to have a grand house like this," Micah said only loud enough for her to hear.

"Absolutely not." She looked at him and shook her head. "It would never be suitable on the ranch. Oh, some of these furnishings would be just fine, but as much dust and dirt as we sweep out of the house on a daily basis, these glorious carpets and tapestries would never do. Just imagine how much cleaning it would take. I'd never get anything else accomplished."

Micah laughed out loud, causing several of the guests to look their way. Charlotte pulled him along to another area of the house. A massive fireplace was the focal point of the next room. Above the mantel, a tall mirror ran all the way to the ceiling.

"Why did you laugh? I was serious."

Micah folded his arms across his chest. "If you had the

money to create a house like this, Charlotte, you could hire an entire staff of cleaners. You would never need to lift a finger. Just think of it. You'd be a grand lady, living in a mansion—a queen in a castle, really."

"I have no desire, and like I said, it would have no place on the ranch."

"I don't know. It could be a nice addition. Besides, you might prefer the city if you gave it a chance. You've only lived on the ranch. You might like city life."

"I lived in Denver to attend finishing school, and I did not care for it at all. It was always noisy and always busy. I prefer waking up to a beautiful sunrise and taking Buck out for a morning ride. I love the way the world around me seems to come alive as the sun makes its way higher and higher."

"Now you're just waxing poetic. What about the wind and all that dirt you were talking about? Or what if your husband wants to live in the city? Maybe he'll prefer town life to the open prairie."

"He doesn't." She hadn't meant to say the words aloud, but now that they were out, she couldn't help but wonder what Micah's response would be. However, Mama chose just that moment to join them.

"I wondered where you two had gotten off to. I've been told that upstairs there are three beautiful tin bathtubs encased in walnut and that we must see them. Also, Micah, I heard the men say there was quite the display in the basement. A Smead furnace, as well as a filtering apparatus and ventilating system. Whatever all that means."

Micah shook his head. "It means a lot of money went into this place."

Mama leaned in. "Indeed, it did, and a waste of such goods if you ask me. Our house is just as roomy, and although I don't have stained glass in my windows, the windows I have do keep out the cold in the winter and the flies in the summer."

"Unless we open them," Charlotte said, amused at her mother's comment.

"I plan for us to put screens over the windows," Mama said as she drew closer to the fireplace. "This is quite the hearth. I wouldn't mind a grand fireplace like this."

"Screens would be wonderful. Just imagine being able to have the windows open and the bugs unable to come in." Charlotte smiled at her mother. "And, yes, it is a lovely fireplace."

"And it is a lovely house. Just not the type of place I'd want," Mama replied and turned toward the stairs. "Let's take a look upstairs. I don't want to miss seeing those bathtubs. That might well be something I would enjoy having at the ranch."

"Our copper tub isn't good enough anymore?" Charlotte asked, following her mother to the stairs.

"Well, it's not encased in walnut," Mama said, glancing over her shoulder before breaking into laughter.

Charlotte and Micah laughed, too, and obediently followed her upstairs.

Micah couldn't help but wonder at what Charlotte had said when he'd questioned her about her future husband perhaps preferring to live in the city. She'd spoken as if she knew who he was. Almost as if she were already married. The thought had caused him a moment of discomfort. That had been completely unexpected. Usually, Charlotte spoke in concise and clear terms. Something he had always appreciated about her.

In fact, he greatly appreciated the Aldrich women and their

sensible natures. So many women he'd met in his younger years and time at college seemed nonsensical compared. He had once commented on that to his father.

"Women can be a real mystery," Dad had told him. "Most have the sole ambition of finding a husband. Their lives depend on it, so they learn all sorts of games to make it happen. Be careful what you say to them, or they might take it wrong, and you'll find yourself in front of a preacher against your will." From that warning, Micah had learned to be a man of few words. At least when talking to women.

Mrs. Aldrich made comments as they continued to inspect the house, but Micah knew that none of this really appealed to her or her daughter. Charlotte had been more impressed by the extravagant tray of desserts being served with a long line of other tasty treats, which had made him smile.

Once they'd partaken of the refreshments and visited every floor of the house, the ladies were ready to go back to the hotel. They had booked rooms through Sunday morning, telling Micah that this way they'd have plenty of time to see to all their business as well as spend a little time exploring some of the new shops and visiting friends. He hadn't really wanted to be away from the ranch so long, but they assured him they'd have some of their hands go over and check on his place. He found it nearly impossible to deny Mrs. Aldrich anything she asked. She had been so good to him.

In every way, she had been a mother to him after his own had passed. It was clear that they needed each other, and he wasn't going to let his pride or discomfort cause him to break this very beneficial union.

"We've missed out on a lot of progress this last year," Mrs. Aldrich said as Micah handed them their wraps. "The great Sarah Bernhardt performed in the opera house last year. Lillie Langtry came just a week later."

"I remember going there when it first opened. Papa wasn't impressed because the play was in French."

"He grumbled, too, about all the money that had been spent and that he had to wear a tie."

Micah chuckled. "Dad said you wouldn't catch him going to an opera."

"No, I don't suppose I would have ever expected that," Mrs. Aldrich replied.

They made their way toward the Inter Ocean Hotel, and as they drew near, a man in ragged clothes popped out of the shadows. Micah put himself between the man and the women.

"Could you spare a coin or two? I haven't had a meal in some time." The man was unkempt and unwashed. The odor was quite strong, and Micah detected the smell of beer mingled in.

"Here." Mrs. Aldrich handed Micah a few coins. "Give him this."

Micah did as she instructed. He never carried a sidearm, although he had a rifle that he tucked under the wagon seat in case of snakes—either the ones that slithered and rattled or the kind that walked on two legs. It was of no good to him now, however.

"Move on with you, Joe," a voice called out. "Stop pestering these good people."

"Just asking for some money to eat, lawdog," the man countered.

The lawman stepped closer, and the tramp backed against the wall, his hand closed tightly around his money. "Just relax. I'm not going to haul you in, Joe."

Micah recognized Bob Vogel. They'd first met when attending the Decker School for Boys, although Bob was nearly nine years Micah's junior. They'd crossed paths a year or two after Micah returned from college, and Bob had told him his plans to follow in his father's footsteps and become an officer for the city's police department.

"Go on now, Joe, and get something decent to eat. Don't waste those coins on drink and smokes."

The raggedy man nodded and scurried off down the street.

"How are you doing, Bob?" Micah asked. He turned to Mrs. Aldrich. "You know Bob Vogel, don't you?"

"Most folks call me Robert these days."

"Of course I know Robert. I'm good friends with his mother and father. How are they doing? I didn't get a chance to see them at the Fourth of July celebration."

"That's because they weren't in town. My sister Carrie's back east. She went to college and then got hired to help with some medical research. They went to visit her." He glanced down the road in the direction Joe had gone. "Sorry if Joe gave you a start. We've had quite a few problems with tramps. They've sort of overrun the city. Sorry that he bothered you."

"He didn't. He's one of God's children just as we are," Mrs. Aldrich replied.

Bob nodded and tipped his hat. "Well, I'd best keep walking. Seems to be a lot of folks out this evening, and I want to make sure they keep the peace."

Once he'd gone, Charlotte put her hand over her heart. "Oh, Mama, he might be one of God's children, but he nearly scared me out of my shoes. If Micah hadn't been here, I think I might have fainted, and you know I'm not given to that."

"You can't let fear rule you, Charlotte. Someone is always in need, and the Bible says we have not because we ask not. That man was just asking. I can't fault him for that."

Micah admired Mrs. Aldrich's kindness, but he saw no reason to take a chance. "Well, let's get you safely back to the hotel." Thankfully, it was just a short distance ahead.

"Things are better in some ways here in Cheyenne," Charlotte began, "and in other ways much worse. I remember when we arrived here how Papa always seemed on his guard when we came to town.

"I'm so glad we don't live in the city. I love our ranch, and that's where I intend to stay. Maybe we should even see about getting a church built out that way. Wouldn't that be nice? We wouldn't have to come all the way to Cheyenne for services on Sunday. Maybe other area families would join us. We wouldn't be a large congregation, but I have a feeling we'd be faithful."

"It would be beneficial," Mrs. Aldrich agreed. "But we can't just hide ourselves away from the world, Charlotte. We did that all last year, and it didn't really serve us well."

Micah couldn't help but agree, although he did so silently. His isolation had only led to feeling sorry for himself and drinking. He'd forsaken every good habit he'd ever been taught, and he'd gotten away from God. Now, as he was working to make his way back, there was still that nagging fear that someone might learn the truth about his father. Still, it had been a year, and no one had questioned the quick burial on the isolated ranch. That was of course due to Mrs. Aldrich giving her word about what had happened. Micah knew, however, if people found out the truth, they wouldn't be so welcoming. It wasn't what they'd do or say to him that gave him real concern, however. It was how they would treat Mrs. Aldrich and Charlotte. If they knew that the Aldrich women had kept the truth secret, there would be much to pay. Already they had to fight to be taken seriously, but if folks knew their word was compromised, it could spell the end of their good reputations . . . maybe even their ability to continue ranching.

If Lewis Bradley had any doubts about Charlotte's feelings for Micah Hamilton before the Nagle party, he didn't now that it was said and done. Throughout the evening he'd watched them together, and they never even saw him. They were so enthralled with each other's company that they hardly noticed anyone around them.

It was obvious that Micah was the reason Charlotte didn't want to marry him. He wondered if her father had known. It wasn't likely, given that he had no concerns about it when Lewis had come to him with the proposition of joining business and pleasure.

Lewis had known his money wouldn't last much longer. His poor investment knowledge had robbed him of much in the early days of his marriage to Willa. However, there had been so much money that he wasn't overly concerned. It wasn't until she died, and then that horrible winter, that things really took a turn for the worse.

He'd been poorly advised. What else could he say? He had no living father to guide him. Not one relative of value or intellect who would know which investments were advantageous and which ones would fail. Even Willa's father was gone.

Someone had recommended a man in Cheyenne who seemed to know quite a lot about the markets and stocks that were being offered, but the man turned out to be a charlatan, and Lewis lost even more money.

Thus, his desperation to team up with Frank Aldrich Sr. had driven Lewis to court the man more than he would his daughter.

Settling in front of his bedroom fireplace, Lewis steepled his fingers as he relaxed his elbows on the arm of the chair. There had to be a way to get Micah out of the picture and force his hand with Charlotte. She wasn't easily intimidated. Lewis knew that much. Micah Hamilton wouldn't be either. Still, there had to be a way. But short of arranging Micah's death, Lewis wasn't sure how he could rid himself of the man.

He let out a heavy breath and gazed at the flames in the fireplace. He was losing money much too quickly. It would soon be common knowledge if he wasn't careful. Already his banker knew there was trouble. Lewis had cashed in some railroad stock and deposited the money to keep things running, but it wouldn't be long before all of that was gone. He'd staved off the man's questions by explaining he was waiting for a big investment deal to pay off. He assured the banker that money was soon to be forthcoming.

Charlotte and her mother had plenty of money. There was money just sitting in the bank with no purpose. Then there were the investments Frank Aldrich had made prior to his death. The Aldrich lawyer had surely told Lucille about their value. And now Charlotte would inherit part of that and even more once her mother was gone. If he could just get his hands on the money, Lewis felt confident he could invest it and double it in no time at all. Already he'd heard about new railroads that were looking for investors. Just tonight he was asked to consider going in on stock for the new streetcar routes. At fifty dollars a share, he couldn't go wrong. The streetcars would run forever. Then there were the expanding utility companies and other business ventures that promised big returns. All were worthy of his attention, but without money those investments were out of his reach.

"But she's got the money," he whispered to no one at all.

That feeling of desperation washed over him again as he pictured Charlotte standing next to Micah Hamilton. She adored him. She looked at him in a way that she had never looked at Lewis . . . probably never would. At least not while Micah was alive.

Maybe it really was as simple as killing Micah Hamilton.

13

Mr. Higgins, I'm so glad to know that you've managed to get to the bottom of everything," Lucille Aldrich said, feeling some of her tension ease.

"As far as I know and can find proof of, there was no written agreement between your husband and Mr. Bradley. This includes, but is not limited to, any arrangement for the ranching business, Mr. Aldrich's investments, and the promise of Charlotte in marriage."

Charlotte heaved a sigh, but it was Lucille who spoke. "So even though Frank agreed that Charlotte and Mr. Bradley should wed, she isn't at all obligated to fulfill that arrangement?"

"No, not at all." Clarence Higgins leaned back in his leather chair. "And even if there had been, it's a simple matter to get out of a marriage in Cheyenne. If you hadn't already heard, we've become famous for divorces. Some call us the Magic City of Divorce."

Lucille shook her head and folded her gloved hands together. "What a sad moniker to have."

"We're also the Magic City of Weddings. Folks who have divorced in Colorado have a long waiting period to remarry, so they come here to get wed again. So many have come, in fact, that Colorado is trying to pass laws refusing to recognize marriages made here by their residents."

"Goodness, what a mess," Charlotte said before Lucille could reply.

She knew her daughter probably had strong thoughts on the matter, but rather than allow them to get caught up in a lengthy conversation, Lucille refocused their discussion. "So we aren't under any obligation to Lewis Bradley?"

Mr. Higgins closed the file in front of him. "None whatsoever."

"Good. We just wanted to make certain that was the case. He's made a pest of himself trying to force Charlotte to carry through with her father's plans to marry."

"Well, I suppose it is possible that Mr. Aldrich could have made a written agreement with Mr. Lewis in private. There might be repercussions if it relates to business dealings. Should he suggest that he has any document of that type, encourage him to come see me, and I can compare signatures and get the details of what was agreed upon. I doubt this to be the case, however, since your husband was a real stickler for doing business through me alone—wouldn't so much as sell a cow without me doing the paperwork. Regardless, he can't force Miss Aldrich to marry him. She's reached her majority."

"That certainly puts my mind at ease." Lucille looked to her daughter. "And I'm sure it helps Charlotte to rest easy."

"I wouldn't have married him even if there had been signed contracts and endless pledges. I won't marry a man I do not love," Charlotte said with a bit of a shrug.

Lucille smiled. She knew her daughter. Once she made her mind up about something, she wouldn't be otherwise persuaded. She loved Micah Hamilton, and it was Micah whom she would marry and no other.

"And you have arranged for the rest of our legal papers to be put into my name and Charlotte's?"

"Yes, of course. I managed most of that last year after our very brief talk at the funeral. The ranch and all of your holdings are legally sound and properly documented. You needn't worry. Charlotte is partnered with you as you requested and will, upon your death, inherit the entirety of your estate."

"Good. That is as it should be." Lucille got to her feet, and Mr. Higgins and Charlotte rose as well. "Then unless there's something else, we will be on our way. It's quite warm."

"Yes, this office can be stuffy, even with the new ceiling fan," Mr. Higgins agreed.

Lucille waited until she and Charlotte were outside before speaking again. She looked at Charlotte. "I hope you feel better now."

"I do. I'm glad you requested the appointment with him when we saw him at the Fourth of July celebrations." Charlotte opened and raised her parasol. "Now if Lewis bothers me again, I will send him straightaway to Mr. Higgins. Being as they're both lawyers, they can speak all their legal phrases and understand each other."

"I wonder if Micah has finished arranging for the saddles we brought in to be repaired."

"You told him to meet in the hotel lobby. My guess is he'll be waiting there for us," Charlotte replied.

They made their way back to the hotel and found Micah reading the newspaper in the lobby. The moment he saw them he jumped to his feet.

"How did it go with the saddles?"

"Old Gus said he'd have the repairs made and ready tomorrow. He'll just put the saddles in the back of your wagon, and when we leave Sunday, we can pay the livery bill, and he'll include it in that."

"Sounds reasonable." Lucille turned to her daughter. "I don't know about you, but after that stuffy office, I'd like a nice long walk."

Charlotte held up her now closed umbrella. "Sounds perfect, and I'll have my own shade."

Lucille gathered her skirt. "I'll go upstairs and retrieve mine as well."

She was surprised when Charlotte handed over her own parasol. "I'll go fetch it, Mama. Please hold this for me."

Lucille dropped her skirt and took the piece. She waited until Charlotte was halfway up the stairs before turning to Micah. "She's under no obligation to marry Lewis Bradley. I thought you should know that before she returns, although I'm sure she will tell you as much herself."

"I couldn't see why she should be. What about the ranch? Did Bradley manage to finagle any of that into his possession?"

"No. Mr. Higgins knows of no contracts. He said should Mr. Bradley come up with something that he says is a signed contract between himself and Frank, we should direct him back to Mr. Higgins. He'd be able to tell if the signatures were truly Frank's, and besides, Frank never signed anything without the lawyer involved."

"I remember that about him. Does he think Bradley would forge them?"

"He's just extra cautious. We were one of the few ranches to come out of the bad winter with assets still in place, and he's heard it rumored that Mr. Bradley is starting to struggle financially. But he had nothing firm on the matter. Just rumors, and we all want nothing to do with those."

"Especially since Bradley's finances aren't our concern. I'm glad, though, that neither of you have to deal with him anymore and can just tell him to leave you alone."

"Mr. Higgins is going to write him a letter and explain

that we talked all of this out and that we know where we stand legally."

Micah glanced back at the stairs, and Lucille followed suit. Charlotte was just starting down. Lucille let her gaze go back to Micah. He seemed to watch Charlotte as if trying to figure something out.

"She is all grown up," Lucille said, looking back at her daughter.

"Yes. Yes, she is," Micah murmured.

She was all grown up. Micah had seen her as the little girl for so long that it still rather shocked him to acknowledge those years were far removed. She had forever been Frank Jr.'s little sister. The tiny blond girl in braids and pinafore aprons. But no more.

"I'd like to walk down toward the capitol building. It will give us a good stretch of our limbs." Mrs. Aldrich raised her parasol. Charlotte did likewise.

Micah offered Mrs. Aldrich his arm, but she took Charlotte's instead. Micah brought up the rear as a watchful guardian might do. He thought of how much these two women meant to him. He would die for them. The thought was rather startling. They were in every way the only family left to him.

"As we saw on the Fourth of July, things have changed so much. This town is nothing like when we first came here," Charlotte said, glancing up at buildings. "Remember how many of the businesses were in tents, Mama?"

"I do. I've been fascinated over the years watching it change, but it seems these last few years have brought even more alterations. I heard we now have a county library. I enjoy a good book when time permits. It might suit me to make a visit there."

"Don't forget, Mama, we were going to check into material for new winter coats," Charlotte reminded her.

"Or you could just buy them ready made," Micah offered. "I've been surprised at how well some of that stuff fits. I just bought myself a couple of shirts."

"You should have told us you needed them," Mrs. Aldrich declared, glancing over her shoulder. "Charlotte and I would have made shirts for you."

"You two have more than enough work already."

"Yes, but we're never too busy for you, Micah."

"It just wearies me here with all the noise and constant change," Charlotte said, not seeming to have heard her mother. "It's different every time we come here. I need consistency in my life. That's why I love the ranch."

"Things change on the ranch all the time. New life being born, animals going to market, things growing and dying." Micah could think of a dozen more examples but left it at that.

"Yes, those things change," Charlotte went on, "storms come, and fires can destroy, but foundationally everything stays fixed. That's what was so hard when Frank and Papa died. Your father too, Micah. That foundation was shaken. Where before it had always been constant. I need that consistency—to know that I have a strong foundation to build on."

"Reminds me of Jesus speaking of the man who builds on sandy soil and the one who builds on rock," Mrs. Aldrich said, smiling at her daughter. "When you were little, you always loved when your father would tell that story."

"That's because he made it fun. He would pretend to hammer and build and then make like rain was coming down. He always pounded his hand down hard on the table to emphasize the house on the sand being destroyed." She smiled back at Micah. "Frank Jr. would imitate him at times, remember? You and he told me that story once when I was afraid."

"I remember that. We were caught out riding and misjudged the weather. Thunderstorm moved in so fast we barely had time to find any shelter." Micah could see it all as if it were yesterday. They were soaked to the skin when they finally made it home.

"Well, the point in my reference is that God is that rock. He's constant and solid. We can build on Him and know that He'll never change because the Bible tells us so." Charlotte's mother glanced at the building across the street. "In another twenty years, that structure might very well be gone. Even the capitol building could change. After all, they're already adding to it. What's to stop them from tearing it all down and completely changing it?" She shook her head. "Nothing. But God is the same yesterday, today, and forever."

Charlotte nodded and drew down her parasol. "Family had always been like that for me too. When we lost Papa and Frank, it felt like my house was on sand, and as the Bible says, great was the fall of it.

"I know people will die and buildings can be destroyed, but the ranch, the land, it remains. It's all so neatly a part of my faith. I didn't realize it until we faced death. I found such strength in my home and the land around me. God and the ranch were my constants. Of course, Mama, you were as well." She leaned over and gave her mother a peck on the cheek.

Micah realized in that moment that he'd had no constant. Even his relationship with God had been meager and weak. Maybe that was why alcohol seemed so appealing. He had felt the immediate calm that it could bring him. Instead of seeking God in prayer or in Bible reading, or fellowship with another believer, he had given himself to a substance that offered only the briefest of comfort.

"And you were a constant," Charlotte said, stopping their

progress to turn to Micah. "I've missed Papa and Frank Jr., but if I'm honest, I think I've missed you most."

Micah was surprised by her boardwalk declaration. He looked around to see who else might have overheard them, but there was no one. People were going about their business with no interest in what the trio might be discussing.

"We should have insisted you join us on the ranch." Mrs. Aldrich reached back and took hold of Micah's right arm.

Charlotte took hold of his left. She smiled up at him with such love in her eyes. "You're stuck with us now, and as Ecclesiastes states, a threefold cord is not easily broken." Charlotte tightened her grip on him. "I think we should find somewhere to have lunch. I'm starving."

"There's Belham's on the next block," Mrs. Aldrich suggested. "I've heard that they're serving lunch these days as well as supper. I say we give it a try."

And just like that, they were off to the restaurant and seated near the window before Micah could offer any protest. Not that he wanted to, but the whirlwind those two women could sometimes create amazed him. Once they decided on a matter, it got done.

"Oh, look, it's Katie Combes. I haven't seen her in ages." Charlotte stood, and Micah did as well out of respect. "I'll be right back." She hurried across the room to where her friend sat with a couple of other women.

Micah reclaimed his seat and smiled at Mrs. Aldrich. "She never seems to tire."

She laughed. "She's been that way all her life. But then, you know that."

Micah nodded. "I do. I thought maybe time would slow her down just a bit."

"It didn't slow me down, and she reminds me so much of myself." Mrs. Aldrich gave a slight shrug. "I don't know that it's a good way to be, but we get a lot accomplished."

"Micah Hamilton, how are you doing?"

Micah looked up to find one of his father's friends standing at his side. "I'm doing well, Mr. Post." He got to his feet and shook the man's hand. Post was a good friend of his father's and just happened to head up the bank where they kept their account. For years Micah's dad had an arrangement to provide Post's family with beef.

"I haven't seen you in some time. I was sure sorry to hear about your father. I had no better friend."

"I know he thought highly of you, Mr. Post." Micah was most uncomfortable in speaking about his father. He glanced at his tablemate. "You know Mrs. Aldrich, don't you?"

"Of course. Lucille, how are you?" He frowned. "We're all much worse off for the loss of your husband and son."

"Thank you for saying so. However, we're getting by, and God has been good to meet our needs."

The man nodded and turned back to Micah. "I'd like it if you stopped by the bank sometime. I'd like to talk to you about your plans."

"I'll do just that."

"Just offhand, do you figure to sell the ranch?" Mr. Post asked.

"No." Micah offered nothing further, and that seemed to put an abrupt end to the conversation.

Post gave a nod. "I must return to the bank, but don't forget to come see me soon."

"I'll do my best." Micah shook his hand once more and waited until Post was nearing the door of the restaurant before he reclaimed his seat.

"Micah, I think the time has come for you to figure out your future," Mrs. Aldrich declared.

"I haven't got the money to set up business at my place. There's so much that's needed, and I took what we had in the bank just to live on after Dad passed away. No bank is going to extend me credit. After the Great Die-Up, no one wants to risk their money. I think about those cows and calves I have—thanks to you and Charlotte—and I don't even know how I can keep them fed through the winter."

"That's all right. I'm going to help you, and you're going to let me." Her words were quite determined.

Micah glanced across the room, where Charlotte was still deep in conversation with Katie Combes. He looked back to Mrs. Aldrich. "What is it you have in mind?"

"My plan is twofold. First, to get you back into the routine, I want you to partner up with us. Come and be my foreman, and we'll give Kit one more chance to take training. If he can't learn or refuses, then you can find another to replace and train. Those boys I hired for a crew have the ability to be good at what they do. You saw them at roundup."

"I did, and you're right. With proper training, they'll do great."

"Then we'll run our cattle together and see that each head has what it needs. I have plenty of hay coming in and that newly fenced pasture close to the house. Close your house and live in the foreman quarters. I will pay you a good salary to work, and you can save it, because I'll also take care of all your other needs just as I would have Frank Jr.

"Second, we'll see to it that all of your heifers and cows get bred without charge, and the steers that are ready for market will go without expense to you, but you will reap the benefits."

"That's hardly fair. I would expect to pay for any expenses you put out."

"No, I've thought this through. Your father was a great help to us at different times, and I made your mother a promise to be there for you and help you both. Frank would want it this way. Frank Jr. would too. Run your cattle with ours, and let's build this herd back up. Charlotte has been shopping more stock, and I know that in five years we can have a fine herd in place."

"So long as there's no drought or bad winter."

She smiled at Micah. "I'll trust it to God. Look, you think about it, pray about it. I'd like you to start work on Monday, but you can wait and give me your answer after church on Sunday."

He laughed out loud, caught completely off guard. He saw the twinkle in her eye, and it amused him all the more. "Are you sure you can wait that long?"

"I am, because I already know the answer."

Micah shook his head. He was already sure what his answer would be as well.

14

After church, Micah felt a great peace in telling Mrs. Aldrich that he would do as she desired and come work her ranch. The pastor had preached a good sermon on God's plans for mankind. The focus, he said, was that whatever a man chose to do with his life, he should do it to the glory of God. He used First Corinthians ten, verse thirty-one for his proof: "Whether therefore ye eat, or drink, or whatsoever ye do, do all to the glory of God."

It didn't much matter if Micah joined up with the Aldrich women or stayed on his ranch fighting to revive it from nothing. What did matter was that he do it to the glory of God. It seemed evident that he could bring God more glory working with others than alone.

"Do I have my answer?"

Micah turned and faced the woman who had become a surrogate mother to him. "I'll do it . . . to the glory of God."

She smiled. "I thought of that too. Seems like God always has a way of getting His thoughts into our heads at just the right time. Now, if you'll excuse me, I'm going to go speak to Mrs. Armstrong before we head back to the ranch."

Several congregants shook Micah's hand and told him

stories about his father and why they missed him. The more they spoke of the man, the more Micah felt guilty for the lie he had told about him. They lauded his bravery and his sacrifice of giving his life for his friend. Twice it was compared to the verse in John fifteen: "Greater love hath no man than this, that a man lay down his life for his friends."

The entire church thought his father had died trying to save Frank Aldrich and his son. They admired Wayman Hamilton and called him great for what he had done. They worked at comforting Micah with those comments, never realizing how much it hurt knowing the truth.

Micah made his way outside to the wagon. It was loaded for the trip home, and so he'd parked it between the church building and a small shed used for gardening tools, hoping no passersby would get the idea to steal anything. He leaned against the stone of the building and tried to clear his mind. Things were about to change, and he couldn't allow himself to be burdened by the past.

Still, the death of his father tormented him like nothing else could. The memories refused to go away. He could still see his father at the bottom of that gully. Blood spreading to soak his wool coat, only to freeze as the sub-zero temperatures hit the dampness.

"Are you all right?" Charlotte asked.

He looked up to find her watching him. How long she'd been standing there he didn't know. "Just remembering."

"Your father?" She moved closer.

Micah studied her for a moment. She wore a stylish blue walking suit made from some sort of lightweight material. Her mother had commented on it being cooler than materials that were generally used to fashion such an outfit. But even so, Charlotte was ridding herself of the jacket.

"Micah, you know you can talk to me. I know the truth

about your father's death, and it doesn't disturb me to hear what you have to say."

"It disturbs me just thinking about it. I feel to blame for so much, but I know if I'd done things differently, he wouldn't be dead. I know, too, if folks around here knew the truth . . . well, things would be a whole lot different. Most would never speak to me again."

"Micah, you didn't mean for what happened to happen. I know that, and so does Mama. Otherwise, she never would've said that he froze to death with Papa and Frank. Your father's death . . . well, it's not that I believe God necessarily wanted him to die that way, but He knew that he would. He is the one who numbers our days. And as Mama has said from the beginning, all three made their choices."

"I just keep thinking I should have done things different. I keep seeing him lying there in the snow. . . . The blood was such a stark contrast to the white everywhere else."

"Micah, you must let it go. You have to allow yourself grace. Your father wouldn't want you to blame yourself. He knew you didn't want him to die."

"I know." He met her sympathetic gaze. "But we all lied. We can't change that. If others knew, it would ruin your mother's life. I might even go to jail."

"But they don't know, and they never will. There's no need for them to know." She took hold of his arm. "Micah, I care very much for you. I pray for you always. You've been so special to my family. I remember being so jealous of Frank because he could spend all his time with you. You two could work together and enjoy your time away from chores together. You remember those camping trips you and Frank used to take?"

"I do. I miss them. We'd go into the mountains and set up our tent. Sometimes we'd hunt, but a lot of times we'd just enjoy the solitude and talk about what we wanted to do with our lives."

"And what did you want to do?" she asked, her voice soft and alluring.

Micah couldn't help being drawn in to answer. "Raise cattle and children. Further establish our father's empires—make our own."

She nodded. "That's all I wanted too. Oh, and to marry the man I love and want to spend my life with."

"You'd have to find him first. I guess I kind of skipped that part. Finding someone with whom you could live a lifetime . . . well, it can't be all that easy."

"Simplest thing in the world, for me," she murmured and looked away.

Micah thought of the things Rich had said about Charlotte's feelings. Was she in love with him? Could she really care for him the way Rich suggested? He cleared his throat. It would solve a lot if he'd just ask her.

"Charlotte . . . do you . . . I mean . . ."

"There you two are. I don't know why it didn't dawn on me that you'd already be at the wagon," Mrs. Aldrich said, coming to join them. "Let's head home. It's starting to get windy, and we'll have to battle that all the way."

Micah forced his question back and helped Mrs. Aldrich into the wagon. Next, he handed Charlotte up before taking the driver's seat. He untied the lines and released the brake.

"Ready?"

The two ladies nodded, and Charlotte met his gaze. She seemed to beg him to finish his question, but Micah knew now wasn't the time. Instead, he looked away and snapped the lines.

Lewis Bradley felt a devilish sense of satisfaction course through his body. He had just overheard Micah and Charlotte talk about the lies they'd told—the deception they'd managed to instigate against the entire community regarding Wayman Hamilton's death.

He wasn't exactly sure what it was they had lied about, but given the discussion, all things pointed to the possibility that Micah had done something to end his father's life. What else would he have to regret in such a haunting manner?

Lewis was nearly giddy as he made his way home. He had planned to get a ride with his neighbor, but he needed the walk to think and plan. First, he needed to know for certain what had happened. If Micah had killed his father and the Aldrich women were hiding this fact, they'd all be in trouble. They'd need a good lawyer to get them out of that trouble, and Lewis would happily represent the women.

He imagined what he might say or do to get the truth out of Charlotte. If he threatened her beloved Micah or even her mother, Charlotte was sure to tell him whatever he wanted to know. She'd have to. She wouldn't want to see either of them in trouble.

There was quite a bit of traffic at the corner as church congregants made their way home. Lewis waited until the street was clear to cross and all the while continued to ponder the matter. If he could arrange to have Micah stand trial for the murder of his father, he knew there would be ways to ensure a guilty verdict. There was still enough corruption in Cheyenne to get what he wanted. He had dirty little secrets on many of the judges and law officials. It wouldn't be hard at all to utilize that knowledge and get what he wanted.

Of course, there was the matter of proving murder. There had been mention of blood. Perhaps Micah had shot or knifed his father. It might have been an accident, but with the right story, it could easily be proven to be murder.

The very idea delighted Lewis more than he could say.

Despite it being the Sabbath, he intended to smoke one of his cigars in celebration when he got home. His aunt would have a fit about it, but that was too bad. She had stayed home from church because Victoria was feverish. And just look at all he'd been able to accomplish. He could never have overheard the conversation between Micah and Charlotte if he'd had to worry about those two.

Lewis smiled to himself. If he could get Micah convicted of murder, then he'd hang, and Charlotte would belong to Lewis. The smile faded. How long would those legalities take? What if he just threatened Charlotte that he'd see Micah charged with murder unless she married him and did so quickly?

By the time he reached his front drive, a plan had started to form in his mind. He wouldn't have to actually get Micah charged if he could accomplish his plan with mere threats. If that was the case, he'd have the information to use later in case it was needed.

Perhaps marriage and blackmail would be enough to see him well set for life. He laughed out loud. For once, going to church had lifted his spirits.

Charlotte tried to enjoy the ride home, but the ruts of the trail seemed rougher and the heat more abominable. What she really wanted was to hear what else Micah had to say. She felt certain that if they'd been left alone just a little longer, she could have declared her love for Micah. She could have explained to him that she'd been completely devoted to him since she was a child and that it would never change. That she loved him and wanted him for her husband—for the father of her children.

"I think we should just head to your place and retrieve

your things," Mama said, bringing Charlotte's thoughts back to the present situation.

"The wagon is full of stuff already. Let's go to your place and get things put away, and I can ride over to my place and get my things. I don't have that much I need to bring. Certainly not a wagonload."

"What are you talking about?" Charlotte asked.

"Micah has agreed to move to the ranch. He's going to take over for Kit and work with you on how you want things run, while hopefully getting Kit to understand what he needs to do to fulfill his job as foreman. I told Micah, just as I'd mentioned to you, that I want him to partner with us."

Charlotte couldn't have been happier with the news. Micah would be available to her twenty-four hours a day. That would make it far easier to get him alone and speak her mind.

She frowned. It would also make it harder if she did that and he refused her. They would have to work day in and day out with that between them. Charlotte couldn't help but turn away from her mother and shift her gaze out across the vast open range. She had wanted to declare her love for Micah for so long, but could she do it now without threatening their livelihood? She needed Micah to straighten out Kit. She needed him to get the cowboys properly instructed.

She heaved a sigh, then realized her mother would wonder at that, especially since she'd said nothing about her mother's announcement.

"Are you all right, Charlotte?"

"Yes. I'm just tired. I didn't sleep very well last night, as you well know. The heat and all was a bother."

Her mother patted her hand, but Charlotte refused to look at her. Mama would know in a heartbeat that there was something more if she saw the unease in Charlotte's eyes.

"You were pretty restless."

"I just wanted to get home. I don't like the city." She hoped that would be more than enough to explain.

"I'll be glad to be there as well," Mama replied. "It was good to get all of that business accomplished and even to see Emma's new house. Goodness, but I can't imagine spending such money on a place to live."

"Neither can I," Charlotte said, hoping the conversation would occupy her mother's thoughts. "If I had an extra fifty thousand dollars, I'd buy more cows and build more barns and build that church we talked about. I certainly wouldn't worry about putting in a furnace system and electricity."

"Well, electricity is rather nice. I was impressed with the ease in which a person can move about in the darker hours."

"Folks ought to be sleeping in the darker hours," Micah joined in. "Otherwise, how are they going to get up at dawn and get their work done?"

"Well, you have to admit city hours and ranch hours are two entirely different things," Mama said with a laugh. "But I'm with Charlotte. I wouldn't spend all that money on a house either, and I wouldn't worry about adding all sorts of fancy luxuries to make my life easier. It's not that hard to light a lamp or candle. It can be taxing to fetch water, but not all that bad now that we have good pumps in place. And, yes, it's difficult to keep a fireplace going without a supply of wood nearby. Sending the boys to the forested areas to cut wood and bring it back here is a terrible chore but not an impossible one." She fell silent, and Charlotte couldn't help but glance over.

Her mother smiled. "Maybe I would spend the money to have one of those fancy Smead furnaces."

"No, don't bother. It requires a ventilation system to be put in as well and piping to distribute the heat. Oh, and coal. You'd have to have coal for the heating. I think wood is better for the time being, even if we do have to drive a hundred miles or more roundtrip to get it. It's a simple matter to cut down a tree. Much harder to mine for coal."

"See, that is just the way of it. You think you've found a way to simplify your life, and lo and behold, there are more complications than you realize."

Charlotte could have offered a comment of agreement, but it wouldn't have had anything at all to do with the furnace system offered by Mr. Smead. Her complications were of an entirely different sort.

15

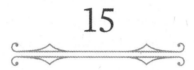

It didn't take much time to get lunch ready. Nora had prepared most everything the day before. Now it was just a matter of warming up the smoked ham or eating it cold. Frankly, as hot as the day was, Charlotte preferred a cold ham sandwich to eating a hot ham steak.

At lunch they discussed the way they would handle things with the cowboys, and by the time Nora was gathering up the dishes, Charlotte was ready to put their plans in motion.

"Nora, would you go out and tell the men we want to meet with them in the front yard?" Mama asked. "Charlotte and I will finish getting the table cleared. Micah, you go ahead and wait for us outside."

Micah nodded and headed out with Nora right behind him.

Mama smiled. "I feel so good about this decision. Finally, I believe we are all going to move forward with the plans God has for us. And you will have more than ample opportunity to tell Micah how you feel."

"But what if he doesn't feel the same way? Before, he could just head home and be done with me, but now he'll have to stay and work with me. I'm less sure about speaking to him now than I was before."

Mama stopped what she was doing and looked at Charlotte for a moment. "You have loved him for most of your life. That isn't going to change no matter what you tell him. It's going to be harder, I think, to work with him every day and try to keep your feelings to yourself. Besides, I think Micah cares for you, and once you put the idea of romance into his mind, then perhaps that will give him permission to explore those feelings."

Charlotte knew her mother was probably right. "I just don't want to run him off."

"I don't think you have to worry about that. Now come on. Let's get these dishes to the kitchen and go speak to the boys."

The men were already gathered when Mama and Charlotte joined them under the shade of the cottonwoods.

"We have changes to announce," Mama began. "Some of them you may not care for, and if any of you are of a mind to leave, you may do so with your pay and no hard feelings."

The men exchanged glances but said nothing. Kit Hendricks was the only one to open his mouth. "What's this all about, Mrs. Aldrich?"

"Ranch improvements," she replied. "We want to rebuild this empire, and to do so we need knowledgeable hands who aren't afraid of hard work. We need a foreman who has more experience than you, Kit, and one who has the ability to train others. That's why I'm putting Micah in charge. Micah has ranched all his life. He knows the duties required and more tricks of the trade than most. He will take over as foreman and our partner. We're going to merge the Aldrich and Hamilton cattle ranches. Kit, you will learn from him and take over for him when he has to be elsewhere. Eventually, if you learn what you need to know, you'll be returned to the position of foreman.

"I apologize for putting you in a position for which you

weren't yet ready. It was unfair to you. Micah will teach you what you need to know."

"I do my job," Kit protested.

"You do part of your job, but even that part is done rather poorly, I'm sorry to say. In order to make this ranch what I want it to be," Mama continued, "I need for the job to be done well. I need the men to respect you. You can't very well teach others if you don't know the job yourself."

Kit's eyes narrowed. "I don't care to have the likes of him bossin' me around."

"As I said, you can stay on and do things our way or leave. I'll pay your salary, and there will be no hard feelings."

Kit looked at Micah and then shook his head. "I quit, then."

"It's a pity, Hendricks," Micah said, squaring off with the man. "You have the ability to make yourself into a good foreman, but you refuse to receive correction or instruction from anyone. There's so much you don't know but could learn."

"I know enough. Mr. Aldrich had no trouble hiring me on."

"But you weren't hired on as a foreman." Charlotte's mother refused to look away. "That was my son's job—not yours. It was never intended to be yours because we never figured to lose Frank Jr. nor my husband. You were hired as a ranch hand. And, as I recall, you had less experience than some of the others, but we wanted to give you a chance."

"The others may have had more experience, but they left you. I stayed," Hendricks countered, his voice full of contempt. "I've been here over two years now."

"And you've learned in part what is required, but you are far from knowing what I need for you to know."

Charlotte heard the exasperation in her mother's voice and stepped in. "He's quit, Mama. No sense in arguing with him."

Kit gave a huff and looked at the other cowhands. "I can't

help it if these ladies don't see the value in keepin' me. Women oughtn't be running a ranch anyway."

"These two are more capable of it than most men I know," Micah interjected.

"I'm sure you've had plenty to do with this, Hamilton." He raised his arms slightly away from his body as if preparing to throw a punch or grab Micah.

Mama stepped between them. "Kit, I won't tolerate fighting, so just go get your things and meet me at the house for your pay."

For just a moment Charlotte held her breath. Kit seemed to hesitate, and she wasn't sure if he would still attempt to go after Micah. He scowled and muttered something inaudible, then backed down and headed for his quarters, cursing as he went.

Mama looked at the others. "Well, are you staying or going?"

The young men looked at each other, and the tallest of the bunch, a boy named Wesley, spoke for the group. "We're staying, Mrs. Aldrich. We don't have any problem with Mr. Hamilton being in charge."

Mama smiled. "Good. I hoped you'd say as much. Please understand me, boys, there's not a one of you who has even reached your twentieth birthday. Some of you have been working with cattle for years already, though none of you were born into ranching. I wasn't afraid to take a chance on you, but you still have a lot to learn. Micah is a good man and a fair one. He will teach you what you need to know to be truly valuable to me in your job. I want to keep you on for good—if you're willing to do things our way. We'll take on more men from time to time, but you'll be my permanent workers, if you want that role. But it will be up to you."

The boys looked at one another, grinning. What she was offering them was a home and job security. For orphans like them, this wasn't something that usually happened. Permanent ranch positions were for family members or men who had years of experience and good reputations.

"I also want you to understand that Charlotte will continue to supervise what you do, along with Micah. She knows more than I do when it comes to running this ranch, and I will expect you to honor and respect her as you would Micah."

"What if they don't agree about how somethin' needs doin'?" Wes asked.

Charlotte immediately spoke up. "Micah's word is final. I won't interfere if he thinks something needs to be done a specific way."

Micah held up his hand. "But we'll also discuss matters. Charlotte has some very good ideas and learned a great deal from her father. I value her opinion and so should you. The fact is, boys, sometimes two folks weighing in on a matter can be better than just one. Even if one of them is a woman. Women are capable and smart, and I'll expect you to respect both of these women as you would me."

Mama nodded in agreement and continued. "And last, but definitely not least, I want you boys in church unless there's a good reason for not being there. We'll have you trade off as to who will stay here on the ranch and who will go each week, but spending time with the Lord is important. If you don't feel you can do that, then say so now. I need godly men working for me."

"My ma would love that you're doing that, Mrs. Aldrich." This came from Jonny, the youngest of the bunch at seventeen. "'Course, she's gone now, but I remember when I was little that readin' the Bible and goin' to church was important to her."

"Well, I figure it's my responsibility to see to your spiritual as well as physical well-being. We're going to be making changes for the better in every way, including your quarters. We'll be doing a few things to improve the living conditions. For now, Nora will continue cooking for you, but in time we may hire in an older man who needs a gentler ranch job." She smiled. "I like to help those in need."

Charlotte had always loved that about her mother. Years ago, Mama had seen a man in Cheyenne who had a bad limp. He was probably fifty years old or more, and he wore the clothes of a cowboy as if they were made for him. Mama had struck up a conversation with him. Before Charlotte knew it, the man was hired on to cook for the ranch hands. His name was Barney, and even though he'd only lived another year, Mama and Papa saw to it that he had a decent burial. In that short time, he'd become family in many ways.

"Do you have any questions?" Mama asked.

The boys shook their heads.

"Good. Now go about your business. Micah will meet with you in the morning."

The boys left, and Micah looked at Charlotte and her mother. "They seem like good men. I think I should be able to work with them. I watched for their reaction when Kit looked like he might fight. None of them were interested in joining him."

"They've been very respectful, Micah," Mama answered. "I think they show great promise, and that's why I want to get them proper training. I think we can have some good, lifelong workers with them."

"I agree." He let his gaze linger on Charlotte for a moment, then nodded toward the corral. "I'll get Duke and fetch my things."

"Are you sure you don't want to take the wagon?"

"No. I'll give it a few days and see if there's anything I really need to bring over. I'd imagine the tools I'd need are right here, and I don't have that many personal items that need to be a part of the move, especially since I won't be here permanently."

"You never know, Micah. You might find that you like living with us," Mama said.

Micah looked at her with a most serious expression. "I already found that out years ago. Yours was the only family I wanted to be with after my ma died. I hated that it was just Dad and me. There was no joy in our house anymore."

"Well, we're going to have plenty here," Mama promised. "You'll see." She turned to Charlotte. "I need to pay Kit, and then you and I will go clean his cabin."

Charlotte nodded and watched Micah head out. She walked in silence with Mama back to the house, where Kit was already waiting by the door.

It took only a matter of minutes to settle with him, and then Charlotte and her mother watched the troublesome man ride away. She had an uneasy feeling about him. He was angry, and angry men often caused problems.

"I think he was the one who burned down the calving shed," Mama said as Kit put his horse into a full gallop.

Charlotte turned to her mother in surprise. "What makes you think that?"

"There was no lantern or other source to start it. Kit wasn't the only one who ever smoked, but he acted so strangely afterward. And in speaking to the boys privately, they all said the same thing. Kit was the only one who had gone to the birthing shed that day. The thing I really want to know is why. Why would he do that? If he burned us out, what did he have to gain by that?"

It was a good question. Why would Kit want to see them destroyed?

Micah returned to the Aldrich ranch after retrieving his clothes and tack. He placed his stuff in a pile by the main barn door and then saw to Duke's needs. Once the horse was properly cared for and turned out into the smallest fenced pasture where the other horses awaited their riders, Micah made his way to the house to see exactly where Mrs. Aldrich wanted him.

"I'm glad you didn't go to the foreman's cabin," she said after inviting Micah into the house. "Charlotte and I went to clean it and found it to be a disastrous mess. Worse than I had anticipated. It will take us a few days to make it livable space. In the meantime, I want you to stay in Frank Jr.'s old room. If that won't bother you too much."

Micah hadn't considered that as a possibility. "I don't suppose it'll be a problem. Thanks."

He had stayed in Frank Jr.'s room on many occasions when they were younger. One summer when his mother and dad had to be away for a time, Micah had stayed several weeks with the Aldrichs, and he had bunked with Frank Jr.

However, when he set foot in the room again, it released an avalanche of memories. Nothing had changed much. Frank's room had always been quite simple. A bed with a wooden trunk at the foot of it.

"You'll have to let us know if you need anything," Charlotte said, coming up behind him.

He turned and looked at her for a moment. She had changed her clothes to a plain blouse and skirt. Her hair was plaited in a single braid down her back with little blond curls framing her face. When he met her eyes, he felt warmed by her gaze.

"Mama wanted to make sure you knew there are towels in the bathing room downstairs. There's hot water for your bath after the sun heats it. Papa built that little water tower for Mama that lets the water warm in the summer. I didn't know if I'd ever told you about it. He did it just the summer before . . ." She let her words fade. "Uh, if you use it, let us know. We have to put more water in the tank for the next person."

Micah searched her face as if looking for an answer. The problem was, he wasn't sure what question he was asking.

"Thanks." He finally forced the word out and looked away. "I should be fine. I'll go get my things."

"I'll come help."

He wanted to tell her no, but for the life of him he couldn't seem to speak the word. He went to where he'd left his stuff by the barn and glanced at the pile.

"I'll put some of this in the tack room. I only need to take my clothes and shaving stuff into the house. Oh, my Bible's there too. I wrapped it in one of my shirts."

She nodded and carefully gathered the clothes. "I'll take these things while you deal with the tack."

He watched her head back to the house before gathering the rest of his stuff. He could almost hear Frank Jr. calling after her to stay out of his room. Frank had loved his little sister dearly, but she could often be a pest to him, and his bedroom was his sanctuary.

Micah put away his things and headed to the house. The grandfather clock in the hall chimed six as he walked through the door. No wonder he was hungry, and something smelled delicious.

"Get washed up, Micah. We're just about to sit to supper," Mrs. Aldrich said as she passed down the hall and headed for the kitchen.

"Yes, ma'am."

He hadn't given much thought as to how this would all work out. He was about to live under the same roof as Charlotte and her mother. Nora too. He hadn't been in the company of women in a very long time. He'd have to really mind his manners.

He went to the washroom and caught sight of himself in the mirror. For a moment, he saw the reflection of his father. His mother had said he was the spitting image of his father as a boy. It only stood to reason Micah would continue to favor him in his adult years. He'd never given it much consideration, however. At least not until now.

Seeing the similarities now was almost more than he could bear. There was a sense of accusation in his reflection. Accusation that he held deep inside.

You should have known better than to leave him alone. You should have stayed with him. You should have . . .

"Micah, did you find everything?" Charlotte asked from the open doorway.

Her voice brought him out of his dark thoughts. "Yes. I'll be right there."

Later that night as Micah tried to fall asleep, he stared up into the darkness and thought of his friend. Frank was the type of friend that came along only once in a lifetime. In some ways the loss of Frank was equal to that of his father. The only difference was Micah knew Frank was in a better place. He had no idea where his father was.

He tried to pray, but it was as if the very question of his father's eternal resting place was blocking his ability to speak. Did God care for those who killed themselves, or did He just toss them aside—send them into darkness to await final judgment?

His father had been a Christian, and up until the moment he took his life, Wayman Hamilton had been a strong man of faith. He had even shared Jesus with other men. Micah had heard him. Micah's own faith had been bolstered by his father's beliefs and Bible teachings.

It hurt so much . . . so deep in his soul.

Had God snatched back His love? Had He removed His compassion and mercy? Was his father forever doomed—

never to receive Jesus's welcome into paradise as the thief on the cross?

Micah sat up and grabbed the pillow. He pounded it several times with his fist, then put it back on the bed before easing back down.

"God, my spirit is overwhelmed by this. Just as it was the day Dad shot himself. Please don't forsake me. I need You."

That was the most sincere and heartfelt prayer Micah had prayed in a long time.

16

Lewis Bradley was not a man to be thwarted, yet for nearly a month his best efforts to get Charlotte alone had been for naught. He'd also done his level best to try to learn what had really happened to Wayman Hamilton. No one seemed to have any information to offer, however. He'd gone looking for Kit Hendricks after hearing he'd been dismissed from his job at the Aldrich ranch but learned the man had left town.

Finally, it seemed his opportunity had come. Charlotte and her mother were at church with a couple of their hirelings, but Micah was nowhere to be found. When Charlotte's mother got caught up speaking to some of her friends, Lewis took the opportunity to corner Charlotte. She was none too happy.

"I have nothing to discuss with you, Lewis. By now I know you have received a letter from our lawyer explaining that none of your arrangements with my father are valid. There were never any signed agreements or witnessed oral agreements. Nothing. So please leave us alone."

"I'm afraid I can't do that. Or perhaps it is that I won't do it." He smiled feeling rather satisfied to watch her expression tighten. "You see, something has recently come to my attention, and I believe it will cause you to reconsider my proposal."

"I have no desire to marry you, Lewis, none whatsoever, and I can guarantee you that I will never love you."

"Because you love Micah Hamilton?"

She looked at him oddly. "Why would you say that?"

"I've seen the way you look at him. You are clearly in love with the man."

Charlotte glanced around at the other congregants and moved farther away before replying. "Even if I am, it's none of your business. Who I court or marry is not up to you."

Lewis had followed on her heels to the side door of the church. He opened the door and pushed her through it. The warm summer breeze immediately offered relief from the stuffy church sanctuary.

Without hesitation, Lewis pressed Charlotte up against the wall of the building. He enjoyed the frightened look in her eyes and the way her breathing quickened. "You need to listen carefully and do exactly as I tell you, or your beloved Micah is the one who is going to pay the price."

Charlotte's eyes widened. "What are you talking about?"

"I know about Micah's father—his death."

The color drained from Charlotte's face, and Lewis felt he had finally managed to grasp hold of power. "That's right. I know everything."

"How . . . how did you find out?"

"It doesn't matter. What matters is that if you do what I tell you, I will remain silent. But if you refuse me, I will let the world know what happened—and I'll start with the police."

She gripped his arm. "No. You can't do that to Micah. He's finally starting to live again. He's been so overwhelmed by grief—"

"And guilt, no doubt," Lewis interrupted. He could see his comment hit the mark as her eyes widened.

She opened her mouth, but Lewis put his finger to her lips. "Say nothing more, just listen. I'm weary of playing games with you. My daughter needs a mother, and I need a wife. You will go home tonight and tell your mother that we are going to be married. I will speak to the pastor and arrange for us to marry immediately.

"I will come to your house tomorrow evening, where we will formally announce our desire to marry and set the date."

"You can't be this heartless, Lewis. Why would you want a wife who will despise you? I would have nothing to do with you. I wouldn't care for your house or your daughter."

"You will or I'll tell everyone what I know and ruin the life of your dear Micah. Who can say what might happen to him? There could be all sorts of legal repercussions." Lewis knew how to manipulate his words to make it sound like he understood what had happened. If he was good enough, he just might get Charlotte to reveal the truth, and then he'd know for sure.

"You'd send an innocent man to jail? That's your idea of endearing yourself to me?"

Charlotte pushed at him, but Lewis stood his ground and kept her pinned against the wall. He leaned in close as if to kiss her. "He's hardly innocent. Oh, and neither is your mother. The games are over, my love. You have no choice in this unless you want to see Micah pay for what happened."

The sound of other people approaching caused Lewis to finally release her. He stepped back, hoping it would appear they were having a romantic moment and nothing more. When several congregants rounded the corner, he gave a smile and tipped his hat in their direction.

Once they'd gone, he looked back to Charlotte, who had tears in her eyes. "Don't cry, my dear. This is really all for the best. At least I know it's for my best." He chuckled and gave a shrug. "And at the moment, that's all that matters."

He walked away then, not even looking back. He knew he had her where he wanted her. She was helpless to refuse him unless she wanted to see horrible things happen to her beloved Micah. Lewis didn't know what their secret was, but apparently it was as bad as he imagined. Micah had probably killed his father in a fit of rage, or perhaps it was even accidental, but the fact that they hid the truth from everyone . . . well, that really was unforgivable. At least, Lewis intended to make it so.

Once he and Charlotte were legally wed, he would decide what to do next. It seemed the information was powerful enough to cause Charlotte to reconsider matters. Lewis would have to find a way to get her to confess all, and then he'd know better whether to see Micah sent to prison or blackmailed.

He went in search of his aunt and daughter. They were waiting in the surrey. Victoria was wailing at the top of her lungs. He looked up at his aunt as she tried to comfort the child.

"What's wrong with her?" he growled, taking his place in the driver's seat.

"She's hot and hungry. You really can be the most thoughtless man at times. Leaving us out here to wait while you tended to whatever business you felt was more important." Aunt Agnes fixed him with an angry glare.

"It couldn't wait." He offered no other explanation and released the brake. "We'll be home in a matter of minutes, and then everyone will be perfectly fine. The cook is certain to have your dinner waiting in the nursery."

His aunt gave a huffing sound and shifted Lewis's daughter away from him. She would be in a snit for the rest of the day, but he couldn't care less. His father's spinster sister was a necessary factor in his life . . . for the moment. Once he married, Lewis intended to send her on her way, even if she didn't have anywhere to go.

He snapped the lines, and the horses moved out. By supper tomorrow, he'd have everything settled. Victoria would have a mother, and he could send his irritating aunt off to one of the other family members. More importantly, there would be money for him to do as he pleased. He frowned. The money part might take time. He needed to come up with an idea for how he could get some cash right away.

The dowry. Aldrich had promised him a dowry of five thousand dollars. Lewis smiled. The dowry would see him through until he could arrange for Charlotte to get her inheritance.

At lunch, Charlotte feigned a headache and problems with the heat and went directly to her room to think. The position Lewis had put her in was seemingly impossible. How had he found out about Micah's father? No one but the three of them knew about the suicide. None of them would ever mention it, even in passing. So how had Lewis learned the truth?

She had no doubt in her mind that he would make good on his threats. He was just that kind of man. She had often heard people talk about how successful he was as a lawyer because he could argue the points of a case until everyone involved was questioning their own testimony.

Falling back on her bed in her dressing wrap, Charlotte fought back tears. Was this how it was all to end? Would she marry Lewis Bradley after all? She had fought against it with her father to the point that her angry words were the last he ever heard from her. She had made it clear to Lewis that she would never love him. Not only that, but he knew she loved Micah. She hadn't even been able to tell Micah about her feelings for fear it would upend the arrangement they had with him.

And everything had been going so well. The ranch was running smoothly. Changes were being made with great success. Mama's cousins from Illinois were scheduled to come next month and help them plot out their crop fields. It had all been going so well that Charlotte had decided to tell Micah about her feelings very soon. Now she could never tell him. At least not if she had to marry Lewis Bradley.

"God, I don't know what to do. This seems to have no other answer but to go through with what Lewis is demanding. How can I marry him—pledge my love and life—when I know it would be a lie?"

She heaved a sigh and fought back the nausea she felt. Just thinking about her situation made her sick. She got up from the bed and began to pace back and forth, then stopped abruptly. She could get by with missing lunch, but if Mama heard her pacing, she'd know it wasn't the heat and a headache that were vexing Charlotte.

The open window beckoned, and Charlotte made her way to it and gazed outside. The summer heat wasn't so bad with the constant breeze. She let the wind blow over her and dry her wet cheeks.

Why did this happen? What was she going to do?

She couldn't talk to Mama or Micah, the only two people she ever went to with her troubles. She had already ranted and railed at God. All the way home from Cheyenne she had sat in silence, but in her heart, she was screaming, praying, pleading for God to make this go away.

If she didn't do as Lewis demanded, not only Micah would suffer but her mother's reputation for honesty would be ruined. People would never trust her as they did now. Mama would face scorn, and no doubt there would be many who would ostracize her completely. And all because she had lied to spare Micah further heartache. What was a person without their good reputation?

A light knock sounded on her bedroom door. She grimaced. "Who is it?"

"It's your mother. May I come in?"

"Of course."

Charlotte turned from the window and went to sit on the edge of her bed. "I was just trying to cool off with the breeze."

"Would you like me to draw you a tepid bath?" Mama asked, coming to stand by her. She reached out and felt Charlotte's forehead. "You don't feel feverish at least, so that's good. I had heard someone mention typhoid at church."

"No, I'm sure I don't have typhoid. The heat just got to me, that's all. I feel better already."

"Then I'll have Nora bring you a tray. You should eat something. I'll make sure she also includes some nice cold lemonade. That new cellar the boys dug is keeping the ice we purchased longer than the old one."

"I'm glad to hear it. It's better insulated, so that makes perfect sense."

Mama gave her a sympathetic smile and touched her cheek. "Whatever it is that's bothering you, just remember nothing is too big for God."

Charlotte knew her mother suspected something other than the heat and gave a nod. "I know and I'm sure everything will come around right."

But she wasn't sure at all.

$\backsim$

When Mrs. Aldrich returned downstairs, Micah was getting ready to head out to the foreman's cabin. He wanted to get his saddle cleaned and to show the boys the proper care of their saddles as well.

"Micah, I wish you'd wait a moment. Do you have the time to talk to me?"

He stopped at the front door. "Yes, ma'am."

"Give me just a minute, I want to ask Nora to take Charlotte a tray." She disappeared into the dining room and in a few minutes returned.

"What's on your mind, Mrs. Aldrich?"

"Let's sit. This will take just a few minutes." She led the way into the front room and took a seat in her rocking chair.

Micah chose a spot in the large leather chair Mr. Aldrich used to use. He knew his widow wouldn't mind. She'd encouraged him to sit there on more than one occasion.

"First, I want to tell you how much I appreciate the job you've been doing. Everything has been different since you took over. Especially the attitude of the boys. They are so much happier, and the quality of their work has improved greatly. At least that's what Charlotte told me yesterday."

"Yes, ma'am, she's right. Those boys are coming right along and are much improved with the way they respond. At first, I thought I might have trouble with Marty, but once he got the hang of what was expected and why we did things that way, then it all smoothed out."

"Sometimes just understanding the why of a thing makes all the difference."

"That's true." Micah shook his head. "There are so many whys that I've never understood the answer to."

She nodded. "Like your father."

"Yes. My mother too. Never did see a good reason for her to die. Started out with a simple cough and runny nose. We all had it and thought nothing of it. Then Ma developed a fever, and the cough deepened, and the next thing we know she's dying from pneumonia. No sense to it at all."

"Death never makes sense to the living. Still, once they're gone, the dead are beyond the cares of this world. We go on asking our whys, but there are seldom any reasonable answers." She gave her shoulders a roll. "I'm getting stiff as

I age. There's no good reason for that either. I'm still just as busy and active as I was ten years ago." She laughed. "Maybe even busier."

Micah knew for certain that he was. There was the sound of someone on the stairs. No doubt it was Nora taking Charlotte her lunch. "How's Charlotte feeling?" Micah asked aloud, even though he'd meant to just keep it as thought.

"She's fine, I think. The heat is bothering her, but I worry that it's something more. She was cheerful and talkative this morning, but after the service she was silent. I tried to get her to talk. I even had one of the boys drive the wagon so I could give her my full attention, but she said very little."

Micah frowned. "Was Bradley there?"

"He was, and I thought perhaps he had talked to her, but I didn't ask. She's always been more than willing to share their conversations with me. I just don't know what might have happened. I suppose it could just be the heat, but somehow, I don't think so."

"No, it really isn't like her." Micah was still concerned that Lewis Bradley had imposed himself upon her.

"Well, I'll try to talk to her again later. I've learned my lesson about letting things go for too long. I should have been there for you sooner, Micah. I can't help but feel that if I'd come to you last summer, you wouldn't have lost this last year."

"You can't know that, Mrs. Aldrich. I'm fairly certain I would have ignored you or anyone else who stopped by. In fact, I know I would have. I did. There were a few folks who tried to offer me their friendship and concern, but I refused it. And given they were already hurting from their own losses from the bad winter, they didn't fight me on it. So I hid away and sought the bottle and didn't talk to anyone. Not even God. Or maybe I should say especially not to God."

"And now?"

"We're on speaking terms." Micah gave a shrug. "From time to time I read my Bible, and I've started to pray a little. And I completely put away the liquor.

"You know, for a little while after Dad died, I thought about going back to church, but then I knew it wouldn't work. The very thing that was killing me was something I could never speak of. I kept thinking of the hypocrisy, of the ugliness that would come if those people knew the truth about Dad's death."

"Oh, Micah, I am sorry. I know what you're saying is true or would have been true for a great many of the congregation. I am so sorry that people believe the way they do about ... such things."

"The worst of it is, I know they're probably right. God probably has nothing more to do with my dad because of what he did."

"I don't believe that, Micah. Your father was a believer. He loved Jesus very much, and every other aspect of his life bore fruit for Him. I don't believe one sin canceled out a lifetime of living for God."

"I know. I don't want to think that way either, but the church thinks that way. I'd heard talk long before Dad's decision. I even believed it myself. . . . I must still, or it wouldn't torment me the way it does."

"I'm so sorry, Micah. We need to pray about it and seek the Scriptures. I know the answers are there."

"Well, no matter what, don't be hard on yourself. You have always been good to me, Mrs. Aldrich."

"Please, I know it may seem strange, but could you just call me Lucille? Mrs. Aldrich is far too formal for our relationship."

Micah had never considered calling her by her first name. He wasn't raised that way, but if it made her happy, he figured it was acceptable. "I will in private, but I think in public it would still be best to keep it formal."

She laughed. "I suppose so, but I'd rather something more intimate. I feel so close to you, Micah. I never thought I could handle losing Frank Jr., but now I see how God has given us each other to help with those empty places in our lives."

Her words touched him deeply. No one else cared for him as much as Lucille and Charlotte Aldrich did, and they showed that each day in their actions. For a short moment, Rich's words came back to mind about Charlotte being in love with him. He looked at Lucille and thought about asking her for the truth. Would she tell him if he did?

"I think I'll go check on Charlotte, but thanks for talking with me, Micah. I really appreciate all that you've done for us." Lucille got to her feet and reached over to touch Micah's shoulder. "We're going to get through all of this . . . together."

17

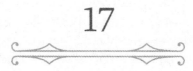

Lucille was pleasantly surprised when Rich Johnson rode up. She had just finished milking the cow and tending the chickens, so her hands were full.

"I come bearing gifts," Rich declared. He motioned to a basket he'd hooked over the horn of his saddle. "Fresh raspberries."

"How wonderful. We all love them, as you know, especially Charlotte."

He climbed down from the large palomino and tied his reins to the fence before grabbing the basket. "I knew she did, but also that you're very fond of them."

"I am." She smiled at his kindness. "Why don't you bring them and come with me to the kitchen. Nora made some oatmeal and bacon, as well as biscuits and strong coffee. Are you hungry?"

"I could stand to eat." He took the bucket of milk from her and motioned to the house. "Lead the way."

Lucille had to admit that Rich was a kind and handsome man. She knew he was courting her in his own way and found his attention rather appealing. She was lonely, even with Charlotte and Micah around. Even with Nora to sit and work alongside. It wasn't the same as having a husband to curl up with at the end of the day.

"Nora, look who's come. Rich has brought us a basketful of raspberries."

"Wonderful. I wasn't sure if there would be much of any, what with the way the sun has been bearing down," Nora said, coming to where Rich held out the basket.

"We had some sunscald, but the boys shaded the plants with a tarp. Took care of that problem."

"That was kind of them."

"Oh, Lucille, it was self-servin'." Rich gave a hearty laugh. "They eat those things like there's no tomorrow. I was lucky to keep a basketful for you."

Nora took the basket. "These will be so good on top of the oatmeal, and I'll still be able to make a pie or two."

"Charlotte down yet?" Lucille asked.

"Haven't seen her." Nora took the berries to the sink and immediately began working with them.

Rich held up the bucket. "Where do you want the milk?"

"Just set it over on the counter. Nora will get to it later after the cream rises." Lucille followed him over and deposited her basket of eggs. "The hens aren't laying as well in this heat, Nora. Only got about two dozen."

"We'll get by just fine," Nora said, giving the basket a nod.

Lucille turned to Rich. "Want to join me in the dining room? We can at least start with our coffee."

"I'll have the food out to you in a quick minute," Nora promised.

Rich met her question with a smile. "I haven't had a woman around to share coffee with in a long time. I'd be glad to share it with you now."

She took the pot off the stove and made her way into the dining room. The table was set for four since Micah and Nora were used to eating with Lucille and Charlotte. Lucille directed Rich to the chair across from hers and poured him a cup of coffee.

True to her word, Nora was soon there with bowls of oatmeal and berries, as well as a pitcher of cream. "Here you go. This will get you started. I'll bring the bacon and biscuits in just a minute."

"Sounds good to me," Rich said before turning to help Lucille with her chair.

Nora returned with the promised food. "Now, if you don't mind," she said, placing the platters on the table, "I will eat a little later. I want to get those berries taken care of."

"That's fine, Nora," Lucille had a feeling she was just giving the couple time to be alone. It was just ten minutes to six, and breakfast usually didn't start until then. At least they could have a little time to themselves.

Once Nora left the room, Lucille reached out her hand to Rich. "Would you mind offering grace?"

He took hold of her hand and rubbed his thumb across the back of it, but his gaze never left her face. "I'd be honored."

A little shiver of delight went up Lucille's spine. It was a feeling she hadn't known in some time. She couldn't help but smile as she bowed her head.

I could get used to this, Lord.

Charlotte came down late to breakfast. She had pinned her hair up in a casual bun and dressed in her work clothes—a split skirt and blouse. It was cooler than some of her other attire and more beneficial for riding. She was relieved to see that Micah had already eaten and gone to work. This was as she had planned, and she felt herself relax just a bit. Better to tell Mama what was on the agenda and then let Micah know later.

Mama was reading the newspaper and nursing a cup of creamed coffee when Charlotte took her seat at the table. She had prayed all night, sleeping very little. She imagined Jesus praying in the garden before His death. She felt that marriage to Lewis Bradley was her death. And in truth, her actions were being done to save others. Of course, her sacrifice was nothing compared to the Lord's, but she found it comforting to know that Jesus understood exactly how she felt.

"Well, here you are at last," Nora said, coming into the dining room with the coffeepot. "I was just coming to see if your mama needed another cup of coffee." She moved to pour Charlotte's mother more coffee, but Mama shook her head.

Charlotte held her cup up. "I'll take some, please." As Nora poured, Charlotte apologized. "Sorry to be so late to the table. I didn't sleep well last night."

"Don't you worry a bit. I've made you some oatmeal with fresh raspberries. Mr. Johnson brought the berries over this morning. They might be just the thing to perk you up."

Charlotte nodded and took up her napkin. "That sounds good, Nora. Thank you so much."

As Nora left the room, Charlotte glanced up to find her mother folding the newspaper. "Did you enjoy your visit with Mr. Johnson?"

Mama met Charlotte's gaze and smiled. "I did. Rich is always so supportive of us. He brought the new freighting schedule and prices for shipping the steers to market."

Charlotte could think of nothing to say and so remained silent. She cherished the momentary quiet. The truth would soon be out, and then there would be no peace at all.

"I'm glad you're feeling better. I am hopeful that you will talk to me about what the problem is and how I can help."

Charlotte shrugged. "There's nothing to discuss. I have

come to some decisions, and those were weighing heavy on me."

"And why should that be?" Mama picked up her cup of coffee.

Charlotte poured cream into her cup and then picked up her spoon. "I suppose because I fear you won't understand the choice I've made. However, I'm asking you to please not question me about it. I've prayed on it a great deal and feel the decision I've made is the right one."

"All right. I will endeavor to understand and not question you on it, but if it's the right choice, then little harm can come from defending it."

Charlotte knew her mother was right, but how could she even begin to explain what she was about to do? Mama knew the truth. Knew that Charlotte loved Micah and would never love another. She would know that Charlotte's decision to marry Lewis Bradley must have come about from some sort of coercion or threat.

Nora returned with Charlotte's oatmeal and another little pitcher of cream. She placed the creamer on the table. "I figured you'd need more. Micah was rather generous with it this morning. That boy does love to pour cream all over his oatmeal. This should set you right as rain." She placed the bowl in front of Charlotte, then picked up the nearly empty pitcher. "I also have a little bacon and biscuits left. Would you like some?"

"No. I'll be fine." Charlotte knew the longer she had to delay what she needed to say, the harder it would be to say it.

"Very well, then. I'll be working outside today to get all those new tomatoes canned. If you need me, just come holler." She seemed to be in such a good mood. Charlotte wished she could say the same. Wished she'd never gone to church yesterday. Never allowed herself to be alone with Lewis.

"So what is it you need to tell me?"

Mama's voice brought Charlotte back to the present. She stared down at the oatmeal and berries. "Lewis Bradley is coming to supper tonight."

"What?"

Charlotte didn't have to look at her mother to hear the distress in her tone. "I said that Lewis is coming to supper tonight. I know it isn't pleasant to you, but it's important." She sprinkled sugar on her oatmeal doing her best to sound like nothing was amiss.

"Why in the world would you invite him to supper?"

She looked up and met her mother's surprised expression. "Because . . . we're going to announce our engagement." She drew a deep steadying breath.

Her mother's mouth dropped open, but not a word came out. Charlotte knew she was going to have to explain, but what could she say? Perhaps if she came at it from the angle of sympathy for Victoria.

"I gave it a lot of thought. And prayer too, as I mentioned. I know that Lewis has nothing binding from his arrangements with Papa, but I also know there must have been good reasons for what Papa wanted. Something that can ultimately benefit the ranch and you. And perhaps more importantly, Lewis's daughter needs a mother. Every time I see her or speak with Lewis's aunt, I pity them all the more."

"Pity is hardly a reason to marry."

"I realize that." Charlotte ignored her mother's worried look and instead focused on pouring cream on her oatmeal. She had to remain strong in this and not burst into tears. Tears that she felt were very much ready to fall.

"What about Micah?"

Charlotte put the pitcher down. "What about him?"

"You love him, Charlotte. You told me that you would never love another."

She couldn't very well lie about that. Mama knew her far

too well. "Micah doesn't need me like Victoria does. Besides, Micah sees me as nothing more than his little sister. I doubt he'll ever see me as more." She sampled the oatmeal.

"Charlotte, I really don't understand any of this. You can't be serious. I know how you feel about Lewis and Micah. You can't go marrying a man just to give his child a mother. You hardly even know Victoria. She's so seldom at church, and when she is, Lewis has his aunt keep her on the back pew and then hurry her out when the service is over." Mama cocked her head slightly as her eyes narrowed. "This has nothing to do with Victoria, does it?"

"I asked you not to question me on this. I know it seems illogical and that you don't understand, but this is what is going to happen. I'm of age and fully capable of making my decisions. You have Micah to help with the ranch, and you won't need me."

"Nonsense. I'll always need you. Charlotte, this isn't something you can venture into lightly. Marriage is sacred. You make a vow to God as well as each other."

"I realize that." Charlotte couldn't hide the sadness in her tone. "I know it is quite serious."

"What has he threatened you with?"

Charlotte felt her breath catch. Leave it to Mama to get right to the heart of the matter. She met her mother's eyes. Mama knew there was more to this than Charlotte was letting on.

"I won't talk about this further. I can't." Charlotte knew if she told her mother the truth that Mama would go to Lewis and confront him. She would explain what had happened with Micah's father and why she had chosen to lie, and then the whole of Cheyenne would know what they had done. Their reputation would be ruined. Mama would probably have to sell the ranch and move back to Illinois, because surely no one would do business with her after that. And then there was Micah. Would he be arrested for lying about his father's death and hiding the truth from the sheriff? Charlotte doubted anyone would understand, and Lewis implied that the law was clearly broken. Micah himself feared that might be the case.

It was unbearable to think of becoming a wife to Lewis Bradley, but even more so to imagine Micah behind bars. Maybe they'd even arrest Mama for hiding the truth about the suicide. The law was funny in what was acceptable and what was punishable.

With this reminder, Charlotte's strength bolstered. She had to protect Mama and Micah. When she looked at it that way, she knew she couldn't make any other choice.

"Charlotte, please don't do this. Please talk to me about what has happened and why you feel you must do this."

Pushing away from the table, Charlotte got to her feet. "I can't and I won't." She hurried from the room before Mama could ask anything more.

She headed outside not at all sure what she was going to do or where she was going to go. She knew she didn't want to run into Micah though. She couldn't bear to tell him just now what she had planned.

Lord, I don't know how to make this all right. I know that marrying Lewis is wrong in every possible way, but if I don't, then Mama and Micah will suffer. Please help me!

Micah barely made it to the house in time for supper. He had gotten caught up talking to the boys in the bunkhouse, and when Nora came out with their supper, he knew he'd have to clean up in a hurry. Charlotte and Lucille wouldn't care that he wasn't dressed in clean clothes, but Micah felt obliged to at least wash away the dirt and change his shirt.

He came into the house and made his way to the dining room, where he heard a man speaking. Surprised by that, Micah slowed his steps and paused just a moment. The voice sounded familiar, but the face it conjured to mind didn't make sense. But there stood Lewis Bradley in the flesh when Micah entered the dining room.

"Micah, I'm glad you could join us," Lucille said, looking pale and upset.

Lewis turned to face Micah. "I didn't realize you let the hirelings eat with you."

"Micah is far more than a hireling. We're running our cattle together for the time," Lucille explained. "It's benefiting both ranches. Micah is a partner."

Still unsure of why Lewis Bradley would dare to show his face in the Aldrich house, Micah walked past the man without a word.

"Evening, Mrs. Aldrich, Charlotte." He glanced at Charlotte. She wouldn't even raise her gaze to him. What was going on?

Just then, Nora came from the kitchen with a large platter. Micah quickly went to help her. He smiled at the heaping pieces of fried chicken.

"This looks wonderful, Nora."

"I know it is your favorite, Micah. I have mashed potatoes and gravy to go along with it, as well as corn, green beans, and sliced tomatoes. Oh, and I made those dinner rolls you like."

"Sounds great." He put the platter in the middle of the table.

"It would seem this meal is given in honor of Micah," Lewis said, not even trying to hide his sarcastic tone.

Nora frowned. "Micah does plenty around here and deserves to have some of his favorites. Besides, they're enjoyed by Mrs. Aldrich and Charlotte, and I'm rather fond of them as well."

"Elite society would agree that chicken is better served to the staff and ranch hands. You wouldn't find it on the governor's table. It's a poor man's food."

"Then it's a good thing the governor isn't eating with us tonight," Micah said, helping Lucille into her chair.

Lewis hurriedly took Micah's example and helped Charlotte into her chair. Micah wanted to say something but held his tongue and helped Nora instead.

Once they were all seated, Lucille looked at Micah. It was then that Micah noticed her eyes were red-rimmed. She'd been crying.

"Micah, would you ask the blessing?"

He nodded and prayed, all the while his mind racing with thoughts. Why was Bradley here, and why had Lucille been crying?

After finishing grace, Micah looked down the table at Charlotte. She was still unwilling to look at him and instead kept her gaze on her plate.

Nora took up the serving fork and acquired a chicken thigh for herself. She handed the fork to Micah while Lucille put a small spoonful of mashed potatoes on her plate before passing the bowl to Charlotte.

Micah served himself two pieces of fried chicken but noted that Charlotte gave the potatoes to Lewis without taking any for herself. Something big was going on, and it put him very much on edge. It was enough to have Bradley at the table, but for the women to act as they were made it clear that things were not right.

He opened his mouth to ask, then decided to bide his time. He glanced at Nora who seemed just as oblivious as he was. Bradley, however, was more than a little smug.

"You really should have more staff here at the house, Mrs. Aldrich. It's hardly fitting to pass the food around the table like a country picnic. It should be served."

"We prefer it this way, Mr. Bradley. If you don't like it, you needn't share our meal." Lucille's words were uncharacteristically harsh.

"Oh, that's quite all right. I can manage for myself. However, I do appreciate a good household staff."

Micah noted that Lucille put a piece of chicken on Charlotte's plate, as well as a roll. Charlotte raised her head and gave her a nod. "Thank you, Mama."

"You haven't eaten since breakfast. I'm worried about you."

"I'm fine. I just have a lot on my mind."

Micah was starting to fear what she might say next. Charlotte was never this quiet, and she hadn't come out to work with the animals or check up on the boys even once. He busied himself with eating but felt on guard every single moment. It was as if the entire room was holding its breath.

"I got the tomatoes canned today," Nora said, seeing that no one else was speaking. "We're going to need to go to town for more jars. I have pickles to make next, and the tomatoes took up far more jars than I'd anticipated."

Lucille nodded. "I have a list of things we need, so perhaps Micah can take us in tomorrow." She glanced at him, then looked quickly away.

Enough was enough. Micah put his fork down. "I don't know what's going on here, but it would be nice to know. I feel like I ought to have my gun cocked and ready. Why is Bradley here when I know he's caused you both nothing but grief?"

Lucille looked at Charlotte, as did Bradley. Charlotte squared her shoulders as Micah had seen her do on numerous occasions just before going into battle.

"Well . . . you see," Charlotte began, then paused to take a sip of water. She cleared her throat and began again. "Lewis has come because . . . we're . . . that is to say . . . " She looked at Micah and then back at her plate. "We're announcing our engagement."

If a gun had gone off and hit him square in the chest, Micah couldn't have been more shocked. He looked at Lucille, who was biting her lower lip as if to keep herself from speaking.

Nora, on the other hand, gave a gasp and turned to look at Lewis Bradley. "I thought that was behind us. What in the world is going on?"

Micah nodded. "I'd like to know that as well."

"The fact is, Charlotte has reconsidered my proposal of marriage," Lewis said. His smug, self-assured attitude was enough to make Micah want to get up from his chair and put a fist in the man's face.

"Is that true, Charlotte?" Nora asked.

"Are you questioning my honesty?" Bradley turned a scowl on Nora. "I won't sit here and be insulted by the household help, even if I do have to endure her eating at the same table."

"That's hardly any of your business, Bradley," Micah countered. "Nora is a part of this family and has more right to be here than you."

His expression changed back to a haughty sneer. "Ah yes, but soon I am to be family. Very soon, in fact. Charlotte and I are to be married right away."

"I can't allow for that." Lucille met Bradley's gaze. "I need Charlotte's help at least until after the steers go to market. She's much too vital to me. We have my cousins coming sooner than I expected to help us with figuring out where we'll be planting crops. Charlotte has all the bookwork to keep and will be an important part of the arrangements." She barely paused for breath. "I don't know why this has happened nor what has changed Charlotte's mind, but she has obligations here first and foremost, and you must respect that."

"I can respect that you have come to depend on her, Mrs.

Aldrich," Lewis replied. "I've no desire to rob you of her company, but it is important that we marry soon. My dear Victoria is most desperate for a mother, and I for a wife. Besides, I have already submitted the engagement announcement to the newspaper."

"You had no right to do that." Charlotte shook her head. "You should have talked to me about it."

Bradley chuckled. "I am sorry, my dear. I was much too excited to wait. I've been anticipating this marriage for nearly two years. You must understand." He looked at Lucille. "When is it that you will have your steers to market?"

"Not before the end of October. That's barely two months away. Surely you can wait that long and allow Charlotte a proper wedding."

Micah didn't know what to do or say. He had no part in this. Not really. Even if Charlotte loved him as Rich had said, she had clearly made the decision to wed another. Whatever the reason was.

"I suppose I could delay until then . . . if . . . well, let's say you were willing to give me Charlotte's dowry now. I could use the money to make changes to the house and ready it for her coming, as well as make other purchases that will benefit your daughter."

"Dowry?" Lucille looked confused.

"Your husband promised me a five-thousand-dollar dowry upon our engagement." He offered no further explanation.

Lucille quickly agreed. "I can get the money tomorrow at the bank and bring it to your office."

"Wonderful." He smiled at Lucille. "Then shall we set the wedding date for the first of November?"

18

Micah hadn't slept much the night before. With Charlotte's announcement that she and Lewis Bradley were to be married, he had found sleep all but impossible. Why was she doing this? She didn't love Bradley. Love had never even entered the conversation. Not only that, but she was clearly upsetting her mother. Lucille had been beside herself. It was a wonder, in fact, that any of them were able to finish dinner.

Breakfast had been no better. Charlotte refused to make an appearance. He and Nora had joined Lucille at the table, but no one was really talking or eating. The only thing Lucille had said was that she wanted Micah to take her into town after breakfast. So now he was hitching the wagon and preparing for the trip.

No doubt, Lucille would want to talk to him about Charlotte, and frankly, Micah was hard-pressed to know what to say. His own feelings toward Charlotte had changed over the last few weeks. Prompted by what Rich had said and Charlotte's own words and actions, Micah had begun to wonder at them having a future together. Now that was no longer a possibility. At least not if she married Bradley.

"Are we ready to go?" Lucille asked, joining him in the yard.

"Yup. Just finished." Micah walked around the horses and came to where Lucille stood beside the wagon.

He helped her up onto the seat and then joined her. "You ready?"

"As ready as I can be."

He glanced at her and noticed her eyes were still red-rimmed. What could he say to ease her misery and worry? He flicked the lines and directed the horses down the long drive. What was there that he could possibly offer to give her comfort?

"I'm surprised Charlotte didn't want to go."

"I told her I wanted her to stay home and help Nora. I needed time to talk to you alone without worrying about her overhearing me."

Micah kept staring straight ahead. "Say what you want to say, then."

"Micah, I can't bear any of this, and I will not allow Charlotte to marry Lewis Bradley. Not so long as there is breath in my body. I don't know what he has over her, but I figure he has threatened her with something."

"Charlotte has nothing to hide. What could he possibly threaten her with?"

"That's what I intend to find out. I'll take Mr. Bradley his money, but I'm going to demand some answers."

"Do you really think he'll willingly give them? If he's forcing Charlotte to marry him, I doubt he's going to easily give up that hold."

"All I know is that I must try. Charlotte won't even talk to me about it. I tried several times last night after Bradley had gone, but she told me to trust that she was doing what she needed to do."

"Is it possible she has fallen in love with him?"

"No. It's not at all possible. She loves you. She's only ever loved you. From the time she was four years old, you have been her focus." The words were delivered as if she were saying nothing more important than what the weather was to be for the day.

Micah looked at Lucille, feeling a sense of elation and disbelief. "She's never said anything to me about it. She used to follow me and Frank Jr. around all the time, but I figured that's what little sisters did."

"Oh, Micah, I don't know what to do. She can't marry Bradley when she's so obviously planned a life with you. She will never love him."

"I wish I'd known about her feelings for me. I mean, I guess I knew she cared deeply, but I figured she felt like she was my sister."

"Do you still feel that way about her, Micah? She mentioned that you only see her as a little sister."

Micah chuckled as his nerves tried to get the best of him. "No, ma'am, I do not see her as my little sister. I might have at one time, but no more."

"Do you think you could fall in love with her? Want to marry her?"

Micah was surprised at the look of hope in Lucille's expression. "It may have already happened. It's only just started to dawn on me, I'm sorry to say."

For the first time that day, Lucille smiled. "Micah, we must stop this wedding. At least I've managed to buy her some time."

"I don't know what we can do if Charlotte is determined to marry him."

"Maybe tell her how you feel. Give her something else to think about. Maybe if she sees what it is she's going to miss out on, she'll change her mind."

Micah considered this for a few moments, then shook

his head. "But whatever Bradley has done to force her hand, whatever he's threatening, it won't go away just because I tell her how I feel."

"But she's in despair over this. I can see it in her eyes," Lucille protested.

"And that despair will only get worse if what you say is true. If she truly does love me and I tell her that I love her too, it's going to be all the harder for her to go through with her decision."

"Good. I want it to be impossible."

"But we both know Charlotte. If she's convinced this is her only recourse, she's not going to change her mind unless the threat is gone. We're back to needing to know what Bradley has threatened to do."

Lucille folded her hands together. "Then I'm going to find out. When I take Mr. Bradley the money, I'm only going to give it to him upon the condition that he explains what he's done."

Lucille sat across from the bank president as he handed her the bank draft. He looked up with a grave expression.

"Mrs. Aldrich, I do wish you would reconsider this. Five thousand dollars is a lot of money."

"Yes, I'm well aware, but it's necessary." She folded the paper and put it in her purse.

"I did see the announcement of your daughter's engagement in the paper this morning. She's to wed Lewis Bradley. Since the draft is made out to Mr. Bradley, I presume it has something to do with that." His stern expression was that of a worried father. Lucille could remember her own father looking at her with such a gaze.

She forced a smile and nodded. "Yes. It's a dowry that my

husband and Mr. Bradley agreed upon. It's a perfectly acceptable practice." She got to her feet, and he rose quickly as well. She had no desire to further discuss the matter. "Now, if you'll excuse me, I must see Mr. Bradley."

She hurried from the bank and found Micah waiting at the wagon. Lewis Bradley's office was very close by, but she didn't want him and Micah to have an encounter. Not just yet. It was hard to know what might happen, and she didn't want to bring about a fight.

"Micah, here's my list. Would you go ahead over to Armstrongs' and get these things?" She pulled the list from her purse. "Nora wanted five dozen quart jars, but I think you'd better see if you can get double that. We still have a lot of canning left to do."

"Sure, but wouldn't you like me to accompany you to Bradley's office?"

"No, I have to do this myself. I intend to get the truth from him, and he might not be forthcoming if you're there. Please just go get these things, then meet me at the Cheyenne Café. We'll have lunch before we head back home."

She could see doubt in his expression and reached out to touch his arm. "Try not to worry. I'm sure nothing will happen to me. Mr. Bradley may be cunning and conniving, but he's no fool."

Micah didn't look convinced but took the list. "I'll meet you at the café, but if you're not there in half an hour, I'm coming back for you."

She nodded. "I understand."

Walking away, Lucille couldn't help but think that this might all just go away if Charlotte and Micah married. Lewis Bradley could hardly force a married woman to leave her husband. Could he?

Lewis Bradley's law office looked rather deserted when Lucille opened the door and stepped inside a small outer office, where an oak desk sat with a typewriter on a stand to the right. The leather chair behind the desk looked well-worn. There were three chairs along the wall in front of the window that faced the street and little else in the room.

Lucille glanced at the door that she figured led to Mr. Bradley's office. Since there was no one else around, she went to it and knocked.

"Come in," Lewis Bradley called.

She opened the door and gazed inside. Lewis sat behind a massive mahogany desk. There was a row of floor to ceiling bookcases behind him and two brown leather chairs placed opposite his desk.

"Come in, Mrs. Aldrich. I've been expecting you. I had heard you were at the bank, and I sent my secretary to lunch early, knowing you would soon be visiting me." He rose slowly. "I'm so glad that you were prompt to see this done."

Lucille stared at him for a moment and then took a seat without waiting for him to suggest it. She held her tongue, trying to think of what she wanted to say. She knew he wasn't going to like her delaying the transfer of the money, but she wanted answers.

"Where's Charlotte? I presumed she would come with you today." He closed the office door and returned to his desk. He didn't retake his seat, however, but stood at the corner only a foot or so away from Lucille's chair.

"She had a great many things to tend to. As I told you, we're very busy at the ranch."

"Yet you brought Mr. Hamilton with you." He looked down at her with his eyebrows raised.

"We had to get chicken feed, canning jars, and several other things for the ranch. It seemed the best thing to do. He's also helping me gather information from the Stock Growers Association since they don't allow women to attend their meetings."

"You've grown very close to Mr. Hamilton, haven't you?"

"He's like a son to me." Lucille knew her tone sounded defensive, and she tried to calm her voice. "He grew up with Frank Jr. and Charlotte. His folks were our best friends."

"Yes, I suppose I knew that." Lewis stared down at her another moment, then finally went to sit at his desk. He smiled. "Now let us move forward with our business."

Lucille steadied her resolve. "Before we do, I want some answers."

Lewis Bradley looked at her in surprise. "Answers about what?"

She could hear the sarcasm in his voice. He knew very well what she was asking. This was all a game to him. "I want to know what you threatened my daughter with to make her agree to marry you."

"Oh, really, Mrs. Aldrich." He chuckled. "You have it all wrong. Charlotte changed her mind because she wanted to honor her father's wishes. We spoke, and I told her how important it had been to him that the Aldrich Cattle Company make a national name for itself. I was an important part of that and didn't like that her father's dream, as well as my own, should be destroyed because of a harsh winter."

"You know as well as I do that she doesn't love you." Lucille expected anger, but Lewis only smiled.

"And we both know that if others stay out of it, love will come in time."

"Not when she's in love with someone else. My daughter loves Micah Hamilton, not you. Nor will she ever love you."

"That's hardly fair to say. Her feelings for Micah are nothing more than a girlish obsession with the dear friend of her brother. She probably holds on to a part of Frank Jr. by pretending to be in love with Micah."

"No, she has loved him for a very long time. Her heart will remain his forever. As her mother, I know this for a fact."

Lewis's smile never wavered, but there was a cold glint in his dark eyes. "I assure you . . . she will forget him."

"I won't argue that point with you, Mr. Bradley. I do want to know, however, what you did to force her to agree to marry you. Once she realized there was no contractual agreement that could force her to wed, she was happy. Just as I was."

Lewis gave another chuckle. "Rather than berate me for loving your daughter, you should be thankful. I'm a man of sterling reputation and can give her a life of ease and splendor. Unlike Micah Hamilton, who will forever battle the ghosts of his past." The sound of the front door opening drew his attention. "That will be my secretary returning from lunch. Now, if you'd please hand over the five thousand dollars, we can conclude our business, and I can get back to work."

Lucille stared at him for a long moment. She could see he would say nothing more, and if she was going to get answers, they would have to come from Charlotte. She reached into her purse and withdrew the bank draft.

She stood and wasn't surprised when Mr. Bradley remained seated. "Here is the bank draft for five thousand dollars. I will expect you to uphold your end of the bargain and wait until November for the wedding. Good day."

Lewis watched Mrs. Aldrich march from his office. She hadn't bothered to close his office door, and so he could see her continue her determined steps to leave his workplace. She was a handsome woman and had she not had a daughter of marriageable age, he might have gone after her for matrimonial purposes. That thought made him laugh out loud.

This brought his secretary to the door. "Did you need something, sir?"

"No. Close the door and get back to work."

"Yes, sir," the middle-aged man replied and quietly closed the door.

Lewis looked at the draft in his hand. He had five thousand dollars. It would allow him to go on pretending to have great wealth. At least for a short time. At least long enough to get Charlotte to the altar.

"And it's not going to be a November wedding, my dear Lucille. When I'm done with Charlotte, she'll be begging me to marry her immediately."

19

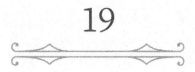

Charlotte had never known such despair unless it was the grief and guilt she had felt over her final confrontation with Papa. Her life was finished as far as she was concerned. For days she had wrestled with her decision to marry Lewis Bradley. She had prayed for long hours, hoping God might show her another way to save her mother and Micah from the shame and the possible legal trouble that would come if people knew about Mr. Hamilton's suicide. But God seemed strangely silent.

Time after time, she had gone to the Bible searching for some Scripture that might show her the way, but nothing seemed relevant. She knew God hated lying and that making a vow to God as she would in marrying Lewis shouldn't be taken lightly. Yet what was she to do?

They had announced their engagement on Monday, and it had appeared in the *Leader* newspaper on Tuesday. Now here it was Saturday, and Charlotte had no better understanding or answers as to how to deal with the matter than she had when first forced to go along with the plan. Mama had been relentless in seeking to know why Charlotte had agreed to marry Lewis Bradley. She had sought Charlotte morning and night with questions and desperation. Charlotte refused to talk to her mother about the situation, however, even knowing she was breaking her mother's heart. She knew Mama spent nights in tears and prayers, and it devastated Charlotte to know she was the cause.

But if I tell her the reason I've agreed to marry Lewis, she'll demand I not go through with it, and she'll sacrifice her reputation of honesty and stand with Micah to face whatever legal issues might come. And who knew how severe the legal trouble might be? They'd both hidden the circumstances of a death.

At the sound of a rider approaching the house, Charlotte went to her bedroom window and looked out. It was Lewis Bradley. He was the very last man in the world that she wanted to see. She sighed and moved to the vanity mirror. She considered her attire and hair. She had chosen a simple high-necked, layered muslin-over-cotton gown. It was nothing special, and she was certain Lewis wouldn't like it. Back when Papa had first entertained the idea of their marriage, Lewis had told her in private that he intended to see her dressed in clothes more befitting her station as his wife.

She smoothed down the bodice, took up a handkerchief, and tucked it in her fitted sleeve. She didn't trust herself not to break into tears.

Drawing a deep breath to steady herself, Charlotte wondered what in the world Lewis wanted. There was no reason for him to be here unless perhaps he wanted to give the appearance of them being close and romantic. It might be his way of trying to convince everyone that they were truly in love.

Charlotte swallowed the lump in her throat at the sound of knocking on the front door. She stepped into the hall and was just making her way downstairs as Nora opened the door to Lewis.

"Good day to you, Mr. Bradley," Nora greeted.

"I've come to see Charlotte."

"I'm here, Nora. You can go ahead and leave us." Charlotte came to stand beside the woman. "Mr. Bradley and I shall take a walk."

"I brought you these," Lewis said, producing a bouquet of hothouse flowers.

He was such a devious man. Here he was pretending to be a romantic suitor, bringing his fiancée a gift of love. She took the flowers and handed them to Nora without even bothering to thank him.

Nora took the bouquet and smelled them. "I'll put them in water." Her words were quite guarded, revealing no joy or delight over Lewis's supposed thoughtfulness.

"Thank you, Nora." Charlotte fixed Lewis with a stare. "Shall we?" She arched her brow but otherwise kept what she hoped was a stoic expression.

"But of course, my dear," he said, opening the screen door for her.

She waited until they were well down the drive before speaking. "What are you doing here?"

"Why, my dear, aren't you happy to see me?" There was a tinge of sarcasm in his voice, and then he chuckled. "Your mother brought me your dowry last Monday."

"Yes, I know."

She stiffened when he took hold of her arm. "That's hardly necessary."

"I think it is. Having you on my arm suggests our desire to be close. By the way, you look quite lovely in that simple country frock of yours, but I can hardly wait to drape you in silks and diamonds."

"Do you suppose that will make up for a lack of love?"

He laughed all the more. "I don't think it will much matter. You'll look very beautiful, and that is all that will be important. People will see you and know that you are mine, and that they cannot have you. Especially Micah Hamilton."

"You will also know that you don't have me. Not in heart and mind. You may force this unholy union on me, but that's the only part of me you'll ever have."

"My dear, that will be quite enough. Because I will also have your inheritance, and you will give me sons."

Charlotte cringed at the thought of bearing this evil man's children. She prayed for strength to keep her word. At least Micah and Mama would be safe. But would they really stay that way? After all, whatever Lewis knew, he would continue to be able to hold that over their heads. There really was no way to make this go away so long as he had the ability to reveal the truth.

"Then I must ask," Charlotte began, "what guarantee do I have that you will remain silent after we are married? You won't even be honest with me about how you found out what you know."

"You have no guarantee. Furthermore, you have only yourself to blame for my overhearing the truth. You and Micah really should find better places to talk than churchyards."

Charlotte's stomach soured. She and Micah had discussed the past that day after church. She was facing all of this because of that one conversation. She frowned. But what had she said that was all that revealing?

Lewis pulled her thoughts back to the present. "I find the idea of waiting until November first to be unnecessary. I can give you a lovely wedding without delay, and so I am planning our marriage to take place on September second. It's a Sunday, and I've already spoken to the pastor. He was surprised, to be certain, but agreed to marry us after the morning service."

Charlotte stopped in midstep and yanked her arm away from his grasp. "I won't do that. Mama asked to wait, and you agreed."

Lewis gazed heavenward and shrugged. "And now I've changed my mind. She doesn't need you." He looked her in the eye. "She has Micah, and they will manage getting the steers to market just fine without you."

"That's not the only thing she's relying on me for."

"Whatever else she needs, Micah will be able to provide. I'm quite sure he'll be more than capable of seeing that the ranch continues to run."

"But as you so neatly pointed out, this is my inheritance. I am responsible."

"And I will take that responsibility from you when we marry. You'll no longer have to make decisions about anything but caring for our home and children. And of course, satisfying me."

His grin was more than she could stand. Charlotte had to hold herself back from slapping him across the face. She started back for the house without considering what Lewis might do.

He easily caught up to her and grabbed her tightly around the upper arm. "You'll mind your manners with me, Charlotte. I can be very punishing to those who refuse to show me respect."

She tried to pull away, but he held on painfully tight. "You're going nowhere until you hear me out. You will tell your mother that we are marrying on the second. You will also convince her that it's your idea. I do not want her visiting my office again, demanding answers about why I'm forcing this on you. I told her this was a mutually agreed upon arrangement and that you are more than happy with your decision. Now it's your job to persuade her of it being the truth."

"But it's not the truth. And now, listening to you, I don't even believe it will resolve the problem."

"And what problem would that be? That I tell the truth

about what Micah did? The truth about your mother helping him to hide it?"

Charlotte raged inside, but on the outside, she became strangely calm. There had to be a way to hold Lewis in check. And then all at once something came to mind.

"You obviously know about my inheritance," she said, trying again to pull away. This time he let her go.

Lewis looked at her oddly. "Yes. I learned that you inherited half of everything, while your mother holds the other half."

"That's right. And here's what's going to happen. I'm going to go to the lawyer and turn my half over to my mother so that she owns everything in full. I'll still be able to access money that I need, but you won't be able to use it as you please. You won't have access to all that wealth you apparently need."

Lewis's eyes darkened. "You wouldn't dare. If you so much as try to arrange that, I'll go to the sheriff."

"No, I don't think you will. See you have something I want. And I have something you want. That makes us equals."

"That's where you're wrong, dear Charlotte." He stepped closer. "I am no one's equal. I have the upper hand in this. Your mother is growing older, and death could be quite near."

Charlotte's stomach soured at the man's flippant talk of death. Would he honestly kill Mama to have their money?

He reached up and took hold of her chin. Charlotte found it impossible to move. It was as if his words had frozen her in place.

"The truth of the matter is this: I am not opposed to doing whatever is necessary to have my way. Refuse to marry me and I will make your loved ones suffer. Marry me and give your inheritance to your mother beforehand, and I will take her life."

"But you can't marry him on the second of September. You mustn't marry him at all," Lucille said, after hearing Charlotte's announcement at supper. "I said and did what I did because I knew it would buy us time."

"But I want to do this, and it is my wedding." Charlotte sounded perfectly at peace with the decision.

Lucille didn't believe there was any peace at all, however. She knew her daughter. Knew that she didn't love Lewis and that none of this had come about of her own accord.

"Charlotte, you must tell us what Lewis has done to cause you to agree to marry him. It's outrageous. You don't love him. You'll never love him. Yes, Victoria may need a mother, but that's no reason to marry a man you despise." Lucille held up her hand to silence Charlotte. "And don't tell me that you've had a change of heart. I know you too well."

Charlotte looked away to stare at her plate of uneaten food. "This is how it is going to be, Mama."

Micah and Nora remained silent, but Lucille could see they were both very uncomfortable. Perhaps it was better to wait until later when she could speak to Charlotte alone. It was her turn to heave a sigh.

"I'm sorry to have reacted so vehemently. It is hardly appropriate at the dinner table." She picked up her fork and stabbed at the meat on her plate. Somehow, some way, she had to prevent this wedding from taking place.

By the end of the meal, Lucille and Micah were the only ones still at the table. Charlotte had gone to her room, her food uneaten, while Nora had gathered the empty plates and headed off to the kitchen.

Lucille looked at Micah and shook her head. "I'm glad you're still here. I don't know what we're going to do."

"I don't either, but I think it's time I had a talk with Bradley."

Micah's words were exactly what Lucille had hoped to hear. She hadn't wanted to ask him to confront Bradley, but now that he had volunteered, she wanted to express her approval.

"I think that's our only hope. Maybe the threat of having to deal with you will cause him to speak openly regarding what's happened. It's obvious that Charlotte doesn't feel safe confiding in us. Therefore, I must believe his threat involves us."

Micah gave a slow nod and got to his feet. "I'll go with you and Charlotte to church tomorrow and then find Lewis and demand to talk privately with him. I'll bring Wes along so he can drive you home."

"Don't let Lewis Bradley refuse you, Micah. I have a feeling this is life and death."

Micah sat thinking about Charlotte and the wedding. He knew more than ever that he didn't want her to marry someone else. He thought about what she meant to him and how much he cared about her. How had he not seen that it was love?

Even now, confessing his feelings to himself, it came as no surprise. If anything, it seemed so obvious that he felt foolish in having even questioned it. He loved Charlotte. He couldn't imagine his life without her in it.

He opened his Bible to Romans eight and started to read. His mind, however, refused to focus on the Scripture. What was Bradley holding over Charlotte? How bad must it be to convince her to give up on her longtime love of him and marry a man she despised?

Micah set the Bible down and started to make a mental list. The only things that Charlotte cared that deeply about were her mother, Micah, and the ranch. The threat had to be against one or all. He wished his father were alive. Talking things out with him had always given Micah insight and understanding. Now he was gone, and Micah didn't even know if he was with God or had been cast into a horrible place where God was clearly absent. Since his father's death, this had been the tormenting question. Could a Christian cause their own death and still maintain salvation? Had Jesus also died for that sin?

So many in the church said no. They said a dead man couldn't repent and ask forgiveness for the sin of taking his life, but Micah had always been taught that Christ had died for all of one's sins. When people accepted Jesus as their Savior and repented of their ways, it didn't mean they just stopped sinning. Man was flawed that way. But they would strive to change and sin less. Still, even those sins yet to be committed had been forgiven when Christ took them on the cross. When people accepted salvation, they accepted that gift of forgiveness for *all* of their sins.

His gaze fell upon the thirty-eighth and thirty-ninth verses of chapter eight in Romans.

> *For I am persuaded, that neither death, nor life, nor angels, nor principalities, nor powers, nor things present, nor things to come, nor height, nor depth, nor any other creature, shall be able to separate us from the love of God, which is in Christ Jesus our Lord.*

Micah read them again for a second time and then a third. He felt the burden lift as his mind began to comprehend the Scriptures he was reading. Nothing could separate people from the love of God, which is in Christ Jesus. Death was at the top of the list.

He glanced over the whole of chapter eight to make sure he understood the context in which those verses had been given. Verse one started with added conviction.

"'There is therefore now no condemnation to them which are in Christ Jesus, who walk not after the flesh, but after the Spirit,'" Micah read aloud. *"No condemnation to them which are in Christ."*

He read verses two and three. "'For the law of the Spirit of life in Christ Jesus hath made me free from the law of sin and death. For what the law could not do, in that it was weak through the flesh, God sending his own Son in the likeness of sinful flesh, and for sin, condemned sin in the flesh.'

"But there will be those who condemn Dad, just the same. They will say he couldn't really have believed if he gave in to hopelessness." Micah glanced upward. "They will say his salvation wasn't real."

Micah felt compelled to continue reading. He caught sight of verse thirty-three. "'Who shall lay any thing to the charge of God's elect? It is God that justifieth.'" He read the next verse as well. "'Who is he that condemneth? It is Christ that died, yea rather, that is risen again, who is even at the right hand of God, who also maketh intercession for us.'"

Tears came to his eyes. Who had the right to condemn his father? God alone was his judge. His salvation in Jesus was assured. His sin had once separated him from God, but Jesus had died once for all, and Wayman Hamilton had asked Jesus to be his Savior. He had sought forgiveness from sin and did his best to live a sinless life.

But then despair had taken his eyes from the Lord and put them on the tragedy around him. His suicide had come through doubt—that age old deception of Satan. A further deception would succeed if Micah chose to believe his father's salvation had been revoked.

He wiped his eyes and fell to his knees. The peace of God

poured over him, and Micah felt certain for the first time that like the thief on the cross, Dad was with Jesus in paradise.

"Thank you, Lord for Your Holy Word. Thank you for taking pity on me and giving me restored hope. Your constant love is all that I could ever want."

For a moment, Charlotte's face filled his thoughts. "Oh, Lord, please help her. Protect her, Father, because I have a feeling things are about to get worse before they get better. Help me to know how to help her."

20

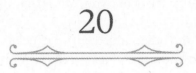

Micah had found it impossible to meet alone with Lewis Bradley. At church, he had refused to speak to Micah, explaining he had plans to discuss with the pastor. After all, his wedding was to take place soon, and there was still so much to see done.

Micah let Wes take Lucille and Charlotte back home and decided to wait around until Bradley was free, but the man foiled him by going home with the pastor for dinner. Micah skipped his own lunch and waited around for Bradley to emerge from the pastor's house, but after three hours and no Bradley, he gave up. Somehow, Bradley must have given him the slip. He made one last effort and stopped by Bradley's house on the way out of town, but the butler told him Bradley was not there.

Today, however, Bradley was approaching the Aldrich ranch in a carriage with two other men in his company. He'd allowed his driver to bring them out and sat chatting away with the other two. Micah didn't know either one, and as they approached, he made his way to the carriage.

"Mr. Hamilton, how nice to see you again," Lewis Bradley

stated as he debarked the carriage. "These are Mrs. Aldrich's cousins Barnabus and Simon Brewster. They arrived sooner than expected, and so I thought it only fitting that I should bring them here to the ranch."

"Good to meet you gentlemen," Micah said as each man joined Bradley. "I'm Micah Hamilton. I know Mrs. Aldrich has been looking forward to seeing you again."

"We've heard a lot about you, Mr. Hamilton," one of the men declared.

"All good," the other added with a chuckle.

"I'm glad to know that. Please call me Micah."

"Where is Cousin Lucille?" the first man asked.

Just then, the front screen door opened, and Lucille appeared. "Barnabus! Simon!" She hurried out to where the two stood and embraced first one and then the other. "I can't believe you're here. You should have let me know you were coming on an earlier train."

"It just sort of fell into place, and we had no chance to send word. We figured we'd surprise you. This fella, here, was at the train station, and when he found out we were trying to find a way out to the ranch, he offered to drive us."

"It was only right that I should," Bradley said with that self-satisfied smirk Micah had come to hate. "After all, come Sunday I'll be a part of the family."

Micah kept his gaze on Bradley the entire time. He could see that the man was more than a little pleased with himself.

"I do hope Charlotte is available to join me," Bradley added. "There are some very important details that I need to discuss with her about the wedding."

Lucille's eyes narrowed as she frowned. "She will want to see Barnabus and Simon."

"Oh, surely that can wait." Lewis smiled. "After all, they'll be with you most of the week. I invited them to stay for the wedding, but they told me they must leave on Saturday. Is Charlotte in the house?"

Lucille said nothing as she stared at Bradley. Her contempt for him was more than evident in her expression. Finally, she gave Bradley a nod but nothing more.

"I'd like to have a word with you, Bradley," Micah said, following him as he headed toward the house.

"I have no time for you, Mr. Hamilton. As you well know, I'm to be married on Sunday and need to speak with my fiancée."

"The wedding is what I want to talk to you about. Actually, the threats you have over Charlotte that have brought about the wedding is what I want to discuss."

Bradley had the audacity to laugh as he kept walking. "Your jealousy isn't at all becoming. There are no threats needed where love is concerned."

"She doesn't love you, and she never will."

This caused Bradley to stop. He turned very slowly, his gaze cold and hard. "You had better hope she does, Mr. Hamilton. Now, for your sake, it would do you well to mind your own business. For a man with secrets in his past, I wouldn't be too inclined to cause me any more frustration."

"So you're threatening her with me. With something you think you know about the past."

"Lewis? What are you doing here?" Charlotte asked, coming from the house. She let the screen door slam shut behind her. She was dressed to ride and stood with her hands on her hips, clearly irritated at the interruption. "Micah? What's going on?"

"It's nothing, my dear," Bradley said, moving to where she stood. He embraced her while she stood stiff and unyielding. "We were just chatting. Now come inside. I have much to tell you. I talked to the pastor yesterday after services, and everything is set. I have even purchased a beautiful gown for you to wear. Far better than anything you own."

Micah wanted to grab Bradley and throw him on the ground. Anything to get him away from Charlotte. It riled him to see Lewis Bradley taking liberties, especially now that Micah had come to know his own feelings for Charlotte.

"Let's walk under the trees," Charlotte said, moving away from Lewis toward the cottonwoods.

Micah stood in place, knowing that if he followed or said anything it would only bode poorly for Charlotte. He whispered a prayer for her and walked back to where Lucille was talking to her cousins in hushed tones.

"I was just telling them about what has happened with Charlotte," Lucille explained.

Micah nodded. "Something Bradley just said makes me pretty certain his hold over her has to do with me. He said something about secrets from my past."

Lucille frowned. "I don't know what to think. Come on, Barnabus, Simon. You must be hungry. Nora's working on lunch, and I must let her know there will be two more . . . possibly three." They headed for the house, and Lucille stopped and called back. "You too, Micah."

Every protest he could think of rose up inside him. He wanted to remain in view of Charlotte just in case Bradley decided to do something untoward. But he knew it was probably best that he go with the others.

Ten minutes later, Bradley entered the house. His expression was clearly one of anger. "I need a horse."

Lucille had seated her guests in the front room while they awaited lunch. Micah had positioned himself at the window but hadn't been able to see where Charlotte and Bradley had gotten off to.

"Why do you need a horse?" Lucille asked.

"Charlotte has taken off on her horse, and I want to go after her. She might come to harm."

"I'll go after her," Micah said, crossing the room.

"It's my place," Bradley protested.

Micah stopped inches from the man. "Perhaps, but I'm the one with a horse."

Without waiting to hear what Bradley had to say, Micah raced to where Duke was corralled and saddled him quickly. He knew basically where Charlotte would go. She had her favorite spots to seek solace. Since she was a little girl, she'd always been fond of a place where the creek forked at the border where their properties joined. He'd try there first.

Duke seemed to anticipate Micah's plan and headed north without much prompting at all. Micah kicked him into a lope on the clear pathway and then slowed when he reached the place where he'd need to leave the trail. It didn't take long to find Charlotte. She was pacing back and forth along the shallow creek and murmuring under her breath.

"Charlotte!" Micah jumped down from Duke and dropped the reins. Duke immediately began to seek grass to eat. "What's going on?"

She was surprised to see him and stopped. "Going on? Nothing's going on."

"You're lying and have been for over a week now. Your mother and I are both worried about you since you've never been one to do so before. You've always been good about speaking your mind in truth."

"I'm telling . . . the truth." She looked away, however, seeming uncomfortable.

"Then tell me why you're marrying Lewis Bradley when you don't love him."

"Papa wanted me to, that's why. I'm honoring him. I told you how bad I felt about arguing with him the day he died."

"And you think this will make up for that?"

"Yes."

"I don't believe you." Micah stepped toward her, but Charlotte backed up a step.

"I must marry Lewis. That's the truth."

"Even though you'll never love him, never care for him?"

Charlotte shook her head. "It's not right of you to say I don't love him. You don't know that."

Micah arched a brow. "Oh really? I have it on good authority that you love me and have most of your life. How can you love him if you're in love with me?"

She flushed red. "I . . . my feelings for you . . . were just a girlish infatuation. It's behind me now."

He crossed the distance between them in two long strides and took Charlotte in his arms. Lowering his mouth to hers, Micah kissed her with all his pent-up passion. He felt her arms go around his neck as she returned the kiss. And just as he felt her melting against him, he pulled away and steadied her on her feet.

"It's behind you, eh?" He grinned, feeling rather delighted with her response. "You feel nothing for me?"

She searched his face for a moment, then burst into tears and ran for her horse. Before Micah could think, she had mounted and was gone. Heading for home and the safety of her room, no doubt.

Micah returned to where Duke grazed and tried to decide what he should do. The kiss had sealed his fate. He knew without any possible doubt that Charlotte loved him, and he loved her. He had never known the kind of feelings that she stirred inside him. No matter what Bradley was threatening her with, Micah knew he had to keep that marriage from happening.

When he returned to the house, Micah learned that Charlotte was locked in her room, crying, and Bradley had left in a huff before she'd even returned.

"I'm afraid I offended him." Lucille gave a shrug. "I told him I wanted the dowry back since he wasn't a man of his word. He told me he was a man of his word, that the change of dates for the wedding was all Charlotte's doing and that she was madly in love with him. I called him a liar."

Micah couldn't help but grin. "Good. Because he is. I kissed her. Better still . . . she kissed me back."

Lucille's eyes widened. "You did?"

"I brought up that she couldn't marry Bradley since she was in love with me. She told me she wasn't—that it had been girlish infatuation. So I kissed her to prove her wrong."

"Good. Now maybe we'll get somewhere." Lucille glanced toward the dining room. "Come have some lunch, and we can discuss what you need to do next."

"Next, I'm going to visit Lewis Bradley. I told him we needed to have a talk, and now we're going to do just that. But I'll take something to eat on the way, if you don't mind."

Lewis Bradley glanced out his bedroom window and saw the approaching rider. He had known Micah would show up sooner or later. He was honestly surprised it had taken him as long as it had. Since overhearing Micah and Charlotte that Sunday weeks before, Lewis had done what he could to establish the details of what happened to Wayman Hamilton. He'd even located Kit Hendricks and brought him back to Cheyenne to work for him. He had asked the man about any trouble between Micah and his father, and Kit had shared about the day Frank Sr. and his son had gone missing. Kit knew very little that was relevant, but Lewis encouraged him to be ready to tell a court of law what he knew. And just for good measure, Lewis embellished the story and went over the details until Hendricks could quote it from memory.

Given Hendricks hated Micah for robbing him of a job, the man was more than willing to lie. It was good fuel for the fire Lewis intended to set. And would be even more effective than the fire he'd hired Hendricks to set at the Aldrich ranch.

The clock chimed five as Lewis watched Micah dismount. He hurriedly rang for the butler, and when he appeared, Lewis was quick with instructions.

"Micah Hamilton is about to knock on the front door. When he does, let him in and show him to the library. Then I want you to go to the stableboy and have him bring the police to the house."

The butler gave him a worried look. "I'll be fine, don't worry. Just have the boy get them here as soon as possible."

"Yes, sir." The knocker sounded, and the butler glanced over his shoulder.

"Go ahead, take him to the library. Tell him I'll be right down."

Lewis listened at his open bedroom door as the butler made his way downstairs. The knocking sounded again, even louder this time. Lewis heard the butler answer the door and greet Micah. Once their footsteps receded down the hall to the library, Lewis made his way to the stairs.

His mind raced with thoughts. If he managed this just right, he could get Micah to tell him what really happened, and then maybe he'd have even more evidence to lay against him. Besides, he had enough dirt on the judge who would likely hear Micah's case. Even if Micah remained silent, Lewis felt confident he could arrange a conviction.

He found Micah pacing as he entered the library. He paused and stopped in front of the fireplace when Lewis entered the room.

"Mr. Hamilton. I would ask what brings you here, but I'm sure I already know."

"I demand that you release Charlotte from the engagement, Bradley." Micah crossed the room to stand directly in front of Lewis.

It took all his gumption to refrain from dodging behind his desk. Lewis knew that Micah could easily take him in a fight, and the man looked angry enough to start punching.

Forcing himself to appear unimpressed, Lewis glanced at the fingernails of his right hand. "And why would I ever do that? I love her, and she loves me."

"She doesn't. She loves me and has loved me most of her life."

"I'm sorry, but you're too late." Lewis took a casual stroll to his desk. He felt better having some space between them, as well as the three-by-six-foot desk.

"What is it you're holding over her, Bradley? You said something about my secrets. Well, I have no secrets. Tell the world whatever it is you think you know, but leave her alone."

"You have plenty of secrets, I'm sure, but one in particular that I know you don't want told." Lewis smiled. "The manner in which your father died."

Micah paled, and Lewis knew he'd hit a nerve. "That's right. I know all about it, and soon the rest of Cheyenne will too. That is, unless you stop pestering me about Charlotte and leave us alone.

"I overheard you and Charlotte talking about the entire

matter after church a few Sundays past. As a man familiar with the law, I know that you are prison bound for what you did."

"And you're using that knowledge to force Charlotte to marry you so that you don't expose me."

"Or her mother. After all, Lucille Aldrich told the sheriff that your father froze to death with her men." Lewis chuckled. "It would seem an entire web of lies has been intricately woven. I would be something of a hero to unravel this and let the truth be told once and for all."

21

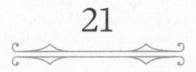

Micah stared at Lewis for a long moment. The man was certain he knew the truth, but Micah was equally certain he and Charlotte had never said a word about his father's suicide. They would never have used that word in public. They knew the dangers of being overheard.

"You're an evil man, Bradley, and you don't know what you're talking about."

"I know enough that you'll soon be on your way to jail and perhaps even execution if I work things just right." Bradley laughed and went to where he kept his whiskey. "Would you like one last drink?"

"I don't drink anymore."

"Pity. It could give you the courage you're going to need." He poured himself a drink. He turned to face Micah once again and lifted his glass. "Here's to the truth."

"You wouldn't know the truth if it punched you in the face. Look, I don't much care what you do to try and hurt me, but the Aldrich women deserve better. If you hurt Mrs. Aldrich, you'll hurt Charlotte as well and ruin their good name. That won't bode well for you."

"Since Charlotte's done nothing but keep the secret, folks

will overlook her part. It's not like she was the one to pull the trigger."

Micah frowned. "What do you mean, exactly?"

"Oh, let's not play games, Micah. We both know exactly what we're talking about. Your father didn't freeze to death with the Aldrich men. You put him in the ground before the truth could be known. Of course, the body could be dug back up to prove the wound that ended his life."

Micah was on his guard. Lewis Bradley knew something, but he couldn't possibly know everything. There was just something about the situation that suggested Bradley was making this up as he went.

"I'm sure you thought you could keep things buried along with the body, but lies have a way of being exposed over time."

"I'm sure you're an authority on that." Micah could see his words had little effect on Lewis Bradley. The man was absolutely delighted by the situation. He knew he was making Micah uncomfortable. Micah just wished he could make Bradley reveal what he knew.

"Well, rather than me going into the details of my father's death, why don't you tell me what it is you think you know."

Bradley laughed. "I know plenty, and soon the entire town will know it as well."

"If everyone knows, then how is it that you plan to control Charlotte with it and force her to marry you?"

"Well, there are several aspects to this matter, as you well know. There's your part in the situation, and then of course her mother's actions."

Micah had had more than enough and was just about to speak when there was a loud knock on the door.

Lewis Bradley smiled and then tossed back his whiskey. "Ah, that will be the law."

Micah turned toward the library door as the butler ushered in not just any lawman, but the chief of police himself, Edward Vogel.

"Chief Vogel, I'm so glad you could come."

Micah extended his hand to Chief Vogel. "Good to see you again."

"Micah." Vogel shook his hand, then glared at Bradley. "What's this all about, Mr. Bradley? Your boy came creating such a scene at the jail that I felt I had to get involved."

"And I'm glad you did, Chief. This is a dire situation. I want you to arrest Micah for the murder of his father."

"Wayman Hamilton died over a year ago when he froze to death."

Lewis Bradley shook his head. "That's only what Micah wanted us to believe. He killed his father, plain and simple. Shot him to death, and I have a witness who can lend credibility to my accusations."

"I did not kill my father." Micah's statement was matter-of-fact, but rage was building within. He couldn't very well reveal what had happened without letting Bradley know the truth. If he could just speak to Vogel in private, then maybe he could explain. Even so, there would no doubt be consequences.

Bradley rang for the butler, and in a moment the man stood beside Vogel in the doorway. "Please ask Mr. Hendricks to join us. You should find him in the carriage house."

"Yes, sir." The butler left as quickly as he'd come.

Lewis Bradley gave an ominous smile. "I don't suppose you counted on Kit Hendricks being around. Once you saw to him being fired from the Aldrich ranch, I found him and hired him to work for me."

Micah held his temper in check. "It doesn't surprise me. You two deserve each other."

It didn't take long for Kit Hendricks to appear. He strode past Vogel and Micah and went to stand close to Bradley.

"You wanted to see me, Boss?"

"Yes, I want you to explain to Chief Vogel what you know about Micah killing his father."

Kit nodded and looked at Vogel, ignoring Micah. "Well, it was a bad day with the blizzards and winds. Mr. Aldrich and his son had gone out to try and save some of their herd. They were gone for hours, and Mrs. Aldrich got worried. She sent me and some of the boys to the Hamilton ranch to let them know the men were missing and get their help for a search.

"We got there and heard Mr. Hamilton and his son fighting. It was a terrible fight with the sound of broken glass coming from inside the house. I heard Mr. Hamilton yell for Micah to calm down. Then there was the sound of scuffling and more yelling."

"And what makes you think that Micah killed his father?" Vogel asked.

"He said he was going to. That was one of the things he yelled as they fought. He said, 'I'm gonna kill you, Pa!' Micah didn't know we were just outside the house."

"We were in the barn when your bunch showed up, Hendricks," Micah said, his hands balling into fists. "And I never once called my father *pa*."

"Better watch him, Chief Vogel. He looks ready to take a swing at Hendricks," Bradley pointed out. Kit took several steps back.

"If I were going to hit anyone, it'd be you, Bradley, for all the misery you've caused Charlotte and her mother."

Bradley looked at Edward Vogel. "See there. What did I tell you? He's violent and intends to do me harm."

Vogel turned to Micah. "What's your version of this?"

"My dad and I were in the barn. Between storms we'd ridden out to see if we could find any of the herd. There were so many dead that it upset my father a great deal. He was angry at the loss and angry that he hadn't listened to advice regarding the winter. The sound of broken glass wasn't glass at all. My dad threw a clay pot against the barn wall in frustration. We weren't fighting. Dad was just raging against all that had happened.

"When the Aldrich hands showed up to announce the men were missing, Dad put aside his frustration, and we went out to search for Mr. Aldrich and Frank Jr. The Aldrich ranch hands were too worried about their own safety, and most resigned their positions and left without helping. Hendricks stayed at the ranch rather than help us locate his boss."

"I was told to remain at the ranch," Hendricks countered. "Mrs. Aldrich didn't release me to go, and I don't take orders from the likes of you."

Micah nodded. "I'd be surprised if you're capable of following orders from anyone for very long." He looked back at Chief Vogel. "Dad and I found Mr. Aldrich and Frank Jr. They'd frozen to death. Dad told me to go get a wagon to bring them back. When Lucille Aldrich and I returned, Dad was dead as well." His gaze never left Vogel's face. "We took Dad back to our place, and I buried him."

"Of course, he would say something like that," Bradley declared. "He's hardly going to admit to killing his father, but Mr. Hendricks overheard the threat. Not only that, but I overheard Micah speaking with my fiancée about the truth of what had happened. He said it was all his fault that his father was dead. Charlotte offered him comfort. You need only confront Charlotte and her mother to get the truth."

"Bradley has been threatening Charlotte to force their marriage," Micah told Vogel.

"He would like that to be the truth because he wants the Aldrich money and my soon-to-be wife. However, I believe you have ample grounds to make an arrest. Then I suggest you dig up the body of Wayman Hamilton. I believe you'll find he didn't freeze to death at all. He was shot."

Time seemed to stand still. Micah met Vogel's stern expression but said nothing. What could he say?

When Micah didn't turn up at supper, Lucille had her concerns. He had gone to pay Lewis Bradley a visit, and she knew very well that things could have gone badly. Mr. Bradley wasn't the sort to take kindly to someone interfering in his plans.

Charlotte had refused to come down to dinner, and so Lucille and Nora shared the table with Barnabus and Simon, discussing the area around them and the potential for a successful farm.

"Water is going to be the hardest part of it," Barnabus was telling her. "It's easy to see why farming is difficult out here. Those university people who've been studying the area say you folks have a very limited amount of rain. Sometimes not even fifteen inches a year. You're only going to be successful by doing something called dry farming."

"Dry farming? It sounds like a contradiction." Lucille took a bowl of succotash offered to her by Nora and scooped some onto her plate. She hadn't been hungry since the change of the wedding date, but she had to at least try to keep up her strength.

"It's becoming more and more necessary as the nation settles in a variety of areas that no one thought was much good for anything. The idea is that the farmer can use what little rain has been given and store it in the ground. The key is deep plowing and planting, or what's being called drilling."

Barnabus continued talking about the techniques, with Simon joining in with a comment from time to time. Lucille was glad to hear what they had to offer, but her mind was on Micah. Where was he?

By the time supper finished, there was still no sign of him. Lucille wondered if maybe he'd just ridden in and gone straight to his cabin. She helped Nora clear the table, then made her way outside and headed straight to the foreman's cabin. She knocked several times and finally just opened the door.

It was dark inside and clearly void of life. She knew from having checked the time in the house before heading out that it was nearly eight. They'd been late to the table that night because of a variety of things, including waiting on Micah's return. But now here it was nearly time for bed, and Micah was still missing.

Lucille stepped outside, pulling the door closed behind her. The last of the light was fading from the sky. Soon it would be dark. Maybe he had decided to stay in town. Maybe he learned there was a stock growers meeting, and he wanted to stick around for it.

She tried to calm her nerves, so she prayed.

"Lord, nothing is going as it should just now. You know I've been praying without ceasing. Please show me what I'm to do. I know I lied about Micah's father, and I pray You forgive me. It was done only with the best intentions. I wanted to save Micah from further grief. I knew people would look down on him if they knew the truth.

"I don't know what's happened in town, but I pray that You keep Micah safe and that I'm not waiting too long to act."

The last time she'd done that it had resulted in the loss of her husband and son. Would waiting bring about tragedy once again? She sighed. It was so hard to just let go of her fears and give it all over to God. After forty some years of following Jesus, Lucille had expected to be better at trusting Him in all things. She drew a deep breath and pushed the bad thoughts aside to continue her prayers.

"And, please, Lord, let Charlotte know that she can talk to me and explain her decision. Let her tell me what's wrong so that we can figure out a way to make things better. Amen."

A heavy sigh escaped her lips as she glanced heavenward. "Frank, I wish you'd never started the arrangement with Lewis Bradley. I wish Charlotte had never captured his attention. But things are as they are, and now we're left to pick up the pieces and figure out what to do next."

She hugged her arms to her body and looked back down the road.

"Please come back to us, Micah."

Charlotte awoke with the sunrise, and for a moment she didn't remember any of the problems in her life. Still groggy, she sat up and stretched, smiling at the memory of Micah's kiss. But then the truth filled in the missing details, and she remembered why that kiss had been given. It wasn't the romantic kiss she'd dreamed of, with Micah pledging his love and Charlotte countering with her own promise to always be his. It had come to prove to her that she was a fool . . . and liar.

She got up and dressed quickly. It was almost impossible to make sense of her life. She prayed but knew that God wanted her to speak to her mother. To be honest with her and tell her why she had agreed to marry Lewis Bradley. She knew, however, what her mother's response to that would be. Mama would want the truth to be told rather than have Charlotte marry a horrible man like Lewis Bradley. Mama would rather be ostracized for her part in the lie than to make Charlotte pay the price.

Her hair was an unruly mess, and after trying several times to braid it, Charlotte finally just twisted it and pinned it in place atop her head. She wished she could just as easily pin her messy life into place.

For several long moments she stared into the mirror. The woman who stared back was full of fear and doubt. She was trapped. Lies had backed her into an impossible corner. How could she even entertain the idea of marrying Lewis Bradley? How could she betray Micah that way—betray herself?

"God, please help me. Show me what to do—right away."

She headed downstairs and could hear men's voices as she approached the dining room. She knew Micah would be there and stiffened her resolve.

I must be strong. I must be brave.

Charlotte entered the room and gazed at the people around the table. Micah was strangely absent. She took her seat and nodded to her mother.

"Morning, Mama."

"Are you feeling better?" her mother asked.

"I suppose so. I am hungry." She glanced at Micah's empty seat, wanting so much to ask where he was.

"He didn't come back last night."

Charlotte looked at her mother. "Where had he gone?"

"To speak to Lewis Bradley."

A chill rushed over her body, and Charlotte shook her head. "Why? Why would he do that?"

"Here we are, just as you requested," Nora said, bringing in a platter piled high with flapjacks. "I hope they're as light as you're used to. The boys in the bunkhouse downed them faster than anything I've ever seen."

She added the platter to the table to join one with bacon and another with scrambled eggs. "I'll fetch the coffee, and we can begin."

Charlotte looked at her mother the minute Nora left the room. "Tell me what this is all about."

"Barnabus, Simon, forgive me, but I need to speak to

Charlotte alone. We'll return as soon as we can, but in the meantime please eat your breakfast." She got up and headed for the hall.

"Are you sure it can't wait?" Barnabus called. "Your breakfast will get cold."

"It's very important," Mama replied, not even turning to face him.

Charlotte followed her mother, not understanding the sudden need for secrecy. "Mama, what's going on?"

"Step outside with me. We don't want to be overheard."

Once they were well away from the house, Mama turned to face Charlotte. The look on her face reminded Charlotte of when she'd come to tell her that Papa and Frank were dead.

"What is it? Please just tell me."

"Micah had asked Mr. Bradley what he was threatening you with, and he made some comment about Micah's past and secrets. I don't know what exactly was said, but—"

Before she could finish the sound of a lone rider coming up the drive drew their attention.

"Micah," Charlotte said and then shook her head as the rider drew near. "No, it's Lewis."

"Oh dear. This is not good."

Charlotte grabbed her mother's hand. "Mama, go inside. I'll speak to him alone."

"No, I won't leave you alone with him. He's obviously up to no good."

"Please, Mama. Just do as I ask. I have a feeling it won't take long, and then hopefully I can tell you what's going on with Micah. If Lewis is behind it, he'll no doubt want to gloat."

Her mother didn't argue, and Charlotte breathed a sigh of relief as she went back into the house. Charlotte's hunger faded as Lewis climbed down from his horse and drew near.

"You look as if you were anticipating my arrival."

She stalked toward him, hands on hips. "Where's Micah? What have you done to him?"

Lewis laughed. "What, no hello or kiss for your betrothed?"

"I want the truth." Charlotte cocked her head to one side as she studied him. "What did you do?"

"It came to mind that your cooperation would be better assured if there were an immediate threat to the welfare of this man you love. I could tell by your paltry attempt to threaten me with the assurance of signing over your inheritance to your mother prior to our wedding that you weren't going to do as I asked. At least not without incentive."

"Micah came to talk to you."

"He did, and I told him that I knew everything and I even had a witness who could see him put in jail for his misdeeds."

"That's a lie. Micah did nothing wrong."

"Oh, but he did. None of you would be acting the way you are had his father died a simple death in the blizzard."

"There was no one to witness Micah's father's death save Micah and my mother. You know nothing. Micah bears no responsibility in what happened."

"Then why all the secrecy, my love?" Lewis drew closer and took hold of her arms. "You see, as a man who has perfected the art of lying for a living, I know when someone isn't telling the truth. But all of that is soon to be behind us. You will marry me Sunday, and Micah will hang for his father's murder."

"But that's not what happened! You can't do this."

He smiled and tightened his hold. "I can and have. Micah is in jail as we speak, and once his trial takes place and the guilty verdict rendered . . . he'll hang."

"Then I won't marry you. I'll never marry you!" She drew her booted foot back and kicked him hard in the shin.

Lewis released her and jumped back with a cry. "You'll pay for that."

"I'm finished with you, Lewis. Get off my land."

He stopped rubbing his leg and looked up at her. "You do this, and your mother isn't long for this world."

Charlotte felt as if she couldn't breathe. She couldn't let him see how he'd affected her, however. She fixed him with what she hoped was a hard, unwelcoming look. "Go!"

He stood looking as if he couldn't figure out whether to fight or leave. Charlotte pointed her finger at him. "Go now, and Lewis . . ." She paused, making sure she had his utmost attention. "If anything happens to my mother, anything to cause her harm, I will give everything on this ranch and in the bank to the church. You aren't ever going to get the Aldrich money."

22

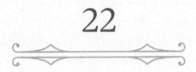

Charlotte marched back into the house with a new determination. The man she loved was facing murder charges, and there was no time to waste. She bounded into the dining room where her mother had reclaimed her seat.

"We need to talk. Now."

Mama smiled and got to her feet. "It's about time." She looked at the others. "Once again, I must beg your indulgence. This is most important. I'll explain later."

This time no one said a word as Mama rushed out. Charlotte led her mother into the front room and turned to face her. "The truth must come out, so I'm not going out of my way to speak to you somewhere else. Soon everyone will know."

"All right. What truth are you talking about? Did you find out where Micah is?"

"Yes." Charlotte shook her head. "It's not good. Lewis has had him arrested."

"For what? Did Micah fight with him?" Mama's expression betrayed her fear.

"No." Charlotte paused a moment. "First, I must apologize for the way I've behaved. I honestly didn't know what else to do, but keeping the truth from you wasn't the right choice."

"I agree it wasn't, but I accept your apology. Now please just tell me about Micah."

"Lewis overheard something Micah and I were discussing at church. We were talking about the past. Micah was hurting over his father. We talked about it, but never mentioned the word *suicide*. We never once said aloud that he had died by his own hand. But apparently the things we did say led Lewis to believe the situation was even worse than that. He believes that Micah killed his father."

"Oh no!" Mama's hand went to her mouth.

"I'm afraid so." Charlotte came to her mother. "Lewis threatened to expose the truth, and I figured he meant the suicide. Instead, he's decided Micah's a murderer. Worse still, he threatened to kill you, Mama, if I did anything to try and stop our wedding from taking place."

"What?" Mama was indignant. "How dare he?"

"It's partially my fault. I tried to bargain with him. Tried to assert that I had as much power in the situation as he did. I threatened to sign over my inheritance to you prior to the wedding so that he couldn't touch a cent of it. He told me if I did that, you would die." Charlotte sighed and met her mother's gaze. "I'm so sorry for all of this. I thought I could manage it. Thought I could somehow save you and Micah both from further pain and shame. However, I think we're going to have to tell the truth about Mr. Hamilton and what happened.

"I know we'll probably be looked down upon for a long time. I don't know what legal ramifications Micah, or even you, will have to face, but the lie has caused us so much trouble."

Mama nodded. "Yes. The truth needs to be told. We should never have lied. God hates lies, and I should have trusted Him to handle the situation. Instead, I tried to fix a problem that hadn't yet become one."

"It's a hard-learned lesson," Charlotte agreed. "But now we have to figure out how to resolve this situation and get Micah released from jail."

Mama nodded again. "I agree."

Micah had never spent the night in jail before now. Waking up and seeing where he was, Micah tried hard to trust the Lord for his well-being. The trouble was, all that had happened was the result of sin. How could God bless that? He had lied about his father's death. But so, too, had Lucille, and it was her reputation Micah had hoped to save. It didn't matter what the folks of Cheyenne thought of him, but she was a good woman with a kind heart. People in Cheyenne thought highly of Lucille Aldrich. Her good deeds through church and the Ladies' Aid Society and elsewhere were well-known. Micah wanted very much for her to maintain those high thoughts. Added to that was her relationship with Rich. What if the man no longer cared about her once he knew she'd lied? Rich Johnson didn't seem like that kind of fella, but Micah didn't want Lucille to be hurt by any of this.

He punched the mattress and sat up. He heard movement in the hall and the voices of men talking. Within a few minutes, a young officer appeared at his cell, tray in hand.

"Breakfast, Mr. Hamilton," the man said.

Micah didn't bother to get up. No sense in making the kid think Micah might rush him. "Thanks."

"Chief Vogel said he'll talk to you after you eat." The young man deposited the tray and left without another word.

The watery oatmeal and coffee didn't look all that welcoming, but Micah prayed thanks over the food and began to eat. He'd eaten worse, to be sure. At least the coffee was strong.

It was hard to know what to do next. No doubt Vogel wanted to talk to him more about the situation, but Micah's thoughts were more on Charlotte and Lucille. Without him there to protect them, what might Lewis Bradley do?

By the time he was tossing back the last of the coffee, Micah felt no better about anything. He knew Edward Vogel was a good man, but if Micah told him the truth of what had happened, he would be obligated to report it all . . . every last detail.

Micah sat on the edge of his cot, thinking about the future. Now that he knew he loved Charlotte and that she loved him, he wanted very much to move forward with marriage. He was confident their efforts in ranching could still prosper, even if some people quit doing business with them. He could imagine them living quite comfortably, raising cattle, and keeping to themselves. If the truth did cause folks to ostracize them, then they'd have each other. Lucile would stay on with them if Rich Johnson decided the truth was too much to contend with, and Micah would see to her having whatever she needed.

"But first I have to get out of here."

He heard voices again and straightened. The young officer returned and opened the door. "I'm taking you to Chief Vogel's office."

Micah nodded and stood. "Should I bring the tray?"

"No, I'll come back for it." The man motioned Micah forward. "Chief Vogel said you wouldn't give me any trouble."

"No, I won't. This is my first time in a jail, and I intend for it to be my last."

The younger man smiled. "I used to be in here all the time. Chief Vogel straightened me out good, and now I'm workin' for him."

They headed down the hall to the door at the far end.

"Seems like a good job to have."

"It is. I like what I do," the man replied. "I definitely prefer not getting into trouble all the time. Made my ma so unhappy, and now that it's behind me . . . she's proud."

Micah smiled. A mother's pride was important to a young man. He knew how much he longed for his mother's approval. Maybe she was up in heaven smiling down on him now. She would know what the truth was and how all he wanted to do was to protect her dear friend. He was certain protecting Lucille was something she'd approve of, but the practical side of her would probably tell him it would never have been needed if they'd just been honest.

The officer led Micah to the hall where Chief Vogel had his office. He knocked on the door, and at the command to enter, he opened the door and motioned Micah inside.

Edward Vogel rose and smiled at Micah. "Morning. How'd you sleep?"

"Cot wasn't very comfortable, but I slept pretty well. However, I told your man here this is my first time in jail, and I hope to make it my last."

"We like to hear that kind of thing from our visitors," Vogel replied. "Have a seat."

Micah took a chair in front of Vogel's desk and sat down. The room was large and had a case of books set against one wall and windows that faced the street on another.

After closing the door, Edward Vogel returned, and rather than take his chair, he simply leaned against the desk just inches away from Micah.

"I was hoping maybe we could talk. I know you, Micah. You're a good man. Your pa was too. I'm less impressed with Lewis Bradley. The man has a ruthless reputation, and it doesn't surprise me that he's somehow tied up in all of this. Still, I'm hoping you can shed some light on the matter. I only locked you up for your own good. I thought maybe a night here would make it a little easier to talk about what happened."

Micah respected the man more than anyone else in town. He'd met the Vogel family when attending Decker's School for Boys. Robert Vogel had been in the school, although he was quite a bit younger. Edward Vogel had been good friends with the headmaster, Charles Decker, so they often saw the men together.

"Chief Vogel, I have the utmost respect for you, and I swear on the Bible that I did not kill my father."

Vogel nodded. "I never figured you did, Micah, but why don't you tell me what did happen and why Bradley thinks you might have."

"I can't without betraying someone I care about a great deal."

"Charlotte Aldrich?"

"No. Not exactly, although she would be very hurt by the situation. It's her mother who I'm thinking of."

"Son, murder accusations are pretty severe, and while I don't think you killed your father, I need to know the truth about what happened. Lewis Bradley isn't the kind of man to just let this drop. And he has Kit Hendricks willing to testify to you having threatened to kill your father, so the law isn't able to just look the other way. And from the way you looked when he mentioned digging up your father's body, I can't help but wonder what we'd find."

"Bradley is jealous. Pure and simple. He's been after Charlotte for years now. He wants her as his wife and had some sort of arrangement with her father for them to marry. But Charlotte refused the idea of marriage. Even argued with her father over the situation. She thought it was all behind her, but Lewis has been badgering her and trying to force her with threats to her and her mother and

. . . me." Micah paused and looked up. "She's in love with me."

"Congratulations," Vogel said, walking around his desk. He sat and leaned back in the chair. "And you love her."

It was more a statement than a question, but Micah answered all the same. "I do. I've only just come to realize it, but there's the truth of it."

"And Bradley knows she loves you, so he needs to eliminate his competition." Vogel nodded and rubbed his chin.

"That's the way I've got it figured. I don't know why he's so determined to marry someone who despises him, except that he must want her money."

"Men have died for less," Vogel replied.

"I know that's true," Micah agreed. "But none of what is being said is true. Bradley is just guessing off bits and pieces of a conversation he heard between Charlotte and me. I was having a hard time, and she was trying to encourage me. Bradley got it in his mind that my feelings of guilt and misery were because I had killed my dad, but nothing could be further from the truth."

"But you won't tell me what the truth is."

Micah shook his head. "I can't because it could cause problems for someone else. It isn't murder, however. You can be assured of that."

"Well then, I'll arrange for a lawyer to come see you. You may not even need him if I can get Bradley to drop all this nonsense and confess that he made it all up."

"The chances of that aren't good, but I'll be praying for you, Chief Vogel."

The older man smiled and gave a nod. "That's much appreciated, son. Much appreciated."

It was afternoon when Lucille and Charlotte made their way to the Cheyenne jail. They were immediately greeted by several officers who refused to grant their request to see Micah.

"We don't allow women to visit the prisoners," the clerk told them.

Charlotte planted her hands on her hips. "He shouldn't even be a prisoner. He's done nothing wrong."

"Micah Hamilton was arrested for murder. That makes him one of our prisoners," the man countered. "Now, I need for you ladies to leave."

"I'd like to speak with the chief of police," Mama declared.

The man shook his head. "Chief Vogel isn't here. He'll be back later, so you could try then."

"Very well." Mama turned to Charlotte. "Let's go until we can speak to Chief Vogel. He's an old friend, and I believe we'll get more resolved with him."

Charlotte didn't want to leave Micah in jail for a moment longer, but there seemed to be no other choice. She followed her mother back outside and took hold of her arm. "What are we going to do?"

"First, we're going to go check in to the hotel in case this takes more than one day. Then we're going to go see the pastor."

"The pastor? Why?" Charlotte didn't know what he could possibly do to aid their situation.

Mama gave her a sad smile. "I want to tell him what happened and ask his advice. He can advise me on what to do. I think, too, that he won't judge me too harshly."

"No doubt others will. They won't understand why we've kept this secret." She shook her head. "No, they'll believe we did it to hide Micah's shame."

"It doesn't matter anymore, Charlotte." Mama gazed

down the street shaking her head. "I don't know why I ever suggested such a lie. I knew it might catch up with us one day, but it seemed the right thing at the time. Micah was so vulnerable and broken. It hurt my heart to see him so shattered."

Charlotte took hold of her mother's arm. "He's stronger now, Mama. But I'm worried about you. When the truth is told, I fear people will treat you poorly. You won't deserve their judgment and ugliness."

"I brought it on myself." She drew a deep breath. "I chose to lie, and even if my intentions were good, it was wrong. It's only right that I face whatever punishment is due."

"I'll be with you, Mama. I'll never leave you, and I know Micah won't either. If they all decide to hate us, then so be it. We can sell out and head north. Montana is a good place, I hear."

"Lucille, you've carried quite the burden." The pastor gave her a compassionate look. She appreciated the lack of condemnation in his expression. "And I can't say that I blame you, given the stigma of the taking of one's life."

"It wasn't my desire to lie, Pastor, so much as to protect. My motive was born of love. God knows this. You must understand, we were close enough to hear the gunshot. Micah couldn't stop it and felt that it was somehow his fault. I knew that if it became public knowledge that his father had shot himself . . . well, people would say things. Condemning things regarding his father's soul. I just wanted to keep that from happening. Of course, I knew it was wrong, but I somehow convinced myself that it was the right thing to do."

"Sometimes our human nature takes charge in that way,

convincing and manipulating until sin seems reasonable, even desirable. And instead, it serves only to make the matter worse. Now Micah is facing false accusations and all because the truth was hidden," the pastor replied.

"And now the truth will be revealed." Lucille glanced at Charlotte. "Micah is stronger and so are we. I suppose it did allow us time for our grief. I intend to speak to Chief Vogel. I will explain exactly what happened and hopefully see Micah released. Then on Sunday, I will address the congregation as you suggested. I don't know if Micah will feel up to speaking or not."

"And I just want to confirm that the wedding is canceled?"

Charlotte answered before Lucille could speak. "It is most assuredly canceled. It was never supposed to happen in the first place."

The pastor frowned. "The entire situation is most concerning. I should probably speak to Mr. Bradley. His actions in this matter reveal a side of him that is most alarming. I would like to know his thoughts on why he's done what he's done."

"My guess, given the way he was insistent on my giving him Charlotte's supposed dowry, is money. I know he's supposed to be quite wealthy. After the death of his wife's father, they inherited a great deal. But money seems to be the driving force with him, so perhaps he doesn't have the money he pretends to have."

"I agree with Mama. I believe this has been solely motivated by financial reasons," Charlotte said. "He never spoke of it to me but has made it clear that he intended to control my inheritance after we were married."

"Well, I'm glad you came to speak to me about all of this," the pastor said, his voice filled with compassion. "I would like to pray with you now if that's all right."

"It's more than all right. I've a feeling we're going to need all the prayers we can get in the days to come," Lucille said, looking to Charlotte. "But I have the greatest confidence in God and know that He is and will ever be our Redeemer."

23

We already told you ladies that you cannot visit the prisoner Micah Hamilton," the police officer said, waving Charlotte and her mother back.

"We aren't here to see Micah, at least not just yet," Mama told the man. "We're here to see Chief Vogel. They said he might be back later in the afternoon, and so we've returned. He's a good friend, so if you would just go tell him that Lucille Aldrich and her daughter would like a word, I'm certain he will allow us to meet with him."

The man looked absolutely exasperated but got to his feet. "Very well, I'll go speak with him, but he's mighty busy, and I doubt he's going to want to spend his time hosting a hen party." He stomped off as though Charlotte and her mother had asked him to collect rattlesnakes by hand.

"He wasn't at all happy with the task you gave him," Charlotte said in a whisper.

"No, I suppose he wasn't, but as my grandmother used to say, 'He'll have to get glad in the same clothes he got mad in.'"

Charlotte smiled and nodded. She longed to see Micah

set free. He didn't deserve this terrible treatment. Lewis Bradley was the one who should have been thrown in jail for all his ugly threats.

The officer returned and behind him followed Edward Vogel. Mama moved forward to greet him.

"Your man wouldn't let us see Micah, and I was afraid he wouldn't allow us to see you either."

Chief Vogel glanced over at the man, who now looked rather sheepishly at them. He gave a little shrug and quickly busied himself with the paperwork on his desk.

"Lucille, it's good to see you again. Why don't you and Charlotte come on back to my office, and we'll talk?"

"Thank you."

They followed Edward Vogel to his office, where he offered them a seat and then took his place behind the desk. Mama leaned forward to immediately engage him with her story. Charlotte had never held more respect for her mother than in that moment.

"I'm afraid that I am the one responsible for all the problems Micah Hamilton is now facing. I've come to set the record straight."

"I see." Chief Vogel eased back in his chair. "I was hoping someone would."

Mama shook her head. "I apologize." She sighed and looked at Charlotte. "This isn't easy, but perhaps it's made just a bit easier because I already confessed it to our pastor. I suppose each time I tell the truth it will be better."

"The Bible says the truth will set you free." Chief Vogel looked nothing but sympathetic. "It doesn't promise it will be easy, however."

Mama chuckled. "You are quite right to say that."

Chief Vogel placed his arms on the desktop and folded his hands. "So tell me what you've come to say, Lucille."

"I understand Lewis Bradley had Micah arrested for the

murder of his father. I'm here to tell you that Micah did not kill his father. I was there when Wayman died . . . by his own hand."

Vogel's eyebrows raised slightly. "Suicide?"

"Yes." She sighed again, and Charlotte reached over to take hold of her mother's hand. "My husband and son had gone out and were caught in the blizzard. I waited much too long to send someone to search for them. Wayman and Micah were the only ones willing to go. I'm afraid our new ranch hands, young boys from Texas, were unnerved by the low temperatures and wind. Anyway, Micah and Wayman set out to search. They found them . . . frozen . . . dead." She paused for a long moment, and no one said a word while they waited for her to continue.

"Wayman sent Micah to our place for a wagon. I insisted on returning with him. I needed to see for myself the place where my husband and son had died. We were nearly there when—when we heard a single gunshot fired. When we reached the gully, it was clear that Wayman had shot himself in the chest. By the time Micah made his way to him, Wayman was dead."

"I am sorry that you had to suffer that. That Micah had to go through it," Chief Vogel said, shaking his head. "A terrible experience to be sure."

"I don't know what got into me," Mama continued, "but I knew how people could be regarding a man taking his own life. I'd seen it happen years before. Even good Christians were cruel, heartless. Some were less so, well-meaning, but still they said and did things that caused more pain than healing."

Vogel nodded. "I've seen that myself."

"So after helping Micah load my husband and son into the wagon, we went back for Wayman. His body had already started freezing. The cold was bitter, and it came to me that we could just tell people Wayman had died along with my men. It wasn't exactly a lie.

"I told Micah we wouldn't speak of the suicide. We would take his father to his ranch, where he could bury him beside Micah's mother without anyone being the wiser." She stopped and clutched her hands together.

"Micah was grief-stricken. You remember how bad it was anyway. All those cattle gone, other people who had died. Everyone had suffered tremendously because of the weather. It was an easy lie to tell, but not done for any divisive or illegal reasons. I just didn't want Micah to have to deal with the attitude I was sure he'd get from other folks on top of trying to deal with losing the last member of his family."

"Things were still bad for Micah," Charlotte couldn't help but add. "We tried several times to go and see him, but he was often gone. Usually off working to clear the carcasses and such."

"She's right. Micah was overwhelmed by all that happened, and I'm ashamed to say that my own mourning kept me from keeping my promise to his dear mother. I told her I'd always be there for him."

"Now, Lucille, you can't be blamed for neglecting a promise while mourning your husband and son. You went through a terrible loss, and you had a daughter who was struggling too. You're one of the strongest women I know, just like my Marybeth. You don't need to feel ashamed or singularly at fault for any of this. Given the same circumstances, who can say what any of us might have done?"

"None of us expected Wayman to kill himself. There was no sign at all. He was a driven man who loved God and served others with great compassion. The best I can figure is that it was all just too much for him. Micah said he'd seen so much death that day, and then to lose his best friend and see Frank Jr. dead as well. I can't help but think he might well have thought it could just as easily have been Micah and might even yet come to that."

"Who can know the torment in a man's mind when he comes to that place where death is more welcomed than life?" Vogel replied.

Tears came to Mama's eyes, which in turn brought them to Charlotte's. She reached over to give her mother a hug.

"All I know for certain is that Micah didn't kill his father," Mama said, pulling a handkerchief from her purse. "He saw the aftermath, but he had nothing to do with the death, and he's remaining silent to protect me from being ostracized for lying about it. But I don't care."

Her voice broke a bit, causing Charlotte's tears to flow even more freely. She'd not seen her mother so full of sorrow and remorse since her father and brother's deaths. Her confessions were bringing it all back.

"I don't know what else I can say or do to see that boy set free, but if anyone deserves to be locked up, it's me."

"No, Mama." Charlotte wept against her mother's shoulder. "You mustn't say that."

"No, you shouldn't say that," Chief Vogel interjected. "It's not true. As you said, you were trying to prevent even more devastating hurt. I knew it had to be something like this. I could tell Micah wasn't lying when he said he hadn't killed his father, but I knew there was something he wasn't saying. Someone he was protecting. He even mentioned it when we were talking this morning." He looked at Charlotte. "Is Lewis Bradley threatening you in order to force you to marry him?"

"Yes!" Her exasperation had to be quite evident. "Lewis wants the Aldrich money. I think if we had married, he would have forced us to sell the ranch and depleted every dime either of us had."

Mama gave a nod and leaned forward. "He's been unyielding in this. I don't know the full extent of plans that he had with Frank, but I don't think those are important to him anymore. I truly believe it has been only about the money."

Chief Vogel considered this for a moment. "Some men never have enough."

"He told me that if I didn't cooperate, if I did anything to keep my inheritance from him, he would kill Mama." Charlotte felt the tears come hot to her eyes. "How could I not agree to do whatever he commanded?"

"Bradley's got a great deal to answer to. But for now . . ." Chief Vogel got to his feet. "I think I've heard enough."

Mama collected herself and drew a deep breath. "Can we please just see Micah for a moment? I want to reassure him that we're here for him and to tell him the truth is out, as it should have been from the beginning."

Edward Vogel nodded and got to his feet. "I think that's only right. Come with me."

He led them to Micah's cell. He was stretched out atop the cot, reading a Bible. When he glanced up and saw them, he jumped up.

"What are you doing here? This is no place for either of you."

"Micah, my dear, I needed to see for myself that you were all right," Mama said, reaching through the bars to take hold of him as he drew close enough. "I wanted you to know from me that I told Edward the truth. He knows all about your father and what happened."

"Oh." He looked at Chief Vogel. "I, uh, well, now you know."

"I do, son, and I understand why you did what you did."

"I'm going to announce it at church on Sunday, Micah. I'd like it if you could be at my side." Mama looked to Chief Vogel. "Will he be out of jail by then?"

"I'm releasing him now," he replied and grabbed the keys. "I'm sure sorry for what you went through, Micah. Sorrier still that you felt you had to lie about it in order to keep people from looking down on you. My wife and I will certainly stand by you through this. And I'll make sure there's no further trouble with the legal system."

"I appreciate that, Chief Vogel. And . . . I'm glad the truth is out. I think it's been just as hard to keep it to myself as it would have been to answer everyone's questions."

"Thank you, Edward." Charlotte's mother rushed forward to embrace Micah. "Forgive me for all of this mess."

He hugged her, but his eyes caught sight of Charlotte. After releasing her mother, Micah came to her. "Are you still certain that you're over your infatuation?"

She walked into his arms and stretched up on tiptoe. "It's no infatuation. I'm completely in love with you. It has always been and will ever be a constant love, Mr. Hamilton. Of that, there is no doubt. Furthermore, I have no desire to ever be over it."

"Good, because I feel the same way." He kissed her then and there, as she had known he would. She didn't care who looked on. This was where she belonged.

The minute Lewis Bradley heard that Lucille and Charlotte were in town, he began planning what to do next. Success was so close he could almost touch it. After hearing they'd had a meeting with the police chief, Lewis knew that he would need to go and speak to the man as well. He wanted to make sure any female conniving and pleas for mercy fell on deaf ears.

"You're not going to like this, Boss," Kit Hendricks said, coming into Lewis's office, "but the sheriff has let Hamilton out of jail. I just saw him walking to the hotel with the Aldrich women."

"What!" Lewis jumped to his feet. "Why is he free?"

"I don't know, but he sure enough is."

Lewis muttered several expletives and grabbed up his hat. "I intend to have a talk with Chief Vogel. You go keep an eye on them and see if they leave the hotel."

He flew past Hendricks and made his way from his office to the police station. Anger didn't begin to describe his range of emotions. He felt overwhelmed with a sense of betrayal and annoyance that culminated in absolute rage. Why couldn't things just go his way this one time?

The clerk at the police station was surprised when Lewis barged into the building demanding to see Edward Vogel. Vogel himself seemed far less concerned. He didn't even invite Lewis to come back to his office.

"I figured you'd come here as soon as you knew Micah was free."

"How could you let that murderer go?"

"Because he's not a murderer," Vogel replied in casual confidence.

"He is. I have a witness."

"You have nothing. I had another talk with Kit Hendricks. Seems some of the details are a bit hazier to him now."

Lewis lifted his jaw a bit and glared at Vogel. "But he's a witness to Micah's threat to kill. There were others there too. If you could find them, I'm sure they'd confirm his story."

Vogel chuckled. It wasn't at all what Lewis expected. "Those cowhands are long gone, Mr. Bradley, and well you know it. What I'd like to know is what your part is in all of this."

Bradley looked at the man as if he'd gone mad. "Wha-what? I only have justice on my mind. I want the truth to be told and the guilty to be punished. That's what's good and fair under the law."

"And you've no other motive for this?" Vogel watched him carefully.

Lewis felt as if he were the one being accused of murder. How dare the man act as though Lewis was the guilty party.

"You should go and dig up the body. It's only been a year and a half. There's bound to be proof there that Micah shot and killed his father."

Vogel's eyes narrowed. "I have all the information I need, Mr. Bradley. However, I would ask you to stick around town. I might have more questions for you to answer. Now, if you don't mind, I need to get back to work."

Lewis forced a smile. "I'll be happy to help in any way that I can, Chief Vogel."

The man had the audacity to ignore his comment. Lewis went to the door and then turned back. "I don't suppose you know if Mrs. Aldrich and her daughter were going to remain in town tonight." The expression on Vogel's face suggested concern. Lewis shrugged. "I thought I might catch up to them and invite them to my home for dinner."

"As I understood it, they were headed to the hotel to get their things and then to the livery stable. They're hoping to get home before dark. Micah is going with them."

Lewis nodded. "Very well. I suppose dinner can wait. Soon we'll be married, and Charlotte's mother will hopefully be living with us, so there will be plenty of dinners together in the future."

"Of course," Vogel replied, his tone sounded a bit too guarded for Lewis's comfort.

He hurried from the police station toward the livery, then stopped. He turned around and went back to his office. If Vogel wasn't going to handle this, then Lewis would take care of matters himself.

"You're back sooner than I figured," Hendricks said when Lewis rushed through the door.

"Is there something you need, sir?" Lewis's secretary looked up from his desk, appearing just as surprised as Hendricks.

"I forgot something. I must get it to prove something to Vogel."

He dismissed them both with a glance and went to his desk, where he took a short-barreled Colt from his right-hand drawer. Let them think what they would. Lewis had it all planned out. He would go to the livery and provoke Micah to fight. In the middle of it all, Lewis would have to shoot him . . . in self-defense. He smiled as he hurried to the livery. Self-defense was perfectly understandable. Hamilton hated Lewis for getting him thrown in jail. Once the deed was done, Lewis would threaten the Aldrich women into supporting him. It was a simple plan. It couldn't fail.

"I'll be glad to get home," Lucille Aldrich said, smiling at Micah. "I'm just so happy to have you with us."

"I have to admit, I wasn't at all sure how God was going to work it out," Micah said, putting Charlotte and Lucille's things in the back of the wagon. "But I had a genuine peace about it. And I slept pretty well, even though the cot was terribly uncomfortable."

"That's because you had no guilt to keep you awake." Lucille patted his arm before letting him help her up onto the wagon.

He turned and looked at Charlotte, who was waiting to receive his help. "And you. You do realize this might have been resolved years ago if you had just told me how you felt."

"I was afraid you wouldn't feel the same. You and Frank Jr. were always talking about your lady loves. I was just the little sister."

"Well, you weren't my sister," he said, leaning over to kiss her once again. Micah didn't figure he'd ever get tired of doing that.

"Get your hands off of my fiancée!"

Micah raised his head and looked past Charlotte to where Lewis Bradley stood glaring. "She's not your fiancée, Bradley."

"This gun begs to differ," Lewis said, pulling a Colt revolver from his coat pocket.

Micah shoved Charlotte behind him. "Put the gun away, Bradley. I'm not armed."

"I've endured all the interference from you that I'm going to take. I don't know exactly what you did to your father, but I still intend to see you pay for his death."

"I've been paying for a long time now, and if you want to hear the full story, then come to church Sunday. Lucille and I plan to be quite open about what happened."

"No. Sunday I'm getting married. It's my wedding day, and you aren't going to spoil it." He pointed the Colt at Micah. "I suppose we could hold your funeral after that."

"Look, Bradley, I'm done with this. You need to stop before someone gets hurt."

"Oh, someone is getting hurt." It was clear he wasn't going to be reasonable. "You should have died before now. None of you deserve to live."

Micah had no way to protect Charlotte and her mother if Bradley decided to start shooting. He prayed silently while looking around as carefully as he could. He didn't want to rile Lewis Bradley any more than he had to.

"You know, Charlotte, I tried to make you come to me. I paid Hendricks to help me—to burn down the Aldrich empire. Well, maybe not everything, but enough that you'd have to come to me to figure out what to do. Charlotte, you should have come to me. But I can take care of everything right now." He pulled back the hammer of the gun, keeping it aimed at Micah. "I've planned this out for a long time now. I want you dead, and since the city won't hang you, I'll put a bullet in you myself."

But before Micah could move, Edward Vogel stepped out from behind one of the stalls. "I think I've heard enough." He looked at Lewis, who was obviously surprised by the chief of police interfering with his plans.

"Vogel! I'm glad you're here. Micah threatened to kill me, and I had to defend myself. The women saw it all. They can and will support what I'm saying." He looked at Charlotte and Lucille and narrowed his eyes. "They will confirm what I've said." Vogel took the revolver away from him and grabbed Bradley by his collar with his free hand.

"I've been here since you left the station. I heard everything. You're under arrest, Lewis Bradley, for intent to commit murder."

24

It was such a relief to be home again. Micah almost chuckled out loud. He was at the Aldrich house, yet he had called it home, and truly that was what it was. He felt a lot of comfort here in this house . . . with Charlotte.

There had been little they had wanted to discuss on the uneventful ride home. It was almost as if all the discussions related to the past had completely drained them of words. When they arrived home, Micah took a hot bath while the ladies saw to supper. When Micah was finished, he went to the kitchen in search of Charlotte.

"Supper's nearly ready," Lucille told him. "I think Charlotte took herself on a little walk. She's probably close by."

Micah found her easily enough. She was walking out under the shade trees. He couldn't help but smile. He remembered that once, years ago when the trees were only half the size they were now, he and Frank Jr. had dared Charlotte to climb one of them. She had severely admonished them saying that she and her mother had worked too hard to get them to grow to threaten the tree's safety by climbing it. She had been most serious about the matter and added with a grin that if they wanted to have a climbing contest, she'd happily challenge them to see who could climb to the top of the barn roof the quickest. Even though she had suggested it, Micah and Frank got into the most trouble when Lucille found the trio on top of the barn. Lucille reprimanded them, reminding the boys that they were older and knew better. Therefore, they bore the lion's share of the responsibility.

"I'm glad you're out here alone," Micah said when Charlotte noticed him making his way to her.

"I was hoping you might join me," she replied, having no idea how alluring she was.

Micah didn't slow his step at all but made his way to her and pulled Charlotte into his arms. At first, he just hugged her close, breathing in the scent of her perfume and cherishing the moment. She was truly the love of his life. He pulled away just enough to press his lips against hers. The kiss was passionate but brief.

"Wouldn't it be wonderful to start all of our conversations like this?" Charlotte said with a sigh.

Micah was hesitant to release her but did. "I can't believe you've been here all this time, and I never really saw you for who you were."

She gazed into his eyes. "And who am I?"

"My heart—the very air I breathe."

"I've felt that way about you for most of my life. I'm glad you're finally catching up."

He ran his finger along her jawline. "I can't help but think of how many years we missed out on just because you didn't do what you usually do and speak your mind."

She stepped back and frowned. "Are you calling me outspoken?"

"On everything but matters of the heart."

Charlotte seemed to consider this a moment and then gave a nod. "I suppose you make a good point."

Micah laughed and put his arm around her. "So what are we going to do about this matter of the heart?"

Charlotte walked with him in silence for several minutes. "I suppose," she finally said, "that will all depend on you."

"Why me?"

"Because the man is the one who usually does the proposing."

They moved beyond the shade of the trees just as the sun dipped below the horizon. The western skies were mottled in hues of orange and yellow against the fading blue.

Micah dropped his hold and turned Charlotte to face him. "Then I'd best get right to work. I don't want another day to pass without staking my claim." He knelt on one knee and reached up to take her hands in his. "Charlotte Aldrich, will you marry me?"

Her expression softened the way he'd seen it do so many times before, never realizing it was love for him that made her look that way. At least not until now.

"I will, Micah Hamilton."

He got up and pulled her close once again. Charlotte wrapped her arms around his neck and lifted her face to his.

"And you're sure you don't need me to build you a castle like the Nagle house?" he asked in a teasing tone.

"Goodness, no." She smiled. "Do you need me to order a bunch of Worth gowns and drape myself in diamonds as Lewis Bradley said needed to be done?"

Micah chuckled. "Hardly." He gazed for a long moment into her blue eyes. "You sure you can be happy being a rancher's wife?"

"Can you be happy being a rancher's husband?" she countered.

Micah moved closer to her lips. "Never thought about marrying a rancher."

"It's all I've ever dreamed of," Charlotte murmured just before Micah's mouth covered hers.

Church on Sunday was a somber occasion. The pastor preached about judgmental people, the Christians who felt it was their duty to make sure everyone else walked a narrow line but worried little about themselves.

"In Matthew seven, Jesus makes it very clear what He thinks about us passing judgment," the pastor continued. "'For with what judgment ye judge, ye shall be judged: and with what measure ye mete, it shall be measured to you again. And why beholdest thou the mote that is in thy brother's eye, but considerest not the beam that is in thine own eye? Or how wilt thou say to thy brother, Let me pull out the mote out of thine eye; and, behold, a beam is in thine own eye? Thou hypocrite, first cast out the beam out of thine own eye; and then shalt thou see clearly to cast out the mote out of thy brother's eye.'"

Charlotte had to admit that most of the congregation looked rather uncomfortable. It wasn't often they got a dressing down from the pulpit, but this time the pastor's comments were well understood. Before Micah, Charlotte, and her mother had even taken their seats, several people had come to ask them about the rumor they'd heard that Micah had been thrown into jail days earlier. The pastor had managed to overhear the last conversation, where one of the nosier ladies of the church had made a point of asking Charlotte's mother why it was she had been seen at the city jail, further commenting that she'd heard someone say Micah had murdered his father. She demanded to know if it was true, but the pastor moved her along to her pew in order to start the service.

Micah reached over and took hold of Charlotte's hand. He squeezed it reassuringly but kept his gaze on the pastor.

"It's easy enough to judge another person. Easy enough to condemn or approve of what others do or say. It takes very little effort to speak our mind about the conduct and choices made by those around us, while hiding away the things we've done, choices we've made.

"Many of you came to church today having heard rumors about members of our congregation, but rather than offer support or encouragement, you came with questions, perhaps even judgments."

Charlotte could hear some shifting of bodies in the congregation. It sounded as though more than a few people were uncomfortable with the direction of the sermon.

"This is a serious matter that must be addressed. We are the church, the living body of Christ. We have accepted Jesus as Savior, doing nothing on our own merit to earn our salvation. It was a gift, free and clear for those who accepted it. However, now that we've taken that gift for ourselves, there is responsibility. Now we are to live a life in Christ, following, emulating, and desiring the things that He desired.

"Jesus calls us to compassion, mercy, and grace. He poured out forgiveness from the cross on the very ones who condemned Him. His example should compel us to pour out mercy and grace rather than condemnation and judgment. His Word tells us that the measure we use will be used on us. This should terrify some of you." He fell silent and looked out over the congregation.

"It should also encourage us to offer grace and mercy, if for no other reason than our own protection. Hopefully, it means more to you than that, however.

"We are one body with many parts, just as the Word says. When one part hurts, we all suffer, whether we realize it or not. Today, I've been asked to let a part of our body speak about something that happened, something that wounded them deeply. I am hopeful that you will extend grace, compassion, kindness, and love because those are the things they are being given by our Savior. Remember the Scriptures spoken here this morning. 'For with what judgment ye judge, ye shall be judged.'"

He let the words sink in for a moment, then turned to Mama and Micah. "Mrs. Aldrich, Micah, would you come forward?"

Charlotte gave Micah's hand one last squeeze and then gave her mother a smile of reassurance. She had offered to come forward with them, but Mama had told her no. She wanted to be able to look to Charlotte for encouragement if things got bad. Charlotte whispered a prayer. Their story wasn't going to be easy to share, but hopefully God would take this sacrifice of obedience and honesty and bless them despite their original choice.

It had definitely taught Charlotte that the truth, although difficult to bear at times, was always the more beneficial to the soul.

After church, Micah found himself encircled by most of the congregation. Most of the women were in tears, and many of the men had the telltale signs of dampness in their eyes. Most came with words of encouragement, and some even offered thanks for the honesty, explaining that they, too, had known family members who had taken their own lives.

Micah felt the final bits of hardness fall away from his heart. It was truly as if a physical band had been removed. The love and mercy they offered was enough to give him real hope for the future. Even the nosy old woman who had confronted Lucille regarding her going to the jail came to Micah.

With an expression of shame, she took hold of his hands. "Micah, I want to apologize if my ways caused you to hide the truth. I would have been one of those to condemn, I'm sorry to say. I want you to know what you said about the eighth chapter of Romans and how we can't be separated from God's love convicted me in a way no preacher's sermon has ever done. I don't want to be one of those things trying to separate someone from God's love, yet I can see how my pride, condemnation, and gossip would have tried to divide. Please forgive me."

Micah fixed gazes with the woman and then surprised her by embracing her. "I forgive you."

He glanced up and caught sight of Lucille. She smiled and gave him a nod. It was almost as if his own ma were standing there. Micah could just imagine her in heaven, smiling down on him in approval, and for the first time, he could imagine Dad standing there beside her.

On the ride back from church, Micah talked to Rich Johnson as he rode along beside the wagon, where Charlotte and her mother were talking about the future.

"We want to be married at the ranch," Charlotte told her mother. "A simple ceremony with friends and family and lots of good food. A kind of roundup without the work."

Mama chuckled. "Well, I like the idea of no work. But since Barnabus and Simon have gone back to Illinois, I doubt we'll have any family who are able to come and attend."

"You and Nora are the only family I need." Charlotte nodded toward Mr. Johnson and Micah. "Of course, Mr. Johnson is like family too."

"What was that ya said, little gal?" Rich asked from atop his horse.

"I said you were like family to me. I was kind of hoping you'd come to my wedding. Micah and I plan to get married at the ranch."

"I'll have to check my schedule. What date did you have in mind?"

Charlotte smiled. "We thought the last Sunday of the month, September thirtieth."

"Hmmm, well, that could be a problem unless I can work out something."

Charlotte had been driving the horses but reined back on the lines to bring the wagon to a stop. "Well, I'd very much like for you to be there. In fact, I thought maybe you could give me away since I have no father to do so. I want it so much, in fact, that Micah and I could change the date if it means the difference between you being there or not." The men paused their horses and exchanged a glance.

"I feel the same way," Micah said, nodding at Rich.

"There's just one thing that might interfere," Rich said a hint of amusement in his tone.

"And what is that one thing, Rich?" Mama asked, looking around Charlotte to better see the men.

"I was just telling Micah here that I had a question I wanted to ask you, Lucille. Seems like your answer might complicate my schedule or maybe fix it up just right."

"And what question would that be?" Mama asked, shaking her head.

"Whether or not you'd like to make it a double wedding and marry me when the children hitch up."

Charlotte turned to her mother. Her mouth had fallen open. The men were already grinning, and Charlotte couldn't help but laugh. She gave her mother a sideways hug.

"Well, what do you say, Mama? I think it sounds like a wonderful way to spend the day."

Her mother still had her gaze fixed on Rich. She nodded. "I'd like that very much, Rich. I think it'd be the perfect way to spend that day."

"Yippee!" Rich gave a holler. "She said yes!"

"I told you she would." Micah laughed. He gazed at Charlotte and shrugged. "I figured they belonged together."

Her heart nearly burst at the joy she felt. "Then I guess we'd better have Rich stay to lunch so we can expand on our wedding plans." Charlotte snapped the lines, and the horses moved out. She couldn't help but smile all the way home. Her mother was going to be loved and cared for, and she was finally going to marry the man she'd loved since she was four years old.

"I felt like I needed to give you this news myself," Edward Vogel said as he took a cup of coffee that Nora offered.

Charlotte and Micah sat opposite the police chief and Mama at the dining room table. Chief Vogel had arrived shortly after lunch and looked more than a little out of sorts.

"The judge dismissed everything against Bradley and Hendricks?" Charlotte felt Micah tense as he continued. "Seems the legal system has failed us this time."

"I thought the same thing. Seems Bradley has dirt on quite a few of our town fathers and the judge. He's been collecting information on folks since he first arrived in Cheyenne," Chief Vogel replied. "At least he's making plans to leave town. He's already put the house up for sale, and I'm told there are three people vying to purchase it. Marybeth said that his aunt told her they were heading back east, where some of the other family resides. She and the baby left yesterday.

Seems Bradley realizes his reputation is ruined here, and it won't serve him well to stick around."

Micah shook his head. "What about the fact that Kit set fire to the birthing shed?"

"He swears it was an accident, and there's no proof to suggest otherwise. Bradley sure isn't going to admit he hired it done. There's still a lot of corruption to overcome in Cheyenne, but it's definitely improved since the early years. We just have to keep striving to weed out the evildoers."

"I can't say that the idea of Mr. Bradley getting off without repercussions sits well with me." Mama looked thoroughly disgusted. "He threatened to kill Micah. He had a gun aimed at him—at all of us."

"I know, and I agree it's not right," Chief Vogel replied. "But I know God has a way of dealing with men like Bradley. One way or another, he'll answer for what he's done."

Mama gave a heavy sigh and softened her expression. "And we need to not judge, lest we be judged. I'm not very good at that when my family has been threatened."

Chief Vogel smiled for the first time since his arrival. "You've got a good heart, Lucille. Your kindness and restraint from judgment is well-known around here. I think God understands where you're coming from." He finished his coffee and then got to his feet.

"I need to be on my way. I have a long ride back to town and a particularly ornery horse that I'm trying to ride the meanness out of so that my youngest can get him in time for his birthday."

Everyone got to their feet and followed Chief Vogel to the front door. Mama stepped forward and extended her hand. "Thank you for coming all this way, Edward."

Just then, Nora came hurrying into the room, waving a bag. "I thought you might like to take home some fresh doughnuts. Made them just this morning, and if you'd been here just a couple of hours earlier, you could have had them for breakfast with us."

Edward Vogel didn't hide his appreciation. He took the bag and immediately peeked inside. "I'm not sure these will even make it back to Cheyenne."

Nora waggled her finger at him. "There is a dozen in there . . . but nobody said you had to share them."

Everyone laughed and followed the police chief outside. Charlotte and Micah remained even after the man and his horse were out of sight and Mama and Nora had returned to the house.

"It doesn't seem right that Lewis could do all that he did and get away with it. I told Mama we should have the lawyer fight him to get my dowry back. That money should be yours."

"I don't want it," Micah replied, putting his arm around her shoulder. "He may have gotten the money, but I got the prize."

Charlotte leaned her head against his shoulder. "Do you think we'll be safe? I mean what if he—" She fell silent when Micah put his finger to her lips.

"There are a lot of what-ifs in life. I think it's always best to avoid them. I've given this all to the Lord, and I trust that He'll take care of us. I'm not afraid for our future. Are you?"

She lifted her head and looked into his eyes for a long moment. "Not with you and the Lord by my side."

Late on the afternoon of September thirtieth, nearly forty people stood gathered under the golden autumn leaves of the Aldrich cottonwood trees to see two couples exchange vows.

A light breeze blew across the open landscape. There was just the right amount of warmth without a hint of clouds in the sky. The day could not have been any more perfect.

Rich's youngest daughter, Emma, had traveled up from Texas, where she lived helping her sister, Clara, with her six children. She had been the Johnson family's wilder child, with a reputation for trouble that many remembered. Still, her father was happy to have her home.

"I think you two make a great couple. Maybe you can travel and have some fun together," she told them the first night they'd all shared dinner together. Mama then surprised Emma by telling her that she and Rich planned to do exactly that and make a trip to Texas after they got the cattle to market. The announcement seemed to double Emma's joy.

Mama and Charlotte stood up for each other, and Micah and Rich were each other's best man. The pastor teased the two couples about the double wedding but praised God for His infinite goodness in bringing love to both.

The ceremony itself was surprisingly short. They'd agreed beforehand that the pastor would ask one bride and groom the pertinent questions before moving on to the second and then joining them together in one final act. Everything happened in perfect order without anyone missing their cues.

"I now pronounce that Lucille and Richard Johnson are husband and wife, and Charlotte and Micah Hamilton are husband and wife. Men, you may kiss your bride."

The crowd cheered as Rich dipped Lucille and gave her a very showy kiss.

Micah gave an ornery grin and winked at Charlotte. "I can't let that old man outdo me." He grabbed Charlotte and lifted her into his arms before settling his lips on hers.

Their guests roared with delight, and Charlotte wrapped

her arms around Micah's neck. "I'll go anywhere you go, my love. Just like I always have."

Micah glanced up with a grin. "But this time, I want your pesky attention and undying devotion."

"It's a good thing, 'cause I aim to see you have it for the rest of your life."

If you enjoyed *A Constant Love*,
read on for a sneak peek of

DESIGNED WITH LOVE

AVAILABLE JULY 2025

I t was a surprisingly warm day for the end of January in Texas. Emma stood dressed in her expensive white Worth wedding gown and waited for the minister to declare that she and Tommy Benton were husband and wife.

Tommy grinned at her, then made a face of boredom, and Emma nearly laughed out loud. At twenty-eight, she supposed that they should take their wedding day with a degree more seriousness, but that wasn't her nature. Life should be one good time followed by another. At least, that was how she'd always seen it—and lived it.

Ten years ago, when the chance to leave Cheyenne for her married sister's ranch in Texas came up, Emma had jumped at it. Some folks in Cheyenne weren't overly fond of her. There were quite a few who'd had their toes stepped on by Emma, and some who bore worse than that. Leaving the area was the perfect solution after breaking her engagement to a local boy in order to take up with another man—a man who soon afterward deserted her. It gave her an easy way to avoid all the folks who thought her worthless and difficult.

Besides, her sister, Clara, wasn't overly demanding. She needed help with her children, and the children enjoyed having fun. Emma was just the right person for rowdy games and horse races. As the children grew up and attended school, Emma had more free time. This allowed her to escape the boredom of the ranch and do what she wanted to do. Clara was usually far too busy with her responsibilities to worry about monitoring her little sister's actions.

Emma did just enough to satisfy Clara and give her the relief she needed, and in turn Clara kept her mouth shut when Emma took off on one of her wild escapades. It was a good arrangement, one that had allowed her to meet Thomas Benton, the youngest of four wealthy Benton brothers, the previous January.

Tommy was sweet—more boy than man. He loved having fun just as much as Emma. He agreed with her philosophy of there being plenty of time to focus on religion when old age was upon them. Youth was supposed to be spent exploring options and opportunities. It was no wonder most adults were sullen and serious all the time. And many were still all bound up by religious rules from the minute they struck out on their own. Emma considered herself lucky to have figured out that such things were a waste of time.

She glanced sideways and saw her father and stepmother. They didn't look all that happy. Goodness, she'd maintained her purity and given them a church wedding, they should be delighted, especially after years of worrying about her moral standings. Her father and mother never accounted for Emma having her own standards—standards that she had refused to yield on no matter how persuasive Tommy had been. That was the reason for the wedding. Emma might love a life free of rules and regulations, but when it came to the physical aspects of love, she was quite guarded. She'd heard far too many horror stories about women who allowed themselves to be compromised. And she had to look no further than her sister to see what a life of marriage and motherhood did to a woman's spirit. Clara said she was happy, but goodness, she never got to do much of anything but see to household duties and child care. Frankly, Emma hoped she never had children.

Tommy didn't care about having them either. He said maybe later, in another ten years or so. Maybe by then Emma would be ready for them as well. Still, being married would put them at risk of that coming sooner rather than later. It was the only real reason Emma had hesitated when Tommy begged her to marry him.

Tommy was saying something, so Emma turned her attention back to the wedding. With the heat, she just wished they'd conclude with the ceremony. Worth gowns were beautiful creations, and this one was no exception, but it was hot, and a simple cotton dress would have suited her better.

Tommy took hold of her hand. "With this ring, I thee wed. With my body, I thee worship. With all my worldly goods, I thee endow. In the name of the Father and of the Son and of the Holy Ghost. Amen." Tommy slipped the ring on her finger.

Emma was impressed with the creation they'd chosen. Tommy had insisted on sparing no expense, and given that he'd inherited a hefty sum of money the previous year, he could afford the best. Diamonds and sapphires set against gold. She'd never owned anything like it, and Tommy had given her plenty of jewelry. One thing about Tommy, he was more than generous with his money. Emma glanced up and met his gaze. This marriage was going to be a happy one. They were good at finding things to do, and marriage would open up even more doors to good times.

The minister, an ancient old man who headed up a church Emma and Tommy didn't attend but had given a large tithe to, pronounced them husband and wife. Tommy pulled her into his arms and kissed her soundly.

"Well, I'm so glad to know that you can keep your word to someone," a feminine voice called out.

Tommy pulled away, and Emma turned to see who was speaking. A woman gowned in black with a heavy veil moved down the aisle toward them. Emma looked at Tommy, who had gone white as a ghost.

The woman lifted her veil aside and smiled. "I don't suppose you expected to see me today, did you now, Tommy?"

"Stella." He barely whispered her name.

"That's right. Stella." The petite blond woman looked at him for a long moment, then turned to Emma. "Did he tell you he'd love you forever? Sweet talk you into doing things you swore you'd never do? Did you lose your innocence to him and then find yourself in a bad way?"

"Young woman, this is the House of God," the minister protested.

"Well, that's why I'm here." She turned back to Tommy. "You took my innocence, all the while promising to marry me. Now I'm carrying your baby, and you've married another."

Emma wanted to do something . . . anything, but found herself frozen in place. Tommy turned back to her with a sad look of regret.

"It'd be best for all concerned if we just ended this family here and now."

Confused by Stella's statement, Emma looked back to her. Somehow, the young woman had produced a revolver and now aimed it at Tommy's head.

When the gun went off and Tommy crumpled to the ground beside her, Emma still couldn't move. She watched as Stella turned the gun on herself as several men rushed her. There was a scuffle, and the gun went off a second time before someone managed to get the piece away from her.

A woman screamed, and Emma turned to see that it was Rosie Benton. Tommy's younger sister. Poor girl. Emma's own family was pointing and starting to cry.

Several people rushed forward to where Tommy had fallen at Emma's feet. For the first time she looked down and could see for herself that Stella's aim had been true. The bullet had pierced Tommy's left temple. Blood pooled around his head. His eyes were still open.

It was only as she studied her husband's lifeless body that she saw the spread of red across the waist of her white wedding gown. For a momentb it seemed unreal. Where had the blood come from?

Emma touched her stomach and realized a hot pain spread across her abdomen. The second bullet had struck her. She looked up to see her father rushing forward. Tommy's brother Colton was right behind him. The men took hold of each of her arms as her knees gave out and the room went black.

It would seem Stella had claimed more than one victim.

"Emma, can you hear me? Emma, please wake up, darlin'."

It was her father's voice. Emma knew it well, and for just a moment she was back home on the ranch outside of Cheyenne. It was early morning, and Papa was urging her to get up.

He was always so cheerful as he called her and Clara. *"Rise and shine, my darlin's."*

Mama would be downstairs fixing breakfast and would send Papa up to wake Emma and her brother and sister. Of course, Papa had been up since before dawn, getting a start on the ranch chores. In the early years, he didn't keep a staff, and Mama didn't have any help with the house or meals. It was just the family, and they all pitched in to help.

"Emma, please wake up."

Fighting against the blackness, Emma struggled to open her eyes. Instead of finding her childhood bedroom, she found herself stretched out on a desk in a small office. Papa held her hand. His expression was grave. Another man seemed quite intent on cutting away her wedding gown.

"Oh, sweetheart." Papa smiled down at her. "I feared I'd lost you."

"What . . . happened?"

She saw her sister crying into a handkerchief while their stepmother embraced her.

"You were shot, Em. The doctor isn't sure how bad it is, but you're losing blood."

Her father's words made no sense. Shot? Then the memory of the wedding flooded back in such a rush that Emma tried to sit up.

"Tommy!"

"Stay still, Mrs. Benton." This from the man who had destroyed her wedding gown. Well, she supposed the bullet had actually done that deed.

"I want to see Emma!" a woman all but screamed from somewhere outside the small room. "Emma!"

"Rosie." Emma had grown quite close to the younger woman. "Let her come to me."

Her father shook his head. "The doctor needs to stop you from bleeding to death. It would just upset her all the more to see you like this. I'll go speak to her."

Emma nodded at her father. "Please tell her I'm all right. Tell her I'll see her very soon."

"I will, Em. I will. You just stay still and let the doctor do what he needs to do."

"I'd like to get her over to the hospital and into surgery. Better lighting and equipment."

Lucille, Emma's stepmother, spoke up. "You think this will require surgery?"

The doctor straightened. "I can't tell just yet. I've got the wound covered and slowed the bleeding."

"The pastor sent for an ambulance." This came from Clara, who came to Emma's side. "Oh, Emma, I'm so sorry this happened."

Emma closed her eyes as the pain became more evident. She supposed the shock of everything had kept her from feeling it too much, and she couldn't help but moan.

"As soon as we get to the hospital, I'll give you something for the pain." The doctor pressed the bandages tight to her body.

It was all too much. Emma could hear the pandemonium and shouts of someone in the other room. Once again, her vision began to blur and rather than fight it, she gave in. She could hear the doctor telling someone that she was losing consciousness from the loss of blood. After that, nothing more.

When Emma woke up the second time, she was tucked away in a hospital bed. She felt her waistline. A thick layer of bandages was beneath the overly large white cotton nightgown she wore. Her vision was somewhat hazy from whatever medicine they'd given her.

"Emma?"

Was that her sister? "Clara?"

"It's me, Em." Her sister took hold of her hand. "The doctor said you're going to be just fine. The bullet sliced across your abdomen. A little deep where it entered. He had to put in quite a few stitches, but said if you'd been standing straight on instead of sideways, you would be dead."

"Tommy?"

Clara's brow scrunched together. "Don't you remember?"

Emma had a vague recollection, but she hoped she was wrong. "She shot him in the head."

"Yes." Her sister's tone was so matter-of-fact. "I'm so sorry Emma. He's dead."

The finality of the words hit Emma harder than she'd

expected. Tommy was dead. His life was over. Just like that. In the blink of an eye. Blink of an eye . . . Why did that phrase ring in her ears? Oh, it was like a twinkling of an eye. She had once asked her father about the phrase after he'd read a passage in Corinthians, and he had told her a twinkling was like a blink. Just that fast. Why had that stayed in her memories?

"I know he's dead. I saw him." She heard herself say the words, but still they made no sense. "Did someone take care of him?"

"Yes. Colton and his brothers arranged to have him taken to the funeral home."

"Who was that woman?"

Clara patted her arm. "It's not important now. Rosie wants to see you. She's beside herself."

Emma nodded. "Please let her come to me."

Her sister left, and Emma closed her eyes. How could so much have changed so quickly? In a blink . . . a twinkling. She was being kissed, and then Tommy was dead. Why didn't the thought bring tears? She cared for him deeply . . . even loved him in her own way. So why couldn't she cry over him?

The door opened, and Rose Benton rushed in. For all her twenty-three years, she was in so many ways so innocent of life. How this must have devastated her. She adored Tommy. She was even set to come live with Emma and Tommy after they returned from their wedding trip.

"Oh, Emma. Emma, I'm so glad you're alive." Rosie bent over and kissed Emma's cheek. "Colton said that Tommy probably didn't even know what hit him, so he didn't have any pain. But now he's dead." Tears came to her eyes. "She shot him dead." She began to sob.

"I know. I'm . . . so . . . sorry."

Rosie stifled her tears. "Oh, Emma, what are we going to do?" She didn't wait for an answer but hurried on. "Does your stomach hurt? I saw the blood on your dress. Your beautiful dress was ruined."

Emma forced a smile. "It's going to be all right, Rosie. It was just a dress. As for the pain, they gave me medicine. I'm sure I'll be fine."

"I was so scared that you had died too. I prayed and asked Jesus to save you, and He did. I would have prayed for Tommy, but Colton said God doesn't bring people back from the dead anymore. I was one of the last ones. But I'll keep praying for you." She sniffed and wiped her face on the back of her sleeve.

"Thank you." For once the words pierced Emma's heart. Mama had told her so many times that she was praying for Emma to yield her life to God. Clara had sometimes mentioned in passing that she was praying for Emma to learn the truth before it was too late.

Was it too late?

A wave of guilty conscience washed over her. Tommy knew about Jesus. They had scoffed at religion and the rules that God laid out for man. Emma had agreed with Tommy that the Bible wasn't for them. Maybe they'd reconsider when they were old and close to death. Now he was dead.

"Emma?" Rosie stroked Emma's cheek with her slender fingers. "Are you scared?"

"I was. I was so scared I couldn't move." Visions of what had happened began to trickle back to mind. The young blond-haired woman all dressed in black—like someone attending a funeral instead of a wedding. A specter of death.

"I screamed. I couldn't help it."

Emma saw the fear in Rosie's eyes. "It's over nowb and you're safe."

"I didn't care if I was safe. I was scared for you and Tommy. I love you so much, Emma." Rosie bent over her once again and pressed her cheek to the top off Emma's head.

"Come along, Rose," Clara said, taking hold of her. "Emma needs to sleep now."

"I'll come back with Colton. He promised we could see you when you're better. He said I could help take care of you."

Emma nodded and gave a wave. The pain was starting to feel more pronounced. Once Rosie had gone from the room, she turned to Clara. "I'm hurting."

"I'll tell the nurse. They said they would give you something when you needed it."

With Clara gone, the room seemed so very silent. Emma couldn't help but think back to Tommy lying dead on the floor. She had been pronounced a wife and just as quickly it was taken from her.

"Emma?" Her father peeked at her from the open door.

"Come in, Papa."

He smiled and crossed the room in two long strides. "I'm so thankful to see you awake. Clara said you were in pain, so I won't stay long. Lucille wanted me to make sure you had everything you needed. Can I bring you anything from Clara's?"

She had moved most of her things from the ranch to the Benton house. She and Tommy planned to get their own place soon, but for the time being, they were moving Emma in to share Tommy's room. Rosie had been so excited.

"I don't know what I need." She moaned and pressed her hands to her stomach.

"Doc says you're very lucky. I told him you were blessed since we don't believe in luck."

"I know. I'd be dead if I'd taken the bullet facing the gun." She could still see the hopelessness in the expression of the young woman who'd shot them. "What happened to her?"

Her father immediately understood. "They took her to the jail. She's there now. Won't say another word. Just sobs." He moved closer to the bed. "Did you know . . . I mean . . . was it a shock to learn that . . . well . . ."

"That Tommy had another woman?" Emma had avoided thinking about that revelation. "Tommy never told me."

"He betrayed you."

"I suppose that's true. I don't know what to make of it all. I can't really even think clearly." She rubbed her eyes and tried to eliminate the image of the woman who'd ruined her wedding.

"I'm so sorry, Emmy." It had been a long time since anyone had called her by her childhood name. "This was supposed to be your happiest day."

Emma nodded, but in her heart, she couldn't help but wonder if justice had been served. They'd made vows to God without either of them meaning a word. They'd even laughed after the rehearsal. Tommy had said he'd never expect her to stay with him if times were bad, and although the thought troubled Emma for a moment, she'd assured him that she felt the same way.

Clara had known Emma and Tommy's feelings on the matter. She'd asked Emma why they bothered with a wedding then.

"Because everyone expects it. You can't go setting up house together or travel together and such without a ring and piece of paper to say it's legal."

That had been Emma's answer. Now as the words came back to her, she was stunned by the coldness and heartlessness of them. What was wrong with her? Why had she ever agreed to marry Tommy that way?

Nearly dying was awakening feelings and thoughts that Emma had fought for years to bury deep inside.

The nurse came in just then carrying a small bottle of medicine. "I've brought something to help you sleep and numb the pain."

Numb the pain. Hadn't that been what Emma had been doing all of her life? Perhaps *pain* was the wrong word. It was more of a void. Her life had always seemed so empty, and yet no matter how she tried, she couldn't find a way to fill that abyss. She was always sure that one day she would find something out there in the world that would make her feel whole and happy.

"Here you go." The nurse handed her a shot glass with a reddish-brown liquid.

Emma lifted her head and reached out for the glass. She instantly regretted her actions and grabbed her waist. "Oh, the pain is so bad."

"Just drink this and you'll feel better in a couple of minutes," the nurse insisted, helping Emma to put the glass to her lips.

The medicine tasted foul, but Emma swallowed it and eased her head back against the pillow. Once the nurse was gone again, Papa stepped forward and took hold of Emma's hand. The look on his face betrayed his own pain.

"I thought I'd lost you."

"I'm so sorry, Papa. This day wasn't what any of us wanted or expected."

"I am sorry about your husband. It's hard enough to lose someone to death, but to have that kind of treachery exposed . . . It's a lot to bear."

"He wasn't treacherous. Tommy just enjoyed life to the fullest. He'd tell you that he had no regrets."

"I wonder if he still feels that way." Her father shook his head. "I know neither of you had much use for God, but maybe now you can see where that gets you. Emma, you have another chance to make things right with God, but that young man of yours . . . well, he made a bad choice, Emma. I'm hoping you won't make the same one."

The medicine was starting to take effect, and Emma could

feel herself drifting away. She looked at her father unable to tell him that his words were taking a strangle hold on her. Without Jesus, Tommy would go to hell. If she died now, she would go there too. She didn't want that . . . not for either of them.

It's too late for Tommy.

Too late.

Tracie Peterson is the award-winning author of over one hundred novels, both historical and contemporary. She has won the ACFW Lifetime Achievement Award and the Romantic Times Career Achievement Award. She is often referred to as the "Queen of Historical Christian Fiction," and her avid research resonates in her stories, as seen in her bestselling HEIRS OF MONTANA and ALASKAN QUEST series. Tracie considers her writing a ministry for God to share the gospel and biblical application. She and her family make their home in Montana. Visit her website at TraciePeterson.com or on Facebook at Facebook.com/AuthorTraciePeterson.